011386956 9

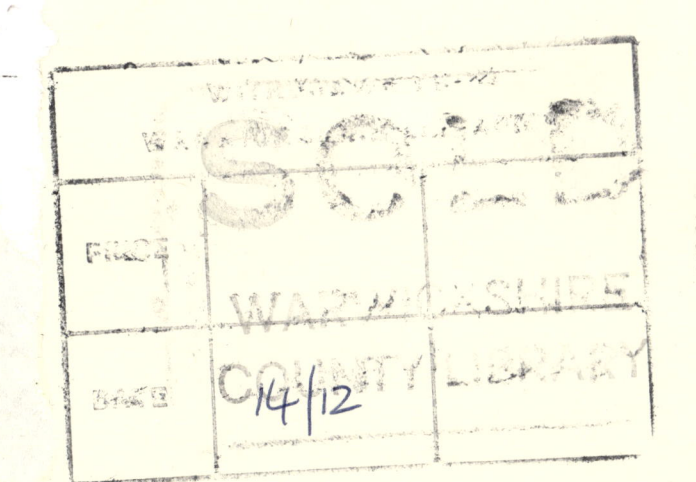

Hallmark of murder

Sprawled in front of the City goldsmith's open safe was the body of a man. Beneath the blood-matted, greying hair a deep wound gaped by the eye socket of the establishment's proprietor, Rodger Newby, the Square Mile's Lord Mayor-elect.

The disappearance of a priceless silver punch-bowl; the unburnt corner of a sheet of deed paper – a new will? – in the shop's fireplace; a bronze statuette wiped clean and replaced on the mantelpiece; the clues accumulate for the baffled City of London police, as do the suspects, mainly in the persons of the luckless Newby's extended family.

'This case is all about money; who has money, who hasn't money, who would like some more,' remarks bluff Sergeant Bragg to his aristocratic colleague, Constable Morton.

As intriguing details of Rodger Newby's private life emerge, the hunt for his murderer takes a dramatic turn with a further fatal shooting, and the case looks wrapped up until a final twist brings the dogged detectives their reward.

Mystery fans of earlier Bragg and Morton investigations will relish this, Ray Harrison's latest Victorian whodunit.

Books by Ray Harrison

French ordinary murder (1983)
Death of an Honourable Member (1984)
Deathwatch (1985)
Death of a dancing lady (1985)
Counterfeit of murder (1986)
A season for death (1987)
Harvest of death (1988)
Tincture of death (1989)
Sphere of death (1990)
Patently murder (1991)
Akin to murder (1992)
Murder in Petticoat Square (1993)

HALLMARK OF MURDER

Ray Harrison

Constable · London

First published in Great Britain 1995
by Constable & Company Ltd
3 The Lanchesters, 162 Fulham Palace Road
London W6 9ER
Copyright © 1995 by Ray Harrison
ISBN 0 09 4744106
The right of Ray Harrison to be
identified as the author of this work
has been asserted by him in accordance
with the Copyright, Designs and Patents Act 1988
Set in Linotron Palatino 10pt by
CentraCet Ltd, Cambridge
Printed and bound in Great Britain by
Hartnolls Ltd, Bodmin, Cornwall

A CIP catalogue record for this book
is available from the British Library

To my wife
GWYNETH

1

'Are the judges stupid, or what?' Bragg exclaimed. 'Not guilty! I ask you! A man was killed, wasn't he?'

'The judge may have been swayed by the evidence of the victim's doctor,' Morton remarked, pausing on the kerb as a two-horse van clattered out of a side-street.

'Huh! All right, so he had a weak heart. He also had a hole an inch deep in the back of his head. You can't tell me he got that by fainting against the railings!'

Sergeant Joseph Bragg and Constable James Morton of the City of London Police were strolling along Cheapside in the weak afternoon sunshine.

'The coroner won't be best pleased, either,' Bragg went on. 'Murder by person or persons unknown was his finding. He will look a fool, to be told that Jenkins died from somebody shaking a fist at him! I tell you what, lad, they ought to go back to the way it was in the olden days – get the jurors together first thing; let them see the body where it lies. As it is, they are too coddled. They don't come up against the violence and the blood. How can they get a proper feel for the thing?'

'That would hardly be feasible outside a village community,' Morton remarked quietly.

'But even in a village it's not much different. All right, the inquest will attract everybody from far and wide – maybe the magistrate's court hearing, too. But the assize court is held miles away, in the county town like as not. Have you ever heard of a juror in a murder trial being drawn from the same locality as the accused?'

'No doubt it is intentional,' Morton said. 'To get away from the impact of the killing, and assess the evidence in the light of pure reason.'

'Well, this morning shows that it doesn't work. That sod Shelford is laughing – at us as much as any! He's got off scot-free; he's got rid of the competition – like as not he will take over the dead man's coal round. And we have been made to look bloody fools!'

Bragg marched on angrily, chewing his ragged moustache. As they paused before crossing into Poultry, Morton caught sight of a newsvendor's stall. There was a placard bearing the words: AUST TEST TEAM.

He felt a sudden spurt of excitement. 'Just a moment, sir,' he said, and dashed across. He came back thumbing through the pages of the *Evening News*. Then his face lit up in delight. 'I am in it!' he cried exultantly. 'I have been selected to tour Australia!'

'Huh!' Bragg glowered at him. 'Do you expect me to cheer, lad?' he said grumpily. 'It'll be another three-month job, like last time.'

'But think of the honour, sir!'

'I'll leave the Commissioner to talk about the honour, if he will tell me how I'm going to keep up with the work,' Bragg growled. 'When will you be going?'

'I believe that we will sail on the fourteenth of November.'

'In four weeks, eh? Well, lad, I'll tell you this – '

There was a sudden commotion ahead; cries of 'Police! Police!' A middle-aged man in a frock coat was on the pavement, waving his arms. A knot of people began to collect. Bragg pushed his way through them.

'What's going on?' he cried.

The man gave him a dazed look. 'It's Mr Rodger . . . he's dead!'

Bragg grabbed his elbow. 'Show me,' he said. 'Constable, clear this crowd away!'

The man went a few yards along the pavement, and stopped outside a shop. Above the windows was painted: *Goldsmiths. Septimus Newby & Co. Est. 1725.* In the windows, on ruckled red velvet, a few large silver pieces were displayed. So, they were not interested in browsers with a few spare bob in their pockets, Bragg thought. Well, that was sensible enough. The City of London was where big money was made. He pushed through the door. It was more like a drawing-room than a shop, he thought. The floor was of polished parquet, with Indian rugs scattered around. There was nothing so utilitarian as a counter. Instead there were three low tables, with upholstered chairs by them. They were set at a discreet distance from each other, so that a murmured conversation would not be overheard. Against the walls were glass-fronted display cabinets of mahogany. Their shelves were filled with silver plate of every description.

'Where is the body?' Bragg growled.

The man gestured to a doorway in the back corner. 'In the office,' he said.

It was a small, square room, with a heavily barred window. A pedestal desk occupied the centre, with more upholstered chairs. A fire glowed red in the fireplace. It was at the same time less sumptuous and more relaxing than the shop. Interest might be kindled by the display out there, but it would be here that the deals would be struck.

In the back corner stood a massive safe, its door ajar. Sprawled in front of it was the body of a man. Blood matted the greying hair above his right ear. A deep wound gaped by the eye socket.

'God Almighty!' Bragg muttered. He beckoned to Morton. 'Here, lad,' he ordered. 'Go and alert the coroner. Get Sir Rufus to give us this case. Then call at the mortuary. See if you can find the pathologist, and get him over here.'

'Monday is surely the day when Professor Burney lectures at St Bartholomew's Hospital,' Morton said.

'Then drag him away! He will only complain, if we move the body before he sees it. And, in my book, this one won't wait.'

'Right!' Morton strode out.

Bragg gazed around the office. There was a table under the window, with a telephone instrument on it. Next to it was a tantalus and a tray with cut-glass tumblers. Two of the glasses had been used – single-malt whisky, by the smell of it. Did that mean the dead man had known his assailant; was connected socially? Or was a more than usually profitable deal being sealed?

He went back into the shop. The assistant was standing by the door, staring vacantly into the distance. Was it shock, Bragg wondered, or concern about his future?

'What is your name?' Bragg asked curtly.

The man turned his head reluctantly. 'Samuel Colley,' he mumbled.

'Well, you went too far, this time,' Bragg said harshly. 'What made you do it? Did he give you the sack?'

A look of incomprehension touched Colley's face, to be overlaid with panic. 'It wasn't me!' he shouted shrilly. 'Why would I call the police, if it was me?'

Bragg pursed his lips. 'All right. So who did?'

Colley numbly shook his head.

'Who is he, anyway? You said Mr Rodger.'

'Rodger Newby, the proprietor of this establishment.' Colley seemed to be recovering his poise.

'So it's an establishment, is it? Nothing so common as a shop!' Bragg said roughly. 'When did you find him?'

'Just now, at a minute past three.'

'As exact as that, eh?'

'Well, Mr Rodger told me not to come back till three o'clock.'

'What do you keep calling him Mr Rodger for?' Bragg said irritably.

'Well, his son, Mr Frederick Newby, manages the Bond Street establishment.'

'That's another shop, is it?'

Colley nodded.

'What is your usual lunch hour?' Bragg asked mildly.

'From one o'clock till two.'

'Is the shop closed then?'

'No. As proprietor, Mr . . . Mr Newby is on duty then. You see, our trade is largely with gentlemen who work in the concerns around this area.'

Bragg snorted. 'So the Bank of England and the Royal Exchange are concerns, are they? Not establishments?'

Colley said nothing.

'Did Mr Newby give any reason why he didn't want you back before three?'

Colley blinked nervously. 'No. Nor would I expect him to do so.'

'I see. You didn't have an easy, trusting relationship, then?'

Colley merely shrugged.

'So, you came back at one minute past three precisely, and

moments later you are yelling blue murder. How come you found him so soon?'

'He was not in the shop when I returned. So I went to his office, to tell him that I was there.'

'Why did you do that?'

'It was my custom. When I have returned from lunch, Mr Newby has habitually left the premises, to attend to his other affairs.'

'I see.' Bragg pondered. 'What happens if you want something out of the safe, after he has gone?'

Colley pursed his lips. 'There is a second key concealed on the premises,' he said reluctantly.

'So Rodger Newby had one, and there was another hidden.'

'That is so.'

'Where is it hidden?'

Colley frowned. 'I am not at all sure I should reveal that,' he said hesitantly.

'If you don't, I'll bloody gaol you for obstructing police enquiries,' Bragg said roughly.

'It is . . . in there,' Colley muttered, gesturing blindly towards the back room.

'Show me!'

Reluctantly Colley turned and walked through the doorway. He kept his eyes averted from the body, and went to the corner of the room at the right of the fireplace. He knelt down and lifted a square of the parquet flooring, to reveal a shallow cavity. In it lay a surprisingly small key.

Bragg straightened up. 'It's a queer way of carrying on,' he said roughly, 'to have a spare key in the same room as the safe.'

'It was not always so,' Colley replied defensively. 'But, two years ago, Mr Rodger left his key at home. As it happened, he needed access to the safe. So certain difficulties arose.'

'And how does that explain anything?'

'Perhaps you misunderstand, officer. The safe does not contain items of value. Mr Rodger kept his records and account books there . . . We go back a very long way, you know.'

'To seventeen twenty-five – or so you claim.'

'Oh, but it's true!' Colley said in an injured tone. 'The records for all those years are there – even a letter from King George the Third, in his own hand!'

'Huh!' Bragg grunted. 'So you keep rubbish in the safe, and all that valuable stuff out on display.'

Colley bridled. 'It is perfectly obvious that most of the plate is too large for the safe,' he said sharply. 'But the premises are made as secure as can be. At night, I put up stout wooden shutters at the windows; the door is double-locked . . . And,' he added waspishly, 'as you well know, a police constable comes down this street every twenty minutes, day and night.'

'Hmm . . . So, you reckon the only time to pinch anything from here would be when the shop is open?'

The street door banged and, moments later, Sir Rufus Stone made his entrance. He was a distinguished Queen's Counsel, who had been persuaded to accept appointment as Coroner for the City of London after his predecessor had been less than impartial in a case with political implications.

'Ah, Bragg!' he trumpeted. 'Thanks to our new telephone system, your message reached me just as I was leaving Vintners' Hall. A happy conjunction of events.' He bent down and peered at the corpse. 'What have we here?'

'What is left of a Mr Rodger Newby, the proprietor of this establishment,' Bragg said sardonically.

The coroner looked up at him suspiciously. 'I hope that you will curb your subversive political instincts, Bragg,' he said, 'or I shall think twice about appointing you as my officer.'

Bragg smiled. 'I doubt if this has anything to do with politics, sir.'

'Be that as it may, I will have you know that Rodger Newby has just been elected as the next Lord Mayor of London. So, at the very least, it is a matter of more than local importance.'

'You may rely on me to be discreet, sir,' Bragg said stolidly.

'Huh! I am not worried about your discretion, sergeant, it is your judgement that concerns me.'

'Don't worry, sir. I will stick to finding out the facts, and leave the judging to your lot.'

Sir Rufus frowned. 'And what do you mean by that?' he demanded.

'Oh, people of education and intellect, with a proper detachment from the blood-and-guts side of it.'

'You seem very jaundiced today, Bragg. But no doubt it will wear off . . . And what conclusions have you come to?'

Bragg cleared his throat. 'This is Mr Colley, who was the deceased's assistant in the, er, establishment,' he said formally. 'He says that Mr Newby sent him off for his lunch at one o'clock, and told him not to come back till three.'

'So he was expecting someone?'

'It seems that way.'

'You have not established the fact?'

'Not yet, sir.'

The coroner swung round irritably to Colley. 'Was he expecting a visitor?' he demanded.

Colley flinched. 'Not that I am aware of.'

'But he must have had a reason for keeping you out of the way . . . Did anyone ring him on the telephone system?'

'There was a call, yes, sir. But that is not unusual.'

'His diary, Bragg. Have you looked in his diary?'

'I've barely been here half an hour,' Bragg said defensively.

'That is no reason for neglecting the obvious!' The coroner strode over to the desk and began to pull open the drawers. 'Here we are!' he exclaimed triumphantly. 'Now, let us see . . . Monday the fifteenth of October . . . Got it!' He pursed his lips. 'Hmm . . . Significant, perhaps, though scarcely revelatory.' He swivelled round, so that Bragg could see the page. It was blank, except for two figures pencilled in – 2 0.

'Two o'clock!' Sir Rufus swung round to Colley. 'Whom was your employer expecting to see at two o'clock?' he asked truculently.

Colley's face blanched. 'I . . . I do not know, sir . . . Mr Rodger did not confide in me.'

Sir Rufus glared at him as if he were a recalcitrant witness. 'Was he habituated to sending you out for a two-hour break at luncheon?' he demanded harshly.

'No, sir. It had never happened before.'

'Well, then!' He turned to Bragg. 'Find the person who kept that appointment,' he declaimed, 'and you have your murderer!'

Bragg took the diary. 'Of course, sir, it may not be two o'clock at all,' he said. 'It could just as easily be twenty. Perhaps Newby had suddenly decided to order some more stock, and jotted down the number so that he would not forget it.'

The coroner snorted. 'Try and rise above your plebeian

origins, Bragg! This is not an emporium for the supply of matches and clothes-pegs! You do not order silver plate in twenties!'

'But there are some quite small items, sir. In fact, there don't seem to be any plates at all.'

Sir Rufus glared at him. 'If you are roasting me, Bragg, you do so at your peril! You know full well that silver plate is a generic term, covering all articles manufactured from sheets of silver.'

'I see, sir.' Bragg suppressed a smile.

Sir Rufus strode over to the fireplace, an infallible sign that he was about to embark on a lecture. Then he checked. 'Someone has been burning paper here,' he exclaimed. 'See that unburnt corner, with the red border? Deed paper, Bragg. Deed paper!'

To Bragg's relief the door clattered open, and Morton appeared followed by Professor Burney, the pathologist. Burney's loose mouth sagged in a grin of anticipation, his round face beamed with pleasure. He nodded at Bragg, then turned towards the coroner.

'Death most unnatural, I am told, Sir Rufus,' he remarked cheerfully.

'That is for you to determine, Burney,' the coroner said frostily. 'You will be giving the evidence.'

The pathologist put down his bag and knelt by the body. He peered at the wounds on the right side of the head and grunted. Then he beckoned to Morton.

'Help me to turn him over,' he said.

With a flicker of distaste, Morton squatted down and pulled at the man's arm. The torso rolled over, the legs flopping after.

'No rigor yet,' Burney murmured. 'Ah, another wound in the back of the head. Pull him over to the window, will you, constable? Where the light is better.'

Burney took a lens and a probe from his bag, then knelt by the head. Morton looked away, as the pathologist began to poke around, his grinning face inches from the wound. Then he twisted the head sideways and peered again at the wounds on the face. He sat back on his heels and looked around the room. With a grunt of satisfaction he got up and went over to the fireplace. On the mantelpiece were two bronze figures, about ten inches high. He picked one up, and his mouth sagged open in satisfaction.

'Here could be your murder weapon, Sir Rufus,' he said. 'You see how this one has the right hand on his hip? I think it might have been the elbow that penetrated the skull.' He turned to Morton. 'Constable, see that this ornament comes over to the mortuary.' He picked up his bag and made for the door.

'What about the time of death, sir?' Bragg called after him.

Burney turned. 'In the last couple of hours,' he said. 'I will take the rectal temperature, as soon as I get him on the slab. That will tell us more precisely.'

'So it could have happened around two o'clock,' the coroner said.

'Oh, yes. That sounds eminently possible.' Burney hurried away.

Sir Rufus turned to Bragg. 'So you see, I was right!' he exclaimed. 'It should not be beyond your competence to find the murderer now. I shall open the inquest on, say, Wednesday – take evidence of identity and discovery, then adjourn. But remember, Bragg, this case must be given the utmost priority, and all the resources necessary to bring it to a satisfactory conclusion.' He nodded and strode out.

Bragg turned to Colley. 'You heard that, sir,' he said. 'So you know what to expect.'

Colley's face was ashen, his eyes vacant.

Bragg stooped and emptied the pockets of the corpse. There was a gold cigarette case, a gold half-hunter watch and chain, a gold cigar-clipper. In an inside pocket he found a personal diary.

'Where are his keys?' he asked harshly.

Colley blinked. 'Er . . . in the lock of the safe.'

Bragg glared at him. 'Right. As soon as the body has been moved, you get off home. But you must be here tomorrow morning, as usual. You needn't open the shop. But I want you to go through the stock, so you can tell us what is missing. Understand?'

Colley looked apprehensively at the body. 'I don't have to – '

'No,' Bragg broke in. 'You sit in the shop until the van from the mortuary comes. When they have gone, put up the shutters and get off home.'

Colley stumbled out of the office.

'I think you had better look after that bronze figure, lad,' Bragg said. 'We don't want it getting lost, do we?'

He went across to the safe, closed the door and locked it. He took the bunch of keys and strode into the shop. Colley was sitting disconsolately on the chair furthest from the office. Bragg showed him the keys.

'Which of these fit the front door?' he asked.

Colley blinked. 'The two Chubb ones.'

'Right.' Bragg tossed the bunch to Morton. 'The constable will be coming back for the bronze figure,' he said. 'Now, who is Newby's next of kin?'

Colley took a deep breath, and let it out in a sigh. 'He has two sons, but I expect his wife is who you want.'

'Where did he live?'

'Seven, Throgmorton Avenue.'

'Just a stone's throw away. Good! Well, we will alert the mortuary, and then inform the widow . . . Make sure you are here tomorrow morning!'

Throgmorton Avenue was a new street, now dividing the Drapers' Hall from its gardens. A brewery's stables and dilapidated old courts had been torn down; spacious terraced houses built in their place. To emphasise its exclusive status, massive wrought-iron gates had been erected at each end of the avenue. It defiantly proclaimed itself an oasis of wealth and privileged domesticity, in the desert of commerce. Not that people were flocking to live there, Morton thought. Perhaps the rents were too high, even for City figures. Or perhaps they no longer wanted to live close to their work. To the undoubted chagrin of the early residents, some of the houses had been let to commercial tenants. Discreet brass plates adorned the entrances of a good third of the houses.

The residence of the late Rodger Newby was at the northern end of the avenue. Bragg led the way up the short flight of steps, to the front door. His knock was answered by a maid in spotless uniform.

'City Police,' Bragg said gruffly. 'Is your mistress at home?'

The girl raised a cheeky eyebrow. 'She's in all right,' she said. 'But I don't know if she's at home to the likes of you!'

'Well, find out, will you?'

The girl seemed disconcerted at the abruptness of the reply. 'Yes . . . all right. Just wait there . . .' she vanished.

Indeed, they were left waiting for five minutes or more. Morton half expected Bragg to go storming in, to ransack the rooms for concealed society women. But instead he leaned on the railing and calmly inspected the houses opposite. Eventually the servant reappeared.

'Will you follow me?' she said pertly. She led them down a corridor to the back of the building, and opened a door on the right.

'The gentlemen from the police,' she announced with a curtsy.

The house's situation was admirable, Morton thought. This floor was elevated some ten feet above ground level. From the bay window there was a clear view over a small lawn and fence, to the gardens of the Drapers' Company. In the spring and summer the outlook would be sheer delight. The room was spacious, with a high corniced ceiling. The fireplace surround was painted white. White bookshelves broke the panels of William Morris wallpaper. There was none of the massive, traditional furniture. Instead, elegant Regency tables mingled with comfortable chairs. A few fine watercolours replaced the usual clutter of pictures. It was all very modern and tasteful, Morton decided. Of a piece with the shop premises.

A woman rose from the window seat. She was in her early fifties, with flecks of grey in her dark hair. Her mouth was set firm, her brown eyes wary. She motioned them to sit. 'I am Elizabeth Newby,' she said with a half-smile. 'Why do you wish to see me?'

Bragg produced his warrant-card. 'Sergeant Bragg and Constable Morton, of the City Police,' he said quietly. 'I am sorry to have to disturb you like this, but I am afraid that your husband has been attacked.'

'My husband? I thought . . .' She stopped abruptly, her eyes staring.

'I am afraid I have to tell you that he is dead.'

Her brows knitted in shocked incomprehension. 'Rodger, dead?'

'Yes, ma'am. He was alone in the shop during the lunch hour. Someone went in and killed him.'

'But why?'

'That's where we need some help. There was no obvious sign of a burglary; though Mr Colley is going to check the stock.'

She was gripping the arms of her chair till her knuckles showed white, but she showed no sign of breaking down.

'Are there any male relatives we can talk to?' Bragg asked gently.

She frowned. 'He has a brother,' she said dully. 'But he is on his way from India.'

'Ah . . . It seems, from what Mr Colley tells us, that you have a son.'

'We have two sons; Frederick, the elder, works for his father, in the Bond Street shop.'

'And the other?'

'Edgar is employed by Pendleton Vintners, in Crutched Friars.'

'Ah, that's nearer. Perhaps you would rather we talked to him.'

A flicker of alarm showed in her eyes. 'No. I am quite able to tell you what you need to know.'

Bragg hesitated. 'You appreciate that our concern is to catch his killer. We want to get as much background as we can, to give us a good start.'

'Yes . . . yes.'

'How long has your husband been principal of Newbys?' he asked.

'Since his father, Sir Thomas Newby, died.'

'How long ago would that have been?'

'It must be almost twenty-five years.'

'I see . . . And Frederick will take over from him, I suppose.'

'Of course. He is our elder son.'

'I suppose no one has been trying to buy the business, or anything like that?' Bragg asked.

She looked at him uncomprehendingly.

'It's a long shot, ma'am, I know. But it has happened that a tradesman has wanted to take over the business of a competitor.

And, when no deal could be struck, the competitor has been put out of the way.'

She flinched. 'You would have to consult Frederick,' she said. 'But I do not believe that, so far as quality silver is concerned, we have any significant competitors in the City.'

'Hmm . . .' Bragg paused to see if she would relax, then: 'Can you think of anyone who might wish him ill?' he asked.

'No!'

Was the reply a little too pat, too defensive, Bragg wondered?

'You see,' he went on, 'it seems to us that your husband knew the person who killed him. He was found in the office, in front of the open safe; it is likely they had drunk whisky together.'

'He would hardly offer hospitality to someone he knew was at enmity with him,' she said with some spirit.

'Yes, that's right, ma'am. So it would have to be a secret enemy.'

'Can there be such a thing?'

'Oh, yes. Your husband had just been elected as the next Lord Mayor of London. I expect a lot of people would envy him that!'

She shrugged. 'I am not really *au fait* with such things,' she said.

'You mean you didn't interest yourself, didn't approve?'

'No, sergeant. I have supported my husband in all his endeavours. Last year Rodger was one of the two nominees, but was not then elected. This year he was. George Pascoe was rejected this year. No doubt he would have been elected next year. There is no blood-letting in City politics . . .' The import of her words seemed to strike her, and she bit her lip.

'Hmm . . . So, your husband did not have any enemies that you were aware of?'

'No, sergeant.'

'Very well, ma'am. I wonder if you can tell us the name of your husband's solicitor?'

She looked up sharply. 'Why should that concern you?' she asked.

'It's just routine,' Bragg said soothingly. 'In the past, legatees have been known to hurry matters along a bit. It's an aspect I have got to cover.'

She twisted her lips. 'Of course, sergeant. Our solicitor is Mr Fummery, of Parkin Cheesewright & Co. You will find them in Chancery Lane.'

Bragg rose to his feet. 'I am most grateful to you, ma'am. It cannot have been easy. May I say how much I admire your composure? I hope we will not need to trouble you again . . . We will let ourselves out.'

Once in the street, Bragg turned to Morton. 'She was a cool one, and no mistake!' he said. 'I don't reckon her world has been turned upside down.'

'She seemed apprehensive when we first arrived,' Morton said. 'But when you mentioned her husband, it was almost a relief to her.'

Bragg grunted. 'You caught it too? I have an idea this may be an interesting case,' he said. 'Now, you get that statuette over to Professor Burney, while I go and think.'

When Catherine Marsden left Cheltenham Ladies College, at eighteen, she had been determined not to be sucked into the vacuous whirl of London society. She told herself that it was nothing at all to do with that chance remark she had overheard. Her godmother, Lady Lanesborough, had been almost commiserating with her mother. She had forgotten the precise words, but it was to the effect that, while Catherine was not pretty now, she might well become beautiful later on. She had been furious at the time. What did it matter if she was taller than average; that her face was somewhat longer than was fashionable? If her chances of making a marriage were to be determined by such trivia, then more fool men! Anyway, she was not going to be trapped in a society marriage of convenience; a position of dependence on any man. She was determined to prove to herself, and to any would-be suitor, that she was capable of carving out a career for herself. Her mother had been as shocked as her easy-going nature would allow. But, surprisingly, her father had supported her. As a society portrait painter, he probably could see the emptiness behind much of the glitter. So, for whatever reasons, he had encouraged her ambitions. It was probably due to his influence that she had obtained a post as reporter on the *City Press*. It was a somewhat parochial newspaper. But, since that parish was the City of London – the financial centre of the empire, if not the world – it was still very influential. She had been working for over three years now. During that time, she had been drawn into several murder cases under investigation by Sergeant Bragg and Constable Morton. She flattered herself that, on occasion, she had supplied the vital information leading to the arrest of the villain. A close personal relationship had grown up between her and James. Nevertheless, she was surprised at his telephoning her. Never before had he alerted her at the beginning of a case. Normally she had been left to hear of it from the papers, or society gossip; had then insinuated herself into the investigation. Not that James was exactly soliciting her aid now. The conversation had been almost furtive. But he had rung . . . Of course, this case was different, since the victim was a prominent City figure – the next Lord Mayor, no less. It was indubitably within her professional sphere of interest; and now she would have a head start over her fellow reporters!

She decided to take a cab to the mortuary. From what James had said, the body would be there by now. On the way she thought about what tactics she would employ. If only the wretched man had got himself killed on a Tuesday, instead of a Monday! Since the *City Press* was only published on a Wednesday and Saturday, there was precious little chance of a scoop . . . But she might catch the national press! She was an occasional correspondent for the *Star*, after all. With its radical leanings, it might jump at a story that hinted at skulduggery in a Tory stronghold such as the City. She paid off the cab in Golden Lane, and hurried towards the low brick building. Suddenly it seemed forbidding and sinister. She had never been in a mortuary in her life. Jame's anecdotes had sometimes given her a *frisson* of excitement; the reality felt different. But she was a reporter, she told herself. Her readers had every right to know what was going on in the City, to be told in detail the circumstances surrounding the murder of the Lord Mayor-elect.

She pushed through the double doors and found herself in a long room. There were no windows, the light coming only from the glass roof. Jutting from the walls were long slate slabs, grey and menacing. Some of them held white-swathed forms. She fought down the panic in her breast. No doubt her father would patronisingly chide her for entering a man's world – say that she should be protected from such things. But women were at the heart of giving life. Why should they be shielded from death?

'Hello!' she called. Her voice echoed from the forbidding walls, but no one came.

'Hello!'

She was wondering what to do next, when the door clattered open behind her and Morton strode in.

'James!' She had a momentary longing to be embraced and comforted.

Morton took off his hat. 'Miss Marsden! Your assiduity does you credit.' He grinned broadly. 'But I fear that you will never be allowed into the holy of holies at the back.'

'Holy of holies?' she repeated inanely.

'The examination room – where the post-mortem is no doubt being carried out at this moment.'

The urbanity of his tone irritated her. She had screwed herself up to come here, and now he was mocking her. 'But you, as a man, will be allowed there,' she said caustically.

'Not as a man; as a policeman. And not out of idle curiosity, but bearing . . . not exactly gifts, but evidence.'

'Evidence! Let me see!'

Morton grinned. 'Not even evidence, merely potential evidence. Dr Burney is of the opinion that Rodger Newby was killed, using a statuette from his mantelpiece.'

'And the parcel you are carrying contains that statuette?'

'Exactly.'

'Well! Let me see it!'

Morton hesitated, 'I really feel I ought not,' he said.

'Stop tantalising me! Anyway, it can do no harm.'

Morton shrugged, then went over to a vacant slate slab and unwrapped the parcel.

Catherine shivered. 'He was killed using that statuette as a bludgeon?' she asked, fumbling in her bag for her notebook.

'That is the view of our elders and betters.'

'It is some sort of soldier, is it not? See, there is a shield with a cross on it, and the hilt of a sword . . . and a dagger on the other hip. But what is he holding in his left hand? It looks like a trumpet.'

'I believe it is an Old English Pipeman,' Morton said. 'I have seen a similar one in Sandringham House, when I was seconded to protect the person of our illustrious Prince of Wales.'

'Why does Dr Burney think that this was the weapon?'

'In his opinion, the projecting elbow will match the wounds in the skull . . . It is quite feasible. It must weigh five or six pounds. Here . . . feel it.'

'No, thank you!' Catherine recoiled in distaste.

'Is our intrepid reporter becoming squeamish?' Morton said teasingly.

'Not at all!. . . Do you think that the results of the post-mortem will be known soon?' she asked.

'I doubt it. Professor Burney is nothing, if not thorough.'

'Then I shall get off a brief report to the *Star*, and do a proper article for Wednesday's *City Press*. I hope that you will help me to flesh out the story.'

Morton began to wrap up the bronze again. 'If I am honest, I would rather you were a thousand miles from it,' he said.

'But you alerted me!'

'I know. It was a typically generous impulse – and ever since I have regretted it.'

Catherine put down her pen and glanced at her fob watch. It was almost half-past five. If she hurried to Lanesborough House, she might inveigle her godmother into some relevant social chit-chat. She and her cronies seemed to have an inexhaustible fund of anecdotes about people in society. Though whether that extended to Lord Mayors-elect was another matter.

She smiled sweetly at the cabby, and he did indeed hurry. It was still some minutes before six o'clock, when she was hurrying up the great curving staircase, past her father's celebrated portrait of Lady Lanesborough, to the drawing-room. She was relieved to see that it was empty, apart from her godmother and Mrs Gerald de Trafford.

'Ah, Catherine!' Lady Lanesborough greeted her. 'You have been neglecting us!'

'Not intentionally, I assure you,' Catherine replied breathlessly.

'Well, sit down. We can have a lovely long chat. We are dining in tonight.'

'Actually, I am in the middle of an article, which must be in tomorrow. But I have stolen half an hour.'

'That will hardly suffice,' Lady Lanesborough said reprovingly. 'I have barely seen you since the end of the Season . . . Are you still involved with that wretched policeman of yours?'

'Hardly involved, godmother. His sister Emily is still a good friend. But now that she has married, I see her less often.'

'Hmm . . . It is time that you were married yourself, child,' Lady Lanesborough said reprovingly. 'But it is such a dull time of year. All the eligible bachelors are off in the country, hunting and shooting.'

Catherine laughed. 'My taste in prospective husbands inclines more towards the aesthetic than the brutish, ma'am.'

'Rubbish! One has to be hard-headed in these matters. With your good looks and your entrée to royalty, you are worthy of an earl, without question.'

'Why stop at an earl?' Catherine said teasingly. 'Why not a duke?'

'No . . . The dukes have all been pauperised. They are having to marry off their sons to American heiresses. You would be far better off with an earl or a viscount . . . But he must have a London house, as well as a country seat, or we will see nothing of you! I will see what can be done in the next three months.'

'Goodness! How very explicit. Why in the next three months?'

Lady Lanesborough dropped her eyes. 'For no particular reason, child.'

'Come along!' Catherine exclaimed. 'You are looking positively shifty!'

'Very well,' her godmother said defiantly. 'According to Lanesborough, James Morton has been picked to play cricket in Australia. So he will be out of the way till April.'

'But I saw him, not an hour ago!' Catherine exclaimed in disbelief. 'He said nothing then!'

Lady Lanesborough raised her eyebrows. 'Well, there you are then,' she said.

Catherine fought down her sense of betrayal. She had refused James's proposal of marriage six months ago. She could hardly now complain, that he should play cricket for his country without consulting her wishes.'

'I have something much more interesting to discuss than men and their silly games,' she said brightly. 'There has been a murder in the City. The Lord Mayor-elect. You may be able to help me with my article.'

The ladies leaned forward expectantly.

'I wonder if you know the people involved. The murdered man is Rodger Newby. He was killed in the family goldsmiths' shop in Poultry.'

'Oh, a tradesman,' Lady Lanesborough said dismissively.

'His father was a Sir Thomas Newby.'

'I know!' Mrs de Trafford exclaimed. 'They have a shop in Bond Street . . . There is plenty of money, I'll be bound.'

'Was that the family that Gertrude Allen married into?' Lady Lanesborough interjected.

'I believe that is so. She was a wealthy heiress in her own right . . . She had sons, as I recall, and perhaps one daughter.'

'There you are, child,' Lady Lanesborough said triumphantly. 'An influential family – though who there is to influence in the City of London, I cannot imagine. They are all high Tory!'

'Do you know, I heard something about that family . . . something recent,' Mrs de Trafford said thoughtfully. 'I have it! You know the Osborne girl – Nancy, I think she is . . . Well, she was being pursued by a shopkeeper from Bond Street! I am sure the name is Frederick Newby. Now, the Osbornes are hardly in the front rank of society, and Nancy is one of five daughters. So the family was not totally opposed to the match. Indeed, I believe Nancy to be quite fond of this suitor. The trouble was that the affair did not seem to advance. The young men were regarding Nancy as unavailable, yet this Newby showed no sign of actually marrying the girl. It was profoundly unsatisfactory. I gather that Nancy refused to allow her father to speak to Newby. Things seemed to be at an impasse. In the end, it seems to have been resolved in a thoroughly inappropriate way. It happened after the end of the Season, so the details have not really got out. But my belief is that the couple got engaged secretly, in September. At least, it is secret so far as his family are concerned. But it does not prevent her from flaunting a solitaire diamond engagement ring.'

'Goodness!' Catherine exclaimed. 'I know Nancy Osborne. I must make it my business to go and commiserate with her!'

2

Next morning, Morton was about to go into Bragg's room, when the Commissioner emerged. Lt.-Col. Sir William Sumner was a short, stiff man, who ran the City Police in an easy, paternalistic way. It had become traditional for the Chief Constables of police forces to be drawn from the higher ranks of the army. The view was that they were used to commanding a disciplined body of men – a skill that could be applied just as easily to a police force as a regiment. It was not totally illogical, since the majority of policemen had served for a time in the army. Though, after the Trafalgar Square riots of 1887, it had been urged in Parliament that the police should promote their own men to take command in future.

As an outsider in police matters, the Commissioner was heavily dependent on his senior officers; and on occasion his trust had been abused. So, as a means of bringing himself closer to investigation work, Sir William had insisted that Bragg – though nominally under the aegis of Inspector Cotton – should work directly to him. Cotton's pride had been hurt, of course. So Bragg had found himself with the worst of both worlds – saddled with the Commissioner's amateurish oversight, while formally reporting through Cotton.

'Ah! Morton,' the Commissioner said stiffly. 'Congratulations on being picked for England! Splendid! Good for the force's reputation. Well done!' He gave a diffident smile and marched on.

Morton went in. Bragg was sitting at his desk, glowering at his empty pipe.

'I see that you have received your tactical orders, sir,' Morton said with a grin.

Bragg scowled at him. 'If you ask me, lad, Sir William is shit-scared. There could hardly be a worse occurrence in City life, than the murder of the Lord Mayor-to-be. I reckon our worthy leader thinks he might lose his job.'

'That would be rather unfair,' Morton protested. 'He could hardly have anticipated the murder.'

'No. But if we don't catch the killer soon, the Common Council will get restive . . . You don't fancy the job yourself, then?' Bragg asked casually.

'Of Commissioner? What a ludicrous notion!'

'Some people wouldn't think so. I've been told, often enough, that you are being groomed for the top job.'

'But that is absurd, and you know it!' Morton exclaimed.

'Why is it? Here you are, from one of the best families in the land, with a degree from Cambridge and all the money in the world, flat-footing it round the streets of London as a constable. Most people would think you were a loony – unless there was a further fetch to it.'

Morton frowned. 'You know perfectly well that I am here by force of circumstances,' he said. 'With an elder brother paralysed by a Dervish bullet, I can hardly hang around The Priory waiting for his death, however inevitable. Indeed, I do not feel welcome there, since I show all too obviously my disapproval at the way the estates are being allowed to go to rack and ruin. Even my parents must realise that the pretence that Edwin can run them from his sick-bed is absurd. But it will not go on for ever. In time, I expect to inherit. Until then I am content . . . And there is always my cricket!'

'Huh! Well, if you are going to be playing pat-ball for three months, we'd better get on with this Newby case. Find us a cab, will you, lad?'

Half an hour later they were gazing at the window of Newby's Bond Street shop. It contained a few pieces of silver plate, but most of the display was of gold watches, necklaces, rings, brooches.

'This is a different kettle of fish, lad,' Bragg said gruffly. 'I've never seen so many diamonds in my life!'

'No wonder they have a grille behind the glass.'

'Come on, lad, let's see what they have to say for themselves.'

The shop was much as the one in Poultry. The same low tables and chairs, the same oriental rugs. This time, the display cases largely contained items of personal jewellery.

A grave, grey-haired man came towards them. 'How can I help you, gentlemen?' he said unctuously.

'City Police,' Bragg said. 'We were wondering if Mr Frederick Newby was in this morning.'

The deferential smile faded. 'Yes, he is in. I told him I could manage perfectly well on my own, but he would stay.'

'Tell him we are here,' Bragg growled.

'I . . . er, yes. Of course, sir.'

He knocked on a door in the back wall, and opened it. 'Some gentlemen here to see you, Mr Frederick,' he said.

There was a murmured reply, and the assistant beckoned them to enter.

Frederick Newby rose from his desk as they entered. He was tall and slim, with dark hair and a long sharp nose. His eyes were red-rimmed, his bearing dejected.

'Sergeant Bragg and Constable Morton, of the City Police,' Bragg said crisply. 'I thought it might be useful to have an early chat.'

'Ah, yes . . . You were the officers who saw my mother yesterday,' he said in a tired voice. 'Thank you for the considerate way in which you dealt with the matter.' He gestured them to sit.

'As you can imagine, sir,' Bragg began, 'it is important for us to fill in the background of a case as early as we can – to get the feel of it.'

Newby nodded. 'Of course,' he said.

'Now, can you tell us about the business? For instance, are the two shops kept separate? Are you a partner, or what?'

Newby took a deep breath. 'I am not a partner; nor am I an employee. As has been tradition in my family, I have worked for my father on the understanding that I would inherit in due course.'

'I see. So I suppose you have inherited now?'

'That will depend on my father's will.'

'Ah. Come to think of it, your mother said as much . . . And are they two separate businesses?'

Newby's eyes narrowed. 'No. They have always been run as one.'

'Since seventeen twenty-five?' Bragg asked.

'No. This branch has only existed since eighteen-sixty. My father was in charge of it then, while my grandfather was at the City branch.'

'Hmm . . . It's just that, to a layman like me, they look to be very different businesses.'

A smile touched Frederick Newby's lips. 'In essence, that is true,' he said. 'Bond Street is at the centre of the fashionable world. So our trade is largely in personal jewellery. A good proportion of our sales are made in the Season, and centred on the Queen's receptions. As you can imagine, we sell a good number of necklaces and trinkets to the débutantes and their mothers.'

'Of course.' Bragg pondered. 'So the trade here is seasonal?' he said.

Newby frowned. 'There is a flat period in the autumn, and after Christmas, naturally.'

'How does that compare with the Poultry shop – or establishment as Mr Colley calls it?'

This time were was more warmth in the smile. 'Of course, the City trade is entirely different. The connection there has, since the beginning, been with the great livery companies. And, in the last century, have been added the joint-stock companies and banks, with their head offices and directors' dining-rooms.'

'We saw, in Poultry, that the stock was mainly silver dishes and the like,' Bragg said. 'But I would have thought that there was a limit to the number of them you could sell.'

'True, but you must realise that they are not necessarily bought for purely utilitarian purposes. Surplus funds can just as easily be invested in silver plate, as kept in a bank. The intrinsic value of the precious metal is always there.'

'You mean, you could melt it down to silver ingots again?'

'*In extremis*, yes. In the meantime, a sideboard of fine silver pieces serves to impress.'

'Hmm . . . So they are bought for show, eh?'

Newby pursed his lips. 'Yes . . . but also for more personal reasons. For instance, the master of a livery company might present, say, an engraved silver dish to mark his year.'

'And perpetuate his memory, eh?'

'Exactly.'

'So, there is a steady trade in the City branch?'

'Indeed there is, sergeant; and, more crucially, little competition.'

'Since the shops are so different, why not treat them as separate businesses?'

'My father would not agree to it,' Newby said curtly.

Bragg paused, then: 'Has there ever been any question of selling either of the shops?' he enquired.

Newby frowned. 'You asked this question of my mother, yesterday. The answer is as she gave it.'

'No one was offering to buy?'

'That is correct.'

'Would you necessarily know, sir?' Bragg asked quietly.

'I would certainly expect to have been told, if any approach had been made.'

'Of course.' Bragg reflected for a moment, then: 'Where do you get your money from?' he asked.

'I do not understand,' Newby said, frowning.

'Well, how old are you now?'

'Twenty-nine.'

'Married?'

'No.'

'But you still need money in your pocket.'

Newby looked at Bragg warily. 'I live in my parents' house. So far as my personal expenditure is concerned, I have received an allowance from my father.'

'I see . . . What about your brother?'

'Edgar? I am sure that a similar arrangement has applied.'

'Am I right in thinking that he works at Pendleton Vintners?'

'That is so,' Newby said curtly.

'Is he married?'

'No. He lives at home also.'

'But he would get a proper salary?'

Newby snorted. 'Since my father was chairman of the trustees who owns Pendletons, I very much doubt it!'

'I see, sir,' Bragg said amiably. 'Now, the goldsmiths' business has been in your family, handed down from father to son, since seventeen twenty-five.'

'Yes.'

'And you have mentioned the livery companies . . . Was your father a member of the Goldsmiths' Company?'

'He was, as I am.'

'You too?' Bragg said in surprise. 'I thought that was something only old men went into.'

Newby frowned. 'It was felt important that I should become a freeman, to preserve the connection,' he said shortly.

'I see. But this mummery is not something you set great store by?'

'Had you asked me my opinion of almost any other of the livery companies, I would have said that they are self-perpetuating relics of medieval trades, with no function in the modern world. That is manifestly not true of the Goldsmiths' Company. No article of gold or silver, manufactured in Britain, can be sold unless it bears an assay mark. Which means that, in the south of England, it must be physically brought to Goldsmiths' Hall to be assayed and stamped.'

'I see. But surely you don't have to be a freeman to have your goods assayed?'

'That is correct.'

'Right . . . Now, your father must have been well up in the City, because he was going to be made Lord Mayor, in November.'

'True.'

'Could that be a killing matter?'

Newby snorted in derision. 'To prevent it, you mean?'

'Yes.'

'I would hardly think so! It costs the incumbent a great deal of money. I would have thought that Mr Pascoe was quietly relieved, to be passed over in favour of my father.'

'You don't see Pascoe knocking him on the head, then?'

'No. However, I cannot imagine anyone wishing to do so.'

Bragg and Morton took a growler back to the City, and went to the shop in Poultry. It was locked and shuttered, but their knock was answered by Colley. In his arms was a weighty ledger.

'How are you getting on?' Bragg asked encouragingly.

'Quite well, thank you.'

'Is that your stock book?'

'Yes.' He stooped and placed it on a table. 'Every individual item is entered there when it is received, and crossed out when it is sold.'

Bragg flicked through the pages. 'I see that, after stock-taking, at the year end, all the stock is entered afresh . . . I suppose that makes sense.'

'Yes, indeed! We have had some items in stock for ten years and more. If we did not bring them forward, we might lose track of them!'

'Hmm . . . Have you ever had stock go astray?' Bragg asked.

'Only once – a silver salver – in all the time I have worked here. We only found it had gone at the stock-taking.'

'When was that?'

'At the end of April this year.'

'I see. Was it valuable?'

'Moderately so. It was antique.'

Bragg walked over to the open display case, and peered at the silver Colley had been checking. 'We have just come back from Bond Street,' he said. 'Can you tell me why the two shops are treated as one business, when the trade is so different?'

Colley glanced at him warily. 'It is not for me to concern myself with such matters,' he said.

'But you must have your own ideas.'

'Well . . . I know there was friction between Mr Frederick and Mr Rodger. You see, Mr Rodger did all the buying, from here. But lines change so quickly in the fashion trade. Mr Frederick would complain that he just wouldn't be able to sell some of the items he was sent. And it was true. In the end, he would have to reduce the prices so much there was barely any profit. But Mr Rodger would not give ground.'

'But, why should Frederick care? As far as I can make out, he was working for pocket-money.'

Colley raised his eyebrows. 'Well, I don't know about that. But it was made clear to me that Mr Frederick would inherit both establishments, in due course.'

Bragg tugged at his moustache in puzzlement. 'Tell me,' he said. 'Why should Frederick get the lot, when there is another son?'

'Mr Edgar, you mean?' Colley said cautiously. 'I know very little about him. He has popped in here occasionally.'

'He works for Pendleton Vintners, apparently.'

'So I believe. Mrs Rodger Newby was a Pendleton.'

'Edgar has his feet in the trough over there, eh?'

Colley shrugged, then turned back to his stock book. Bragg stooped and picked up a smaller ledger from the table. 'What is this for?' he asked.

'In it we enter non-stock items – plate brought in for repair, watches needing regulating.' He took the book. 'See, we enter the item when it is brought in, and the number of the customer's receipt. Then, when the repair has been paid for, and . . .' He checked, swivelled round and rushed to one of the display cases.'

'It's gone!' he exclaimed in alarm. 'The Malpas bowl has gone!'

Bragg took him by the elbow. 'What is the Malpas bowl?'

'A silver punch-bowl, made by Paul de Lamerie! It is priceless! Oh, my God!'

'How big was it?' Morton asked.

'About fifteen inches across, and nine deep.'

'If it was a de Lamerie, it would indeed be valuable.'

Colley slumped on to a chair. 'I only put it in there because it was too big for the safe,' he said. 'Whatever will happen now?'

'I expect it will be covered by your insurance,' Bragg said dismissively.

'No! Only our stock is covered. We expect articles brought in by customers to be covered by their owners' policies . . . Oh, my goodness!'

'Perhaps Mr Newby sent it to the repairers, without mentioning it,' Morton suggested.

'But that's just it! The bowl was not here for repair; it was brought in for valuation. You see, Mr Rodger was an expert on English silverware. He was on the plate committee of the Goldsmiths' Company – and you cannot get higher than that! He was very interested in the bowl; said he must show it to Mr Frederick. And he told me to look through recent auction catalogues, for sales of de Lamerie pieces.'

'Perhaps it is in the Bond Street shop, or at their house,' Morton said. 'In any case, I cannot see how you can be held personally responsible, if it disappeared between one and three o'clock yesterday.'

'But how do I know it did?' Colley asked plaintively. 'How can I prove that?'

Catherine Marsden was shown to a sitting-room in the Belgrave Square house of the Osbornes. It was on the very edge of society's little village, and hardly sumptuous, but the square was pleasant enough. Catherine reminded herself of how privileged she was, to be able to look out from the Park Lane balcony of her parents' house, over the lush green of Hyde Park. Recently the avant-garde in artistic circles had taken to decrying portraiture as sterile and uncreative; as something the camera could now do better. Her father had shrugged off the criticism. He could still demand a thousand guineas for a portrait, and people were pleading to be painted by him. Nevertheless, Catherine became very irritated on his behalf, when she compared the liveliness and charm of his portraits with the tense wooden images produced by photographers.

The door opened, and Nancy came into the room. Her eyes were red, and a handkerchief was clenched in her hand.

'Oh, Catherine,' she wailed. 'What a dreadful thing to happen!'

Catherine rose and put her arms round the girl. 'Everything will come right in the end,' she said inanely.

'I only heard an hour ago! Papa said he was dreadfully battered.'

'Stop dwelling on it so,' Catherine said sharply.

'I can't help it . . . Frederick and I were . . .'

'You were engaged to be married – I know.'

'But, you see, his father did not . . . Now it seems so wicked to have deceived him.' Nancy sniffed. 'Another year and it would have been all right. Once Frederick had turned thirty, his father would have agreed . . . My fiancé is such an honourable person, Catherine. He said that, when he went into the firm, he accepted he would not marry until he was thirty. He said it was a promise he dare not break, or we would have nothing! I told him I did not care. He laughed and assured me that my father would.'

'And, would he?' Catherine asked quietly.

'Papa? Well, I suppose he would.' Nancy sniffed. 'Naturally he would want me to have a secure, comfortable married life . . . And I am not clever like you. You are independent; you have an interesting job, can hold your own with your male colleagues.' She dabbed her eyes. 'I . . . I am just a chattel!'

'Now you are being silly,' Catherine said sharply. 'I would have thought that, if anything, Rodger Newby's death has brought your marriage nearer. After all, Frederick is his own man now.'

'Yes . . . but you see, Frederick promised me he would approach his father again . . . And now this has happened!'

Bragg and Morton went through the mortuary and into the examination room. There were windows on the back wall, giving on to a yard cluttered with disinfectant carboys. Under the window was a long bench, with instruments and specimen jars on it. In the corner was a glazed white sink, and next to it a cabinet containing books and bottles. In the middle of the room was a slab, on which the eviscerated body of Rodger Newby lay. Burney was bending over the head, probe in hand. He looked up.

'Ah, Sergeant Bragg,' he said cheerfully. 'Just in time . . . And Constable Morton too! I hear you are playing for England in Australia. Well done! Now, we want at least four centuries from you!'

'He will be away long enough, without wasting our time now,' Bragg said irritably. 'Is there anything you can tell us about Newby?'

Burney straightened up, a shamefaced grin on his face. 'Why, yes . . . He was in good physical condition, for someone in his late fifties; would have gone on for another twenty years. I was just about to test my theory about the statuette . . . Perhaps you would hand it to me, constable . . . Thank you. You will appreciate that it had been wiped, and returned to its place on the mantelpiece; which argues a methodical assailant, who was not afraid of discovery. However, I was able to obtain material from the crook of the arm. Teichmann's test indicated the presence of human blood. All that remains is to apply the elbow to the depression in the skull. Help me turn him over, will you, constable?'

With a grimace of repugnance, Morton pushed at the shoulder of the corpse and it rolled over.

Burney picked up the statuette from the bench and gently placed its elbow into the wound on the back of Newby's head. 'Yes,' he murmured. 'It fits exactly. And this area of bruising was caused by the impact of the hip.' He straightened up. 'Well, sergeant, I shall inform the coroner that death was caused by blows to the skull, utilising this bronze statuette as a weapon.'

'It suggests that the assailant did not come prepared to murder though,' Bragg said.

Burney gave a loose smile. 'To you, that may have relevancy,' he said. 'To me it has none. Now, I assume that you will take care of the bronze . . .'

Bragg and Morton took the statuette back to Old Jewry and locked it in the cupboard, then they walked to Throgmorton Avenue. This time the maid was more subdued.

'She has company with her,' she said. 'Just a minute.'

Soon they were being shown into the sitting-room at the back of the house.

Mrs Newby rose to greet them. She was wearing a black dress, heavily trimmed with crape. Her cheeks were flushed, her mouth clamped in an angry line.

'I am sorry to trouble you, ma'am,' Bragg said quietly. 'I thought you would be wanting to make the funeral arrangements.'

She let out a pent-up sigh. 'Of course, sergeant.' She gestured to a second woman, who was sitting on the window seat. 'This is my widowed sister, Mrs Harvey,' she said abruptly. 'As you would expect, she is a great comfort to me at this time.'

'I have just come from the mortuary, ma'am,' Bragg said quietly. 'You can tell the undertakers that they will be able to collect your husband's remains tomorrow.'

A flicker of pain crossed her face. 'Very well.' She gestured reluctantly to a settee. 'Please sit down.'

'Thank you, ma'am.' With his solemn demeanour and ragged

moustache, Bragg's face looked positively lugubrious, Morton thought.

Bragg waited while Mrs Newby composed herself, and looked covertly at her sister. Mrs Harvey was younger, slimmer and prettier. She caught his eye and looked away. Bragg noticed that she was wearing a large diamond ring on her right hand. So she was not short of a penny, herself. He turned to Mrs Newby.

'Have you made any plans about the funeral?' he asked solicitously.

'I understand, from Frederick, that the interment will be on Friday morning,' she said bleakly.

'At Manor Park cemetery?'

'Yes. In addition, the Corporation of the City has expressed a wish that there should be a memorial service, on Wednesday of next week.'

'Very proper, too,' Bragg said. 'Him being so eminent.'

'But it does prolong the distress for the family,' Mrs Harvey broke in. She had a warm, musical voice. When she smiled, Bragg thought, her face would light up.

'It is what he would have wished for – indeed, expected,' Mrs Newby said sharply.

Mrs Harvey bowed her head.

'I was surprised that your son, Frederick, was working this morning,' Bragg remarked.

Mrs Newby raised an eyebrow. 'It is what his father would have wanted. And there is nothing for him to do here.'

'Of course . . . Now, you said that your second son, Edgar, works at Pendleton Vintners. Am I right in thinking that you two ladies were Pendletons, before you married?'

'That is so. I was Elizabeth, and Mrs Harvey was Alice Pendleton.'

'From what Frederick said, ma'am, the vintners' business is run by a trust. Does that mean you didn't have any brothers?'

'That is correct.' Elizabeth was becoming edgy. 'But I hardly see how that is relevant to my husband's death!'

'I expect you are right, ma'am. But it is useful for us to have the full picture . . . And I gather that your husband was the principal trustee.'

'I have not seen the documents, but I believe that is so.'

'Our father was something of a martinet,' Alice Harvey broke in with a smile. 'And he firmly believed that a woman's sphere was as a wife and mother.'

'You did not even have children,' Elizabeth said tartly.

Alice did not reply.

'And who were the other trustees?' Bragg asked Mrs Newby.

'It was utterly stupid!' Elizabeth exclaimed. 'Apart from Rodger, the trustees were the vicar of St Olave's church for the time being, and the senior partner of Parkin Cheesewright & Co. for the time being.'

'It does sound unusual,' Bragg agreed. 'So the family now has no say in what the trust does?'

'For my part,' Alice said, 'I shall be content if my current income from the trust is maintained. But, as my sister has said, I do not have the encumbrance of children.'

'So the ladies were not at ease with each other?' Catherine asked, putting down her coffee cup.

She and Morton were in the sitting-room of her parents' house, having dined in the restaurant of the Savoy Hotel. Mrs Marsden was ensconced in a chair by the fire; reading a novel, but alert for any furtive impropriety between them.

'Mrs Newby has received a terrible shock,' Morton said. 'One could hardly expect her to act normally. But the friction seemed to arise mainly from the fact that Mrs Newby has children, and Mrs Harvey has none.'

'In which case,' Catherine said, 'it seems strange that Mrs Newby was sniping at her sister. But, perhaps she was no more than giving vent to her own grief.'

'Yes . . . However, it will all come out in the end.'

Catherine looked at him with a sardonic smile. 'You know, of course, that Frederick Newby was secretely engaged, in defiance of his father's wishes.'

'Engaged? To be married?'

'What else?'

'Good heavens! From what he told us, he is virtually penniless, and will remain so till he is thirty.'

'Would have remained so . . .'

'You are sure of this?' Morton asked in growing excitement.

'His fiancée is Nancy Osborne, a friend of mine.'

'That puts a different complexion on things! I am most grateful.'

Catherine cocked her head. 'But it was my duty to inform the police. After all, you will need to solve the crime quickly, if you are to sail to Australia in four weeks' time.'

'Ah.' Morton looked crestfallen. 'Yes . . . I was going to tell you, of course.'

'Of course . . . I am surprised it did not burst out of you yesterday, when we met at the mortuary.'

'My apologies,' Morton said ruefully. 'Your presence drove every other thought out of my mind.'

'All else, except corpses and bronzes and battered heads,' Catherine admonished him. 'Sometimes I do not know why I put up with you!'

3

When Morton arrived at Old Jewry, next morning, he found Bragg grumpily scraping out the bowl of his pipe.

'You know, lad,' he said, 'the coroner is right about my plebeian prejudices. In Dorset, where I come from, it's people that matter. Power isn't important, because there is nobody to have power over. And, when you live on cabbage and potatoes, money isn't all that important either.'

Morton laughed. 'You forget, sir, that I have been privileged to visit Bere Regis. I have fond recollections of succulent roast pork, lamb chops, and the finest sirloin of beef I have ever tasted!'

'All right,' Bragg said crossly. 'But you know what I mean . . . I have no patience with the Newby lot. How old is that Frederick? Knocking on thirty! He lives at home with his "Mamma" and his "Papa", and holds out his hand for pocket-money . . . And for why? It isn't that he wants it that way. It isn't filial duty. I bet he hated his father . . . No, it's because, if he licks his father's arse, he will get the business. And, later on, he will put his son through the same; and so it will go on.'

Bragg jabbed a pipe cleaner into the stem of his pipe. 'I reckon I ought to turn this case over to you, lad. You might understand them.'

'I am sure,' Morton said evenly, 'that you are in no way prejudiced, and that your common-sense perceptions are what is needed in a case such as this.'

'But you are closer to that world; to being in the wings all your life, and hobbling on to the stage as an old man.'

Morton laughed ruefully. 'I could hardly put it more graphically,' he said. 'However, Frederick Newby is not wholly subservient. He has thrown off the shackles to the extent of becoming engaged. According to Miss Marsden, the event has been kept a secret from his parents. Nevertheless, the young lady in question flashes her diamond ring around society drawing-rooms.'

'Hmm . . . She sounds like a breath of fresh air.' Bragg stowed his pipe in his pocket and got to his feet. 'Come on, lad. We had better get off to the inquest.'

When they arrived at the coroner's court, they found the room already crowded. Catherine's report of the tragedy in the *Star* had evidently alerted the national press. Morton could see her at the centre of an animated group of men. No doubt she was cultivating obligations among her peers. The body of the court was occupied by City men, clad in frock coats and stiff collars. Their conversation was more muted; the murder was too close to home for comfort. Morton looked around. None of the Newby family seemed to be there.

The coroner's desk was on a high dais, with the City of London's coat of arms resplendent in scarlet and gold behind it. To the left, the coroner's clerk was swearing in the jury. On the right was the witness-box. Bragg and Morton squeezed themselves on to one end of a pew-like bench.

At precisely ten o'clock, the clerk rapped on his desk to call those present to order. The coroner billowed out of a side room and ascended the dais. He glared about him until the hum of conversation had died away, bowed to the court and sat down. He adjusted his wig, glanced at his papers, then nodded to his clerk.

The clerk jumped to his feet. 'In the matter of Rodger Newby deceased,' he announced, and sat down again.

'The court will take evidence of identity,' Sir Rufus pronounced.

An usher approached someone sitting at the middle of the front row. He stood and was led to the witness-box. It was Colley. The usher placed a bible in his hand, and he stumbled through the oath.

Sir Rufus leaned forward. 'Please give your name and address to the court,' he said curtly.

'Samuel Colley, sir; of twelve, Latimer Street, Stepney.' The clerk laboriously transcribed the answer into his book. It was not a particularly salubrious neighbourhood, Morton thought; though that was hardly a cause for suspicion in itself.

'Have you been shown the body of a man, by the mortuary attendants?'

'Yes, sir.' Colley's face was strained, his eyes blinking.

'And did you recognise the deceased?'

'Yes, sir.'

'Who was it?' the coroner asked testily.

'Mr Rodger Newby, my late employer.'

'Very good. You may stand down.'

Colley stumbled down the steps of the witness-box and found his way to his seat.

The coroner cleared his throat to still the murmur of conversation. 'I will now take evidence of discovery,' he proclaimed.

The usher went again to Colley, and guided him to the witness-box. There was an amused murmur from the benches, instantly quelled by the clerk's gavel.

Sir Rufus glared around him, then: 'Please give your name and address to the court,' he directed.

'Samuel Colley, of twelve, Latimer Street, Stepney.'

'Very well. Please relate to the court the circumstances in which you discovered the body of Mr Rodger Newby.'

Colley seemed to be stupefied. He was gripping the edge of the witness-box till his knuckles showed white. 'I . . .' he began. 'I had been to lunch . . . I came back at three o'clock, because – '

'There is no need to go into irrelevant detail,' Sir Rufus interrupted. 'What did you find when you returned?'

'I, er . . . The shop door was unlocked . . . which was as I expected.' The coroner glared at him, but restrained himself. 'I went into the shop . . . I remember one of the glass cases was open. I walked across and closed it. Then I went into the office, to hang my coat behind the door . . . And I saw Mr Rodger lying on the floor in front of the safe. I rushed across. He was all battered about the head . . . I felt for his heart, but he was dead. So I ran out into the street and called for the police.'

'Thank you, Mr Colley,' Sir Rufus interrupted. 'That is enough.'

The usher showed Colley once more to his place, and a hum of conversation arose. The clerk finished his record of the evidence and reached for his gavel. 'The court is adjourned *sine die*,' he proclaimed. 'Please stand.'

Sir Rufus rose to his feet, bowed to the court and stalked out.

'Quite a performance,' Bragg observed sourly. 'As good as Gilbert and Sullivan!'

'The law's due process must be observed,' Morton said. 'Or civilisation as we know it would collapse!'

'If you ask me, lad, there is not much to be said for civilisation as it is – at least, not for most of us.'

They waited in the rapidly emptying courtroom. Then the coroner appeared, divested of his wig and gown. 'Ah, Bragg,' he said. 'I trust that you are making progress. I will not keep the case adjourned for ever!'

'I understand, sir,' Bragg said submissively. 'Of course, we cannot go blundering about in our usual way. These people are quality; we have to respect their feelings.'

'Pah! When you begin to talk about showing respect, Bragg, I know you are floundering.'

'Not quite, sir. But the City is a bit special. Outsiders have to tread warily.'

'Nonsense, man! Justice is not partial. As my officer, you can demand aid and succour from the highest in the land.'

'Yes, sir . . . Do I gather that you are connected with the Vintners' Company?' Bragg said innocently.

'Indeed I am.'

'I see. Are your family in the trade, then?'

Sir Rufus glared at him. 'No, Bragg. I am a freeman by redemption.'

'Sounds like a religion!'

'Redemption is an antique term. It merely means that, not

being connected with the wine trade, I paid a sum on my admission.'

Bragg raised an eyebrow. 'I see . . . At any rate, you can tell us about these livery companies.'

'No doubt, though I do not regard myself as an authority. However, I have eaten a good number of livery dinners!'

'To say nothing of the wine, eh? The other day, sir, someone described the livery companies to us like this. He said that they are self-perpetuating relics of medieval trades, with no function in the modern world.'

'That sounds thoroughly subversive! However, in some cases – such as the Tallow Chandlers – the connection with modern industry has become somewhat tenuous.'

'Then, how is it that they still run London?'

'Not London, Bragg – the ancient City, the Square Mile only.'

'Even so, that hardly seems fair.'

'Fair?' Sir Rufus exclaimed. 'When has government had anything to do with fairness? You are talking like a socialist!'

'You have got to admit, sir, that there is a lot to be said for elections.'

'Oh, there are elections, if that is what troubles you.'

'That's funny. You see, I have lived in the City for more years than I care to remember. But no one has ever asked me to vote for the Lord Mayor . . . For a Member of Parliament, yes. But never for anybody connected with running the City.'

'Ah well, I suppose you deserve a modicum of enlightenment . . . In olden times, members of the trade guilds used to wear distinctive clothes, or liveries. Consequently they became known as livery companies. Now, every year the members of the livery companies assemble in Guildhall to elect two Sheriffs for the City of London, who will serve for the ensuing twelve months. At the same time, they nominate two candidates for the office of Lord Mayor.'

'Mrs Newby said as much. She said that George Pascoe was passed over, and her husband elected.'

'Do not interrupt, Bragg! I shall lose the thread of my argument . . . In fact, the actual decision on which of the two candidates became Lord Mayor lies with the Court of Aldermen. And the aldermen are elected by the ratepayers. So, you see, it is all thoroughly democratic.'

'Except that the big ratepayers are businessmen, and live in country mansions well away from the smoke and the stink.'

Sir Rufus snorted. 'Keep your puerile remarks for less pressing occasions, Bragg. The task I have laid on you is to determine the identity of Rodger Newby's killer. From the substance of your ramblings, it would appear that you have not the slightest idea of how to begin.'

'That would not be true, sir,' Bragg said quietly. 'The family have to be under suspicion, with so much money around. But other people could have a motive.'

'Such as?' the coroner demanded.

'Well, sir, would you kill to make sure you were made Lord Mayor?'

'I, Bragg? A bencher of one of the Inns of Court! The idea is ludicrous!'

'I expect it is,' Bragg said meekly. 'But what if you were the one of the two candidates that did not get endorsed by the Court of Aldermen?'

Sir Rufus gave him a penetrating gaze. 'Pascoe? You think he might have done it?'

'As I said, we are just feeling our way. Now, Mrs Newby told us her husband was the one passed over last year. She made it sound as if it was automatic that he got the nomination this year. But, looking back, it has not often worked that way.'

'Pascoe! . . . Well. I am bound to say that I was surprised to discover he was one of the candidates. I will admit that I did not vote for him – nor for Newby, either.'

Bragg looked at him straight-faced. 'So you don't look on this livery business as well-fed mumbo-jumbo?' he said.

'Good God, Bragg! I begin to feel that I should take you off this case! Your objectivity is seriously in doubt.'

'I would not accept that, sir,' Bragg said mildly. 'It's just that I do not like to start off with unwarranted assumptions.'

'Huh! Well, as to Pascoe, he is a sound man, of course. A working fishmonger, with a sizeable wholesaling business in Billingsgate Market. He was Prime Warden of the Fishmongers' Company a few years back. The salt of the earth, from what little I have seen of him.'

'You mean, not refined enough for people of quality?'

'Rubbish, Bragg! The City is not peopled with snobbish idlers, as you seem to think. It is the commercial heart of the world! Ability and acumen are what count; birth is nothing. You ought to find that comforting . . . There was no reason in the world why George Pascoe should not have achieved the office of Lord Mayor – except that a majority of the electorate preferred Newby.'

'So, what will happen now?'

Sir Rufus frowned. 'I confess that I do not know . . . and, being a lawyer, my instinct is to look for precedent. I assume that there must be another election. Though whether the livery, having already proposed the two candidates required by custom, can now propose a third, must be open to question . . . An interesting point, Bragg. Now, be off with you! I am appearing in court this afternoon. I, too, have a living to earn.'

Bragg and Morton took a hansom to Lower Thames Street. Billingsgate Market was built like a railway terminus, Morton thought, with its cast-iron pillars and glass arcades. They were directed to a small wooden cabin, half-way down one aisle. It bore a signboard proclaiming *Pascoe*. Marble slabs were marshalled around it, heaped with different kinds of fish. Wooden boxes were piled close by. Men with blue and white aprons were passing between the slabs, selecting fish to box.

'Where is George Pascoe?' Bragg asked of one of them.

The man jerked his head in the direction of the cabin, and went on with his work.

Bragg knocked on the door of the cabin and went in. It was barely large enough to hold a desk and chair. A heavily-built, grizzled man in his sixties was seated there, leafing through a bundle of papers. He had taken off his jacket; his shirt-sleeves were rolled up his muscular arms. He did not look up.

'Mr Pascoe?' Bragg said.

'Just a minute . . . I have to sort out the orders from this pile.'

Bragg shrugged his shoulders at Morton as the man went slowly through the papers, extracting some items, ignoring others. Finally he reached the bottom, gathered up the orders and got to his feet.

'I'll be with you just as soon as I've got rid of these,' he said. He went out of the cabin, passed the bundle of papers to one of the men, and came jauntily back.

'That's me finished for the day,' he remarked, resuming his seat. 'Mind you, I was out of bed at four!'

'City Police,' Bragg said, showing his warrant-card.

'Oh, yes?'

'Are you Mr George Pascoe?'

'Yes.'

'What is your address?'

'Thirty-two, Newcomen Street. Behind London Bridge station.'

'South of the river.'

'Yes.' Pascoe smiled. 'I can walk here in twenty minutes, at five o'clock in the morning . . . Now then, have you come about those boxes of halibut?'

'No, sir. It is about the death of Rodger Newby.'

Pascoe became grave. 'Ah, I see. A bad business, that.'

'You knew him, I gather.'

'Of course!' He looked up perplexed. 'He had just been elected as the next Lord Mayor. He was a very prominent man.'

'Yes. It was between you and him, we understand.'

'That's so. He missed out last year. It was only right that he should get it this year.'

'Hmm . . . It doesn't really work like that, though, does it?'

'Like what?'

'That the discarded candidate gets elected next year.'

Pascoe looked up cockily. 'I don't know. I'm a fishmonger not a historian.'

'But a very prosperous and influential fishmonger.'

'Maybe.'

'I gather that you have been Prime Warden of the Fishmongers' Company.'

He smiled with pride. 'That's right.'

'The top of your particular tree, unless you had got to be Lord Mayor.'

'Well, it would have been nice, but I've lost nothing by it. You don't sell more fish because you have the gold chain round your neck.'

'Whereas Newby might sell more silver?'

'Here! I'm as sorry as the next man about what happened to Rodger. We were good mates.'

'You were also rivals for that gold chain.'

Pascoe sighed as if to a backward child. 'Look,' he said, 'it's nice being in the Fishmongers'. That's where I belong. And I enjoyed my time as Prime Warden, though I was no great shakes at the speeches. But it didn't matter; I was among friends. I never should have agreed to put up for the Lord Mayor's job. But I was over-persuaded. I tell you, I was relieved when Rodger Newby got it. Entertaining toffs and royalty is more in his line.'

'So you will not be looking to step into his shoes?'

'What, as Lord Mayor you mean? No! I reckon they will start all over again. My hat won't be in the ring, I can tell you!'

'I see. Thank you for your time, sir. By the way, where were you around two o'clock last Monday afternoon?'

'When Rodger copped it, you mean?' He cocked his head on one side and narrowed his eyes. 'I remember! I took one of my wife's eel pies to a mate of mine. He has a stall in Whitechapel Market. Some damn stupid van driver took the corner too close, and knocked it all arse over tip. Hurt his leg bad.'

'And what is your friend's name?' Bragg asked, getting out his notebook.

'Going to check up on me?' Pascoe said chirpily. 'Right. It's Albert Smith of Stutfield Street, next to the Spotted Dog.'

Bragg elected to walk to Chancery Lane. Although a cab would have been considerably quicker, he seemed to need to purge his system of some irritant. He pounded along the pavements unspeaking, occasionally grunting to himself. But once over Fleet Street, he checked his pace.

'And what did you think of our friend Pascoe, lad?' he asked.

'I do not know enough about City politics to judge,' Morton said. 'If you start from the premise he proposed, that the Lord Mayor's function is to entertain royalty and visiting notables, his attitude seems entirely reasonable.'

47

'Except that, if he had believed that all along, he would never have put up. After all, the Prime Warden of the Fishmongers' is pretty high up the ladder. There must be more to him than he is letting on. So why not go right to the top?'

'The simple answer to that question is that not enough people voted for him.'

'And why did they not? Or, more importantly, why did he think they had not?'

'Who knows?'

'You are being thick, lad!' Bragg said irritably. 'It was easy enough for Pascoe to become the Prime Warden of the Fishmongers' Company . . . All right, I am not saying he didn't have to lobby his friends, and lick a few arses. But he was a working fishmonger, in a big way of business. In a sense, he represented what the Company was all about. But making the jump to Lord Mayor was a different matter.'

'Surely you mean a different kettle of fish?' Morton chaffed him.

Bragg ignored the sally. 'Pascoe as good as told us,' he went on. 'When it got to the stage where it was against Newby, he couldn't compete. However hard they pretend to be unbiased, Newcomen Street hardly has the same ring to the City fathers as Throgmorton Avenue.'

'But would that necessarily lead Pascoe to commit murder?'

'I don't know, lad. But you saw that long scratch on his arm? I reckon that was only a couple of days old . . . Ah, Parkin Cheesewright & Co., was it? Then, here we are.'

They climbed a steep flight of stairs, and were confronted by an enquiry room. A young woman in a crisp, white blouse was sticking stamps on a pile of envelopes. To her right was a telephone instrument.

'City Police,' Bragg grunted. 'I want to have a word with Mr Fummery.'

'Have you an appointment?' she asked with a smile.

'No.'

'You see, Mr Fummery is running late. He had to go to an inquest this morning.'

'So did we, miss. I want to talk to him while it is still fresh in his mind.'

'Is it about poor Mr Newby?'

'Yes.'

She drew in her breath. 'Ooh! I will tell him you are here.' She slipped from her stool and whisked out of the room.

Morton expected some approving remark about young women being an improvement on superannuated male clerks, but none was forthcoming. They waited several minutes, Bragg becoming increasingly restless, then the girl returned.

'If you will follow me,' she said brightly, 'Mr Fummery will see you now.'

She led them up a flight of stairs to the floor above, her slim ankles visible under the hem of her skirt. She ushered them into a room with a view over the rooftops. An amiable-looking man, with mutton-chop whiskers and a shock of white hair, rose to greet them.

'I believe that I saw you in the coroner's court, this morning,' he said genially.

'Sergeant Bragg and Constable Morton, City Police,' Bragg said. 'Mrs Elizabeth Newby told us that your firm are the family's solicitors.'

'Indeed we are. Please sit down, gentlemen . . . A most regrettable affair, as you no doubt agree.'

'We are trying to get the business into focus,' Bragg began. 'Now, can you tell us if the premises in Poultry and Bond Street are owned by the Newbys, or leased?'

'Most certainly leased.'

'Do you have a copy of the lease for the shop in Poultry?'

Fummery smiled. 'From long experience, I know that violent deaths lead to relentless inquisition,' he said. 'On hearing of the manner of Rodger's death, I had all the files brought to my room forthwith.' He picked a file from a bundle on his desk, and rapidly flicked through its contents.

'No,' he said. 'I have a note that the lease was prepared by the landlord's solicitor. My function was merely to check and approve it. I see that it has another three years to run.'

'And the Bond Street shop?'

Fummery turned a page. 'Ah, it comes up for renewal in six months. I must make a note about that.'

'We found the unburnt corner of a sheet of deed-paper, in the fireplace at the shop,' Bragg said. 'At least, Sir Rufus Stone said it was deed-paper.'

'I would not care to dispute the point with him,' Fummery said jovially.

'Could anyone gain from burning the leases?' Bragg asked.

'It is difficult to see how. Such an act would certainly not invalidate the contract subsisting between the parties. And I should add that, in each case, the landlord is a property company of substance and integrity.'

'Hmm . . . That's a blind alley, then . . . Suppose it was Newby's will?'

Fummery's eyes narrowed. He swivelled round and gazed out of the window for a time; then he swung back. 'After you went to see Mrs Newby, on the day of the tragedy . . . and I must say that she was appreciative of the considerate way in which you broke the sad news to her . . . she wrote to me expressing her desire that I should do everything in my power to assist the police.'

'That was good of her. What were the provisions of Newby's will?'

Fummery's brow furrowed. 'I must say that the resulting position regarding Rodger's will is not free from difficulty, because our client had given notice of his intention to change it.'

'What was the position up to that point?' Bragg asked.

'I should begin by saying that Mrs Rodger Newby was a Pendleton, of the wine-merchanting family.'

'We do know that, yes.'

'Well, she and her sister are the principal beneficiaries of a family trust set up by old Nathaniel Pendleton. Mrs Newby's income from the trust has been considerable, so Rodger did not feel it incumbent upon himself to provide for his widow by way of testamentary disposition.'

'So what was in the will?' Bragg asked, trying to curb his impatience.

'The entirety of the goldsmiths' business, both at Poultry and Bond Street, was left to Frederick as the elder son. Edgar was bequeathed securities, including a holding in the Consolidated Fund. A holding, I might say, of considerable value. The household effects were to go to Rodger's widow.'

'So, where is the difficulty?'

Fummery pursed his lips. 'Well, it is my duty to reveal to the

Probate Court that Rodger Newby intended to change his will. Indeed, gave me specific instructions in that regard.'

'Indeed? What was the new will going to be? Everything to some fancy piece?'

'Good heavens, no!' Fummery said in a shocked tone. 'Rodger Newby was a man of unblemished character.'

Bragg snorted. 'All right. Go on.'

Fummery considered for a time. 'I can see no point in obfuscation,' he said at length. 'You are bound to come at the truth in your investigations . . . The fact is that Edgar Newby has been a great disappointment to his parents. He has been employed, as you may know, by Pendleton Vintners, which is owned by the Pendleton trust. There have been difficulties over there, accusations of dishonesty.'

'Against Edgar, you mean?'

'Alas, yes. Rodger had reluctantly come to the view that his younger son was unfit to be the recipient of a large legacy. A week ago, he instructed me to prepare a new will . . . I endeavoured to dissuade him from such an extreme action; but Rodger was not to be swayed, once he had made up his mind.'

'Can you tell us the terms of the new will?' Bragg asked.

'In the circumstances, I feel it is my duty . . . Edgar's sole inheritance was to be an annual sum of five hundred pounds. Rodger intimated that the executors could easily purchase an annuity contract in that amount, so leaving the residuary estate unencumbered.'

'And what was to happen to the rest?'

'It was all to go to Frederick.'

Bragg whistled. 'That would hardly promote family harmony! So, what will happen now, if it is the will that has been burned?'

Fummery frowned. 'It is a matter of some complexity. I am of the view that counsel will have to be consulted . . . Had Rodger not indicated his firm intention to change his testamentary dispositions, the original will might well have stood. You see, the accidental destruction of a will would not invalidate it, provided that there was reliable evidence of its existence and its terms.'

'Such as your office copy.'

'Exactly. Equally, were a testator to die between giving

instructions for a new will and actually executing it, the former will would still stand – on the basis that the testator might have changed his mind.'

'Right. I understand that.'

'But if, before signing the second will, the testator deliberately destroyed the first, it would be taken as a firm indication that he intended it to be null and void.'

'I see. This is a tangle!'

'If it is accepted by the court that Rodger Newby himself destroyed the will, then he would be regarded as having died intestate, in the first instance. However, following the Lord St Leonard case, the whole subject is in a state of flux. In that case – and he was at one time Lord Chancellor, and head of the judiciary – no will could be found on his death.'

'He did not believe in them for himself, then?'

'Not at all, sergeant! His daughter, who was herself an eminent lawyer, insisted that her father had made a will. Indeed, she was able to give the court a most exact account of its provisions. Now, the point is this. Although no testamentary document could be produced, the court nevertheless gave effect to the daughter's recollection of the alleged will.'

'But she was a lawyer – one of them. She wasn't a shop-keeper,' Bragg said sardonically.

'Yet the precedent exists, you see. The frontier might be pushed back further, to embrace the situation in which I find myself.'

'Hmm . . . So, at worst, Edgar could find himself with what he would regard as a miserable five hundred a year, and a brother who was as rich as Croesus?'

'That is so.'

'It bears thinking on. And I don't suppose Rodger kept his intentions to himself . . . Now, what would happen if he were held to have died intestate?'

Fummery shrugged. 'Why, one-third of the estate would go to the widow, and the remainder would be divided equally between Frederick and Edgar – the last thing that Rodger would have wanted.'

*

'This is a rum case, lad,' Bragg said, putting his glass on the beer-stained table. They were snatching a quick lunch in a pub near St Paul's cathedral.

'I mean,' Bragg went on, 'what kind of person would wipe that bronze and put it back on the mantelpiece?'

'Do I deduce, from your use of the word "person", that you are not excluding the female gender?' Morton asked with a grin.

'Well, why not? It sounds more like a woman, to me.'

'An interesting hypothesis. But which woman? None that we have yet met, I'll be bound.'

'You cannot see his wife knocking him off his perch, then?'

Morton frowned. 'I must grant you that she would be resolute enough. She received the news of his death with admirable sang-froid.'

'Talk bloody English!' Bragg interrupted. 'If you mean she was as calm as the sphinx, say so.'

'An admirable simile, sir. However, there is so far not the slightest suggestion of a motive for murdering her husband.'

'There is always motive enough between married folk,' Bragg growled. 'I was barely married two years myself, but we had shouting matches enough! It doesn't take much to go too far.'

'You exaggerate, surely.'

'Well, maybe not in your lot. I expect the toffs can't raise their voices, because of the servants. But it doesn't stop them hating.'

'There is not the slightest evidence to support that theory,' Morton said. 'Anyway, Elizabeth Newby would hardly have made an appointment to see him at the shop.'

'Women can be devious, as you will discover,' Bragg said darkly. 'For my money, she had a motive.'

'Elizabeth Newby?' Morton exclaimed. 'Why on earth should she take against her husband?'

'For the usual reason . . . to protect her favourite child.'

Morton shrugged. 'You are far ahead of me,' he said.

'A woman is always fascinated by a touch of wickedness; it adds spice to life. You think of a wild child in a family; it will be that one the mother favours.'

'You mean Edgar?'

'According to Fummery, he is a bad lot. And Rodger Newby seems to have agreed with him. Let's assume that Rodger decides to change his will; tells his wife as much. So she comes down to the shop, to plead in private for her chick's birthright. And when Rodger won't give way, she clocks him with the statue.'

'That is amazing, sir,' Morton said admiringly. 'And you are able to deduce all this from the fact that the bronze was wiped and put back! Even Sherlock Holmes could never rise to such heights!'

'All right,' Bragg said crossly. 'How do you read it?'

'I would have to agree that Mrs Newby was remarkably self-possessed,' Morton said reflectively. 'However, that is probably her nature. I thought her sister seemed more relaxed, less remote.'

'Well, she would, wouldn't she? It was not her husband that had just been murdered.' Bragg took another gulp of his beer, and wiped his moustache on the back of his hand. 'To my mind, lad, this case is all about money; who has money, who hasn't money, who would like some more.'

'The two sons, then.'

'Well, it would be easy to go along that road. But, if you do, you are assuming they knew that their father was going to change his will.'

'Frederick would have gained by the change. He would be unlikely to murder his father at that point.'

'But suppose, for a minute, that nobody in the family knew about the new will. Where are we then?'

'We do not have enough information about Edgar to form a judgement. As for Frederick, we know that he was under pressure from his fiancée, and perhaps her family.'

'Yes . . . Well, I don't know how hot-blooded this lass is. But Frederick doesn't seem to have a lot of go in him. He had done as his father wanted all these years. He would have waited a bit longer, surely?'

'Even a dullard must have a breaking-point.'

'Maybe. But, for my money, Pascoe is the favourite, at the moment.'

Morton laughed. 'I must confess,' he said, 'that I had judged him as nothing more than an also-ran.'

'That's because you are a nob. Things don't matter to your

sort, like they do to real people. But, put yourself in Pascoe's shoes. He is an ordinary working Londoner. And by working, I mean up at four in the morning . . . He has built a prosperous business, he is an important man in the trade. And, as such, he gets the chance to join the Fishmongers' Company. A whole new world opens up to him. He goes to ceremonies and banquets, in lavish surroundings – he's even a bit special in their terms, too. Because most of them will be like Sir Rufus – have bought their way in. Whereas he is a real fishmonger, with the smell of Billingsgate on his clothes!'

'Do you really see that as significant?' Morton asked with a smile.

'Yes, I do. These redemption buggers are only playing at it. When Pascoe sets foot in that Fishmongers' Hall, he feels part of a tradition stretching back to the Middle Ages. It becomes important to him; he works at it, he wants to succeed. And he does succeed. He goes through the various offices, and eventually becomes Prime Warden – the top of the tree. And then somebody says: "Why not have a crack at Lord Mayor?" Well, why not? He has already gone much further than he dreamed was possible. So he has a go. He spends all his free time sucking up to people, canvassing support . . . And you have to, lad, make no mistake. I've looked through Newby's private diary. There was barely an afternoon, but what he had a meeting with somebody or other in the City . . . Anyway, all the arse-licking pays off. Pascoe is put up as one of the two candidates. Think how proud he must have felt! Him, a working fishmonger, no education to speak of, with a chance to be top of the greatest mercantile and financial centre in the world . . . It's only when he has lost, when it all comes crashing down, that he realises he never had a chance of winning; he was only put forward for election to keep the proletariat quiet.'

'Not money, then, but position,' Morton said thoughtfully. 'So, do you intend to arrest him?'

'Not yet, lad. We'll give him a bit more rope.' Bragg put a couple of coppers on the table. 'Let us go and see how our friend Colley is getting on,' he said.

*

The two detectives walked to Poultry, and were surprised to see the shutters removed at Newby's shop. Bragg pushed open the door, to find Colley absently polishing a silver tray.

'So you decided to open, then?' Bragg said brusquely.

Colley looked up defensively. 'Mr Frederick thought we should. He said the . . . happenings might bring in some casual trade.'

'Sounds cold-blooded to me.'

'Maybe. But the profit on some of these articles would pay my salary for a month.'

'Huh! Have you finished the stock check?'

'Almost . . . Oh, yes! I was forgetting. There was something else missing! A modern silver tankard.'

'I noticed you recovered your memory at the inquest,' Bragg said grimly. 'Was it because you were under oath? Are you not too sure how you will get on in the hereafter?'

'I, er . . . It had slipped my mind that the show-case was open,' Colley stammered. 'What with everything else.'

'Can you give us details of the tankard?' Morton intervened soothingly.

'Yes.' Colley went into the office and brought back the stock ledger. He opened it where a folded piece of paper protruded. 'It was a glass-bottomed, plain tankard, five inches high,' he said.

'Any distinctive style?'

'How would I know?' Colley asked in a hurt tone. 'We have a lot of them . . . I only knew it had gone, because of the stock number.'

'You will have to explain.'

Colley put the ledger on a table and beckoned to Morton. 'See . . . When stock comes in from the makers, we give each item a number, and enter it in the book. And we scratch the number on the bottom of the article, where it can't be seen.'

'I understand. And presumably you delete the number in the ledger, when a sale is made.'

'Exactly. When I had ticked off every item in stock, I still had one number unticked. So I knew it had been stolen.'

'Can you give us details of the hallmark?' Morton asked.

Colley referred back to his ledger. 'It was made in Birmingham, so it has the anchor mark,' he said. 'There will be the lion passant, for silver, and a letter S for eighteen ninety-two.'

'Any maker's mark?'

'It was made by James Walker.'

Bragg intervened. 'How come this great man in the Goldsmiths' Company buys his stock from Birmingham, instead of London?' he asked roughly.

'Well . . . tankards are what one might call industrial items. They make them there in quantity, just as they make china in Staffordshire.'

'While, in London, they are still in the Dark Ages, eh?'

'I would not agree there,' Colley said with some spirit. 'And as for the Goldsmiths' Company, it draws its members from the whole country.'

'I see, sir,' said Bragg, suddenly emollient. 'Now, we would like to know what is in the safe.'

'I told you. It is mostly old records.'

'Are the leases of the two, er, establishments in there?'

'I never saw them here. I expect they are kept by Erlanger's Bank.'

'I see . . . What about Rodger Newby's will?'

'Well, he was looking at it recently, when I went in. He said he was thinking of changing it.'

'Ah . . . Anything in it for you?'

Colley's face reddened. 'He told me I would get a little something.'

'Buying your loyalty, was he? How much were you worth?'

Colley passed his tongue nervously across his lips. 'It was two hundred pounds,' he said.

'That's a fortune! A couple of years' wages. Why would he promise you that? Had you some hold over him? Catch him with the shutters up and his trousers down?'

'No! Nothing like that!' Colley said irritably. 'He felt he could not rely on his sons. You have to realise that Mr Rodger had very clear views on how everything should be done. He valued continuity. He could not accept that the young want to change things.'

'You mean Frederick and Edgar?'

Colley hesitated. 'Well, Mr Frederick used to make suggestions for the Bond Street establishment. He said he wanted to take the buying into his own hands; that tastes were changing. But Mr Rodger would have none of it.'

'What about the other son, Edgar?'

'Oh, they have had nothing but trouble from him . . . I have heard . . .' Colley lowered his voice, 'that he gambles – on the horses! Mr Rodger said that he would have to take the two boys in hand.'

'Hmm . . . Maybe they got in first with the big stick! Right, then, find me his will.'

Colley looked shocked. 'I don't know that I should,' he said.

'Well, if you don't, we will turn out the whole bloody safe. Then you will have to put it all back, won't you? King George's letter and all!'

Reluctantly Colley turned and went into the office. He took a metal tray from the bottom shelf of the safe. He slid the contents on to the desk, and went through them.

'It's not here!' he cried in alarm. 'See! The envelope is empty.'

'What about the other envelopes?'

'They are insurance policies. It ought to be in this one.'

'Perhaps he had the will out, and put it back in the wrong envelope,' Bragg suggested.

'Yes, that must be it.' Feverishly Colley went through the other envelopes.

'No. It is not here!' he exclaimed. 'Now what will happen?'

Bragg and Morton hailed a cab. It took them beyond the City's eastern boundary, away from the wide streets and towering buildings, into an area of decaying brick tenements and rutted lanes. This was Jack the Ripper country. Within a stone's throw from here, four prostitutes had been killed and hideously mutilated. The maniac responsible was still at large.

They stopped the cab and got down. On the corner was a pawnbroker's shop, its three balls hanging drunkenly above the doorway. The window was so encrusted with dirt, it was impossible to see inside. Bragg burst through the door. The shop was empty. At the jangle of the bell, a head peered suspiciously from a curtained alcove behind the scarred counter.

A fringe of yellowish-white hair surrounded a bald head. The flaccid face was a mottled pink, threaded with purple veins converging on the nose. A pair of rheumy eyes peered at them suspiciously.

'Why, it's Sergeant Bragg!' he cried in a hoarse Scotch voice. 'I thought it must be the other lot.'

'Other lot, Jock? What other lot?'

'The Metropolitan Police.'

'Got some hot gossip for them, have you?'

'No, Mr Bragg, I've been done!'

'That must be a new experience for you, mate. What happened?'

Jock looked around furtively, and lowered his voice. 'Someone brought in a diamond necklace . . . It was a nice young woman, too. Very upper-crust sounding. She told me she was going to live in America, and had been left it by her mother. I took pity on her, I suppose. Anyway, I gave her seventy pounds for it.'

'Seventy pounds!' Bragg whistled. 'That's a small fortune!'

'I know,' Jock said plaintively. 'Of course, it was old-fashioned . . . I sold it on through the trade. It was only fit for being broken up, and the stones reset.'

'I bet,' Bragg said sarcastically. 'These old-fashioned diamond necklaces are not worth the keeping, are they?'

'But that's just it,' Jock said with a grimace. 'It turned out they weren't diamonds at all! They were paste!'

Bragg laughed. 'It's a change for you to be worsted, Jock! Good luck to her!'

'That's not very nice, Mr Bragg. My buyer was not very pleased – though he had looked at the article here, in the shop. He was taken in as much as I was.'

'Offer to go halves with him,' Bragg said jocularly. 'And get your windows cleaned! Now, then, have you handled any silver recently?'

Jock looked up with a pained expression. 'Now, you know the people in this area are not flush with family heirlooms,' he said.

'We are looking for a silver tankard – Birmingham, eighteen ninety-two. Made by James Walker.'

'Nothing special about that, sergeant.'

'So we are told, Jock. But the second piece is – a silver punch-bowl made by Paul de Lamerie.'

Jock blinked. 'Paul de Lamerie?' he said casually. 'Yes, I think I have heard of him.'

'If you are offered it, I want it,' Bragg growled. 'Get the person's name – their real name, mind – and pay whatever is asked . . . And if I ever find you've sold it on, I'll strangle you with my own hands.'

4

Bragg and Morton had barely got to their office, next morning, when the Commissioner wandered in.

'Ah, Bragg . . . I wondered how things were going on the Newby case,' he said diffidently.

'As well as I would expect, sir,' Bragg said. 'But it's early days yet.'

'Hmm . . . I had hoped that you would have a clear grasp of the thing by now . . . a suspect perhaps.'

Bragg tugged at his moustache thoughtfully. 'A suspect? Well, it could have been the person who burnt the will, or the person who stole the tankard – though they might be one and the same. It could have been the son who stood to inherit, or the son who would not. It could be Pascoe, whom Newby beat to the golden chain . . . and we have a few odds and sods who don't fit in anywhere at the moment.'

A pained expression crossed Sir William's face. 'I, er . . . you must realise, Bragg, that I am under considerable pressure to solve this case. The Common Council are wrestling with the problem of how to go about electing a replacement. But they have made it clear that they want this enquiry well out of the way by the time of the installation.'

'I see, sir. How long does that give us?'

'The ceremony will take place – must take place – on Friday the ninth of November.'

'A good three weeks, then?'

'Yes.'

'And the City fathers won't mind who it is, so long as we arrest somebody?'

The Commissioner flushed pink. 'Now, you know full well that is not the case!' he said irritably.

'What if they go and elect Pascoe, and he turns out to be the murderer?'

'God forbid! That would be a catastrophe!'

'Are you saying, sir, that we shouldn't look too hard in that direction?' Bragg asked innocently.

'By no means! The City Police have never been tainted by political jobbery, and they must remain so!'

'Thank you, sir. It is good to have someone firm and resolute at the head of the force.'

The Commissioner gave a half-smile. 'Thank you, Bragg . . . And you will keep me informed of progress?' He turned and marched out.

'Poor bugger,' Bragg remarked. 'He's a nice enough chap. I expect he was all right in the army, where you can do everything by numbers. But he's out of his depth here . . . What time is it, lad?'

'Twenty past nine.'

'Then let us go and see what kind of a cook Mrs Pascoe is, before her husband gets home.'

They took a cab over the river and into the tangle of streets behind London Bridge station. There was the usual pattern of bay-windowed houses occupied by the well-off, and meaner terraces where those who served them lived. But, to Morton's eye, the whole area was in decline. Compare Newcomen Street to Throgmorton Avenue, and there was substance in Bragg's gibe about Pascoe's being destined to lose the election. However unprejudiced City men might claim to be, it was not hard to believe that they would turn up their noses at a fishmonger from Newcomen Street.

Number thirty-two was better kept than the other houses around. There were bright curtains at the windows, the brass door furniture gleamed, the step and the pavement in front of it had been recently scrubbed. Mrs Pascoe answered their knock. She was a dowdy little woman in her late fifties. She looked at the two men apprehensively.

'Sergeant Bragg and Constable Morton, City Police,' Bragg said. 'May we come in?'

She hesitated, then led them into a sitting-room overlooking the street. The contrast with Elizabeth Newby's house could hardly be more marked, Morton thought. The walls were covered in dark floral paper; aspidistras adorned the corners, gilt-framed prints the walls. A circular table with a chenille cloth occupied the centre of the room, while the rest was taken up with a haphazard collection of chairs and sofas.

'It was your husband we really wanted to see,' Bragg remarked expansively.

'But he won't be home for an hour,' she said sharply.

'Ah, I see. Never mind . . . And are you looking forward to being the Lady Mayoress, ma'am?'

She twisted her mouth ruefully. 'To be honest with you, I was not sorry when George didn't get it. I would have done my best, of course, because he had set his heart on it. But my stomach goes funny at the thought of shaking hands with all those posh people!'

'Well, ma'am, you might still have to. Now that Rodger Newby is dead, your husband is the favourite. You will be Lady Pascoe in a month, I'll be bound!'

'If it's what he wants, sergeant . . .' She gave an excited smile. 'I am so proud of him!' she said. 'He can do anything he sets his mind to!'

'And he is proud of you, Mrs Pascoe. He was only telling us about your cooking. He said your friends can't praise your eel pies enough!'

She smiled modestly. 'Well, they are nice, though I suppose I shouldn't say as much . . . I put sherry and herbs in. And top it off with a puff pastry crust.'

'It sounds a real treat.'

'In the last one I made, I put in a whole glass of brandy instead! It was a bit special. I made it for one of George's friends. He'd got himself hurt, with a van overturning his stall.'

'Was that Jack Arnold, of Stepney?'

'No! Albert Smith. He has a stall in Whitechapel Market.'

*

Bragg and Morton took their leave of Mrs Pascoe, and walked over London Bridge to Crutched Friars. The premises of Pendleton Vintners, on the corner with Seething Lane, were not at all pretentious, Morton thought. When they pushed through the door, they found themselves in a small, dark office. There was linoleum on the floor, and the globe over the gas-light was thick with dust. On the right was a scarred oak counter; behind it, rough deal shelving on which wine bottles lay in pyramids. To the left was a large pedestal desk, littered with bundles of papers.

'Bang that bell, lad,' Bragg said. 'See if we can raise somebody . . . You know, this takes me back a good few years. My first job – after driving a cart for my father, that is – was in a shipping office in Weymouth. Not that they shipped fine wines, or anything like that. But there was the same look of organised clutter. To you and me that lot looks like a hopeless jumble, but I bet the clerk could lay his hands on any bit of paper you wanted.'

'Their efficiency seems to end well before the point of answering their bell,' Morton said.

'Ah, well. The retail side will be no more than a courtesy to the passing customer. They won't make their profits that way.'

The door in the back wall opened and a short harassed-looking man came in. He was wearing a dusty frock coat; his white collar had been scrubbed until the points were frayed. He eyed them warily.

'Yes, gentlemen? How can I help you?' he asked.

'City Police,' Bragg grunted. 'We are looking into the murder of Rodger Newby.'

'I thought as much,' he said peevishly.

'Were you expecting us?' Bragg asked.

'Not exactly. But when two midgets like you come in, well. . .'

Bragg took out his notebook. 'And, what might your name be, sir?' he asked.

'Ward . . . Thomas Ward.'

'What is your function here, Mr Ward?'

'What do you want to know? My official title, or what I actually do?'

Bragg smiled. 'Both, if you wouldn't mind.'

'Well, when I took the job it was supposed to be office manager. But if I didn't keep my eye on everything else, nothing would get done!'

'I see . . . Of course, the business passed to trustees when old Nathaniel died.'

'Yes. I suppose it sounded, in his head, as if it would work; a lawyer and a businessman as trustees.'

'To say nothing of the parson, to pray for you all!'

'But, in fact, nobody is properly in charge.'

'Do you ship wines yourselves?' Morton asked.

Ward raised an eyebrow. 'You've got a posh accent,' he said. 'You could almost pass for a gentleman . . . No, we buy from a good shipper, though. It means we don't need to have a fortune tied up in stock. His warehouse is just down by the Custom House.'

'But you have a warehouse of your own, surely,' Bragg said. 'You haven't got room to swing a cat here.'

'We keep some stock at the back. You would be surprised at the number of people who still take the odd case home with them, in a cab. But, yes, we do have a small warehouse, in French Horn Yard.'

'And Edgar Newby runs that, we gather.'

Ward bridled. 'He does no such thing! If he does anything, it is on the selling side.'

Bragg smiled. 'I have worked in family concerns myself,' he said sympathetically. 'It's not easy.'

'Well . . . you daren't say much, because it's you that would get the sack.'

'But certain things have gone wrong, I gather.'

'It's not for me to say . . . But I do know this; nothing was ever really done about it.'

Bragg nodded sympathetically. 'What is the record system here?' he asked.

Ward sighed irritably. 'Do you really want to know?' he asked. 'I can't see it has much to do with Mr Rodger's death.'

'Please, sir. We never know what will help and what will not.'

Ward crossed to his desk and picked up a handwritten letter.

'Here is an order from a man in Belgrave Square,' he said. 'It is for four cases of Château Margaux eighty-nine.'

'For laying down, no doubt,' Morton remarked.

'I expect so. It is a first-growth claret.'

'Indeed. And a good year.'

Ward looked at him quizzically. 'Yes . . . Anyway, what happens is that we prepare an invoice for the customer. If we are delivering the wine, instead of the customer taking it himself, we make a copy of the invoice and send it over to French Horn Yard.'

'They write out the despatch note for the carrier there, I suppose,' Bragg said.

'That's right. And they make two copies of it. One stays with the cellarman, and the other comes here. Once I get that, I know the delivery has gone and I can send my invoice.'

'Hmm . . . Seems foolproof,' Bragg remarked. 'Is Edgar Newby in?'

'If he is, it will be at the warehouse,' Ward said. 'I have as little to do with him as I can manage.'

Bragg and Morton walked the hundred yards to French Horn Yard. The original Tudor inn had been torn down a hundred years ago. On the frontage, now, was a large brick building, occupied by a company of household removers and storers. A *porte-cochère* led from the street to an area at the rear. In the olden days the coaches would have rattled through an archway to discharge their passengers here, feed and stable their horses. Now the coach-houses and stables had been swept away; in their place stood a range of workshops and warehouses. Above the door of one of them was a sign, *Pendleton Vintners*. Bragg led the way inside. It was a strongly built structure, lit only from the roof. It would not be easy to steal anything bulky or weighty from here, Morton thought. Along the walls were stacks of wooden wine-cases. Others formed islands about the floor. He strolled towards one end of the warehouse. Here were case upon case of great clarets – Lafite, Margaux, Haut-Brion. On the opposite wall were fine burgundies. The stock in this warehouse alone must be worth a small fortune.

Now Bragg was bellowing for attention. In answer, a young man appeared from an office half-hidden by wine-cases. He sauntered towards them, a supercilious smile on his lips.

'Mr Edgar Newby?' Bragg asked courteously.

'Yes.'

'We are City Police officers . . . Sergeant Bragg and Constable Morton.'

'Of course you are.' The tone was almost mocking. 'Mother told me of your visit. I wondered how long it would be, before you came here. I began to feel quite slighted, that you should have seen my brother two days ago, and not yet called on me . . . But, of course, he is the elder.'

'Does that rankle, sir?' Bragg asked.

'No. Why should it? I am not cut out for pomp and circumstance.' He strongly resembled Frederick. But he was slighter in build, with a thinner face and a petulant, sneering mouth.

'We are, as you know, investigating the death of your father,' Bragg said evenly.

'His murder, you mean.'

'If you like, sir . . . I confess that we are a bit stumped, at the moment. It looks as if someone came into the shop, while your father was in the office. This person saw his chance. Here was priceless silver all round him, and nobody there to stop him. We reckon he opened one of the cabinets, started to fill his bag – we know that two pieces are missing – when your father came out into the shop.'

'But his body was found in the office,' Newby objected.

'True enough. But it could have been dragged there. You see, with this kind of attack there is usually blood at the scene – a pool of it . . . Not this time, though. Considering the way your father had been battered, there was very little blood.'

Newby was unperturbed. 'Poor Father,' he said sneeringly. 'And Jesus Christ was worth thirty pieces of silver.'

Bragg was taken aback at the callous irreverence. 'Do I take it that you and your father did not get on?' he asked.

Newby shrugged. 'By his lights, I suppose he tried to be honourable and just. But he was trapped in mid-century. He was the paterfamilias of his own youth. He expected everyone to bend to his will. And, of course, poor old Frederick had to . . . Do you know, he has had to keep his engagement to Nancy Osborne secret! If my father had found out, he would have cut my brother out of his will.'

'Then you would have got the lot.'

Edgar snorted. 'I doubt it. But the possibility must surely remove me from the area of suspicion.'

'Have we cause to be suspicious of you, sir?' Bragg asked quietly.

'None in the world! But I am sure it would be a convenient hypothesis for you. The wranglings between my father and me are well known.'

'We have caught the odd remark, yes.'

'Then, you will have realised that my sin consisted in being beyond his power. Fate decreed that, as the younger son, my future lay with this business, not my father's. Not even he could disregard my grandfather's will.'

'But I thought he was one of the trustees,' Bragg said.

'That is true. But the probity of Fummery, and the sanctity of Canon Wilkes, meant that he could not have his way.'

'I see . . . And where were you exactly, between one o'clock and three, last Monday?'

Edgar gave a sardonic smile. 'You must understand, sergeant, that Pendletons' trade relies heavily on sales to institutions like the Inns of Court, livery companies, gentlemen's clubs and the like. In the past, we have had a secure connection. But this is now being eroded, particularly by West End wine merchants. It is an important part of my function to socialise with the officers of these institutions. On Monday lunch-time I was doing precisely that.'

'I see, sir. Well, I think we ought to have it on the file. For the sake of completeness.'

'Of course, sergeant. I was with Edward Palliser, the owner of the Moulin Rouge club.'

'Where is that, sir?'

'In Windmill Street, of course . . . Soho.'

'And who else was there?'

'Oh, we did not lunch in the club. There would be nothing doing at that time of day. No, we met in a pub in Covent Garden, over a pork pie . . . The Three Pigeons, I think it was. We talked for an hour or so, from a quarter to two. Then I came back here.'

'I see, sir,' Bragg said sourly. 'And this Edward Palliser will no doubt confirm your story.'

Edgar gave a supercilious smile. 'Oh, yes, sergeant,' he said. 'I am certain that he will.'

After lunch Bragg and Morton strolled over to the shop in Poultry. They stood while Colley wrapped a silver card-tray and respectfully presented it to the customer. When he had ushered him out, he turned to the policemen.

'I thought I had seen the last of you,' he said plaintively.

Bragg smiled. 'Oh, no! You won't get rid of us till we have caught the murderer . . . And was Frederick right?'

Colley frowned. 'I don't follow . . .'

'He said there would be a rush to buy here, after the murder. Sounds ghoulish to me. But people are peculiar, aren't they?'

'Well, we have been busier, yes.'

'Hmm . . . Have you finished the stock-taking?'

'Yes. And there was nothing else missing.'

'Right. So we are looking for a silver tankard, and this Malpas punch-bowl . . . Now, Rodger Newby told you he wanted to show it to Frederick. Did he say why?'

'No. But he seemed very intrigued by it.'

'Do you think he did show it to his son?'

Colley pursed his lips. 'I doubt it,' he said. 'Mr Frederick has not been here, to my knowledge, since Mr Malpas brought it in. And I know the bowl has been here all the time.'

'So there is a Mr Malpas, is there?' Bragg remarked.

Colley looked surprised. 'Of course there is!'

'The way you talked I thought it must be a national treasure. Who is this Malpas?'

'A country landowner from Suffolk.'

'Do you have an address for him?'

Colley went into the office and returned with the repairs book. He flipped over the pages. 'Mr Henry Malpas,' he said, 'of Great Melford Hall . . . I believe it is near Sudbury. I do hope – '

The street door opened, and a tall, bronzed man strode into the shop. He smiled familiarly at Colley. 'Is my brother in?' he asked, making for the office.

'No, Sir John!'

He swung round at the sharpness of Colley's tone. 'Ah, perhaps he is at Bond Street . . .'

Colley looked across at Bragg.

'We are police officers,' Bragg said. 'We are here because Mr Rodger Newby was murdered, on Monday.'

The man looked incredulous. 'Murdered? But why? By whom?'

Bragg disregarded the questions. 'Would you be his elder brother, sir?' he asked.

'Indeed I am!' He looked very like Rodger would have been in life, Morton thought; with the same beaky nose and high forehead.

'I thought you were in India, sir,' Bragg said.

'So I was, or in transit from there. I arrived at Southampton on the *Clan Macnab*, early this morning.' His voice was strong but pleasant, his accent very much of the ruling class. 'Poor Elizabeth!' he exclaimed. 'How is she taking it?'

'Very well, so far as I can see.'

'Yes . . . a remarkable woman, inspector.'

'Sergeant . . . Sergeant Bragg. This is Constable Morton.'

'A sergeant?' he exclaimed. 'Forgive me, but I expected someone considerably more senior. I am not inexperienced in these matters myself, having been a magistrate in Calcutta for a good deal of my working life. But no doubt things are different in London.'

'No doubt at all, sir,' Bragg said gruffly.

'Ah. I see I have got off on the wrong foot,' he said with a wry smile. 'I am sorry. Nevertheless, I do offer my services. Please feel free to call on me.'

'Thank you, sir.'

'Have you any suspects?'

'Some silver is missing. We think a cracksman saw the shop was empty. He slipped inside, then realised that your brother was in the office. So he went in, killed Rodger, then looked through the stock at his leisure.'

'And when did this occur?'

'Between one and three o'clock in the afternoon.'

'I see.' He turned to Colley. 'And where were you?' he asked. 'I wager that my brother did not give you a two-hour lunch break!'

'He made me stay away for that time, Sir John.'

'Curious! Ah, well, sergeant, it is your case – though it is also my concern. I must go to Elizabeth and give her my support . . . Who is running the business, Colley?'

'Well, sir,' Colley said deferentially, 'I suppose it is Mr Frederick. So far, he has left this end to me.'

'Yes, yes, of course . . .' He turned to Bragg. 'I am staying at the Royal Hotel. Do you know it?'

'The new one, by Blackfriars Bridge.'

'Excellent! If you need me, I shall be at your service.' He turned and strode out.

When Bragg and Morton got back to Old Jewry, the desk sergeant greeted them with a broad grin.

'A young woman in your room, Joe! Wouldn't take no for an answer. Wait all night, she would. Not been getting her into trouble, have you?'

'At my age? I'm not quick enough to pat my landlady's bum! Who is it?'

'Nothing to get excited about, Joe – at least, not for you.' He glanced speculatively at Morton. 'It's that newspaper reporter, Miss Marsden. I knew you wouldn't mind.'

Morton sprinted up the stairs, with Bragg trailing behind. 'Miss Marsden! This is an unexpected pleasure,' he said with a smile.

'Thank you, James! However, it is to Sergeant Bragg's chivalry that I must appeal.'

'Chivalry?' Bragg said cautiously.

'I need to be extricated from the clutches of an ogre, in the shape of my editor, Mr Tranter.'

'Then leave the *City Press* and we can all live happily ever after,' Bragg said drily.

'Give in to improper pressure? Never!'

Bragg hung up his overcoat, then crossed to his desk. 'What pressure are you talking about?' he asked.

Catherine seated herself gracefully on a chair by Bragg's desk. 'As you know,' she said, 'I was able to get a piece about the Newby murder in the *Star*, on Tuesday morning. A veritable scoop! At that point Mr Tranter, the editor, seemed pleased. I did a somewhat less lurid account for Wednesday's *City Press*, which he accepted without question. He seemed quite exhilarated, to have something sensational that we could legitimately concern ourselves with. He even agreed that I might do some research into the family, for a follow-up article after the memorial service. I was delighted, as you can imagine. Then, this morning, it all changed.'

'In what way, miss?'

'Just after eleven o'clock, I was summoned to the presence. Now, Mr Tranter is by nature a charming, inoffensive man; and above all, a rational man.'

'Which means that you can usually get your way in an argument!' Morton said with a grin.

She frowned, then ignored him. 'This morning he was almost uncouth. He did not even invite me to take a chair!'

'No more did I, miss,' Bragg said. 'Yet here you are, sitting at my desk anyway.'

'But Mr Tranter is my superior, not a friend . . . In brief, he told me that my article in yesterday's edition had excited a hostile reaction in certain influential quarters. He was very defensive. In the end, he agreed that I might write a piece for Saturday's edition; but it must confine itself to the repercussions of Rodger Newby's death on the Lord Mayoralty.'

'On who will be chosen in his stead?' Morton asked.

'Nothing so interesting! He believes that the present situation has never occurred before. He set me to look for a precedent.'

'And has it?' Bragg asked.

'I can half answer your question! I have gone backwards through the records for three centuries. In all that time, a similar situation has not arisen.'

'But why should the possibility cause him concern?' Morton asked. 'It could hardly impinge on the value of Newby's murder as current news.'

'It is not that,' Bragg said. 'If you ask me, the City fathers don't want anyone talking about the murder. They just want to forget it. And do you know why? They reckon Pascoe did it! To have one candidate for Lord Mayor murdered, and the other strung up for doing it, would set them back a thousand years.

What price the fur-trimmed gowns, the golden chains and knee-breeches then? Who would believe they are harmless old fogeys whose word is their bond?'

Catherine sighed. 'So, what ought I to do?' she said.

'Why ask us?'

'It was just that I thought you might have some information for me, which would change the situation.'

'No, miss. At the moment, it's just one big mess. All I can tell you is that two items of silver, a tankard and a punch-bowl, were missing from the shop. Not that it takes us a lot further. A silver salver went missing in April, but nobody was murdered over that . . . But, I'll tell you what. Since Constable Morton is going to play pat-ball in Australia, regardless of whether this case is finished or not, I'll give you a strand of your own to unravel, if you like.'

'What is that?' Catherine asked cautiously.

'Well, a man called Malpas brought in the punch-bowl for Newby to value. He was the experts' expert on silver, we gather. Now, Colley said that Newby was very intrigued with this bowl. On the face of it, that's not surprising, because it was made by a man called Paul de Lamerie.'

'In the rococo period.'

'You know about these things too, do you, miss?'

Catherine tossed her head. 'A little,' she said.

'Yes . . . I suppose you would. Anyway, he told Colley to look through recent auctioneers' catalogues, to see what de Lamerie pieces had been sold.'

'Presumably to establish current prices.'

'I expect so, miss. Now, I would like you to do that for me, if you will.'

'It seems a less than exhilarating occupation,' Catherine protested. 'However, I can scarcely refuse you . . . I will ask Stanley Rainham to help me. He is the silver expert at Phillips, Son & Neale, in Bond Street. I am sure he would be fascinated.' She glanced across, and caught the mulish look on Morton's face. 'But I cannot see how it will reveal who murdered Rodger Newby.'

'Well, if it doesn't, it will have kept you out of mischief . . . Talking of which, we had Newby's brother come bursting in on us, at the shop.'

'He had only one brother,' Catherine said sharply. 'I am sure that he is in the Indian Civil Service.'

'That's true, miss. Just got off the boat, this morning. Walked into the shop expecting to see his brother.'

'Poor man!'

'Sir John Newby, he said he was.'

'That is the man. He and Rodger were twins. It is rather interesting, really. From the particulars in *Who's Who*, they were treated very differently. John was sent to school at Eton; Rodger was a day-boy at the City of London School. John was groomed for a glittering career administering the empire; Rodger was consigned to life as a shopkeeper.'

'It seems hardly fair,' Bragg said. 'Anyway, John did well, if they gave him a knighthood.'

Catherine gave a knowing smile. 'As to his career, I cannot comment. But the title was inherited from his father, Sir Thomas Newby. It is a baronetcy.' She glanced at Morton, then rose to her feet. 'My impression is that you feel I should bow to my editor's wishes. Very well, I will do so. But I shall expect to be told of any developments!' She swept confidently out of the room.

Bragg tapped out his pipe in the ashtray. 'You are going to lose that young woman, if you don't stop buggering about,' he said gruffly. 'She's not going to wait for ever. You would look bloody silly, if you got back from Australia to find she'd got wed.'

'Would you have me throw away my freedom?' Morton said lightly. 'Surely, it is only necessity that drives a man to marriage?'

'Don't talk bloody nonsense! Being married makes you feel good about yourself. You are part of the natural scheme of things, not just an onlooker. For the couple of years before my wife died, I felt like a king! All right, I was only a police constable, living in a married quarter. But it was something I had worked for. It was a little world we had made together. Maybe I should have realised she wasn't as excited about it as me. Perhaps, on balance, she would have been happier in a county force, living in the country – especially with a child on the way. But I tell you, lad, when she died I lost more than a wife and son. I lost my own self-respect too, my own special place in the world. Ever since, I've been on the fringe of things; looking from the outside, on other people living the sort of life that should have been mine. I wouldn't want you to throw away your chance.'

Morton gazed out of the window. 'At the end of the opium case,' he said quietly, 'a bare seven months ago, I did ask Miss Marsden to be my wife. It was at an inopportune moment. She was overwrought from the death of her friend, and she mistook my motives. She thought that my proposal arose out of a desire to protect her, rather than from deep affection. So she declined to marry me . . . Yes, I still hold her in the highest regard. But I, too, have my pride. Were she to refuse me again, that would be the end of the matter. So, you see, I must be certain of my ground next time . . . After all,' he added flippantly, 'a plodding police constable should think twice, before aspiring to the hand of a society beauty who has touched hands with the Queen!'

Bragg snorted contemptuously. 'Well, I suppose you know your own kind best,' he said. 'Now, since you are likely to be a baronet one day, you might be able to talk sense about that.'

'You refer to Sir John Newby?'

'Well, not him in particular. Tell me when they were started, what's so special about them.'

'Goodness! Well, we must go back to the Middle Ages, when the king and his barons held great estates; when political and military power were synonymous. Below those hereditary nobles were the knights, who were the cavalry of the day. They were often landless, and attached themselves to the noble houses.'

'So the knights were not barons?'

'Precisely. And, as each knight had to personally prove his valour before being dubbed, his title was not hereditary.'

'So, where do the baronets come in?'

'Essentially, they were invented. King James the First needed money for a settlement scheme in Ireland. So he revived an ancient title. He sold a baronetcy to any gentleman who would pay him a sum of slightly less than four hundred pounds.'

'Huh! But it would be a lot of money, in those days.'

'True – though I gather that one could pay by instalments! However, the great attraction was that the title was hereditary.

Unlike a knighthood, once you had made the investment, the head of the family would henceforth be entitled "Sir".'

'The title would go to the eldest son?'

'Yes.'

'It sounds a bit disreputable,' Bragg said sourly.

'Perhaps. But I gather that the king had no difficulty in raising his money. So snobbery is not a phenomenon of our times only.'

'I see . . . And is that where your family's title comes from?'

'Indeed no! One of my ancestors distinguished himself at the battle of Blenheim, under the Duke of Marlborough.'

'So it was earned, was it?'

'We like to think so.'

5

A bitter wind was blowing from the east, when Bragg and Morton reached the Manor Park cemetery. They were glad to shelter by a clipped yew tree. A gardener was brushing up leaves that had fallen on the avenue leading to the chapel. Rodger Newby might not have died in his bed, but everything still had to be tidied up for his funeral. When he had collected a small pile of leaves the man would hastily stuff them into a sack, lest they were scattered again by the wind.

'What time is it, lad?' Bragg asked, his hands deep in the pockets of his overcoat.

Morton pulled out his gold half-hunter. 'Five minutes to eleven,' he said.

'God! I hope they are on time, or we shall freeze to death . . . I wonder who will come.'

'Family only, I would think. The hierarchy of the City will save itself for the memorial service, on Wednesday.'

'Well, make a note of those who do come.'

Morton laughed. 'This is your theory that murderers go to their victims' funerals, is it? I honestly cannot remember an instance where it actually happened!'

'It did happen once – when you were in your cradle.'

'That hardly forms the basis for a rule! We could be safe in the Metropolitan fug now, instead of courting influenza.'

'Your generation is too soft, lad . . . Hello! Here they come.'

Morton looked towards the Gothic stone archway. A glass-sided hearse, drawn by four black horses with nodding black plumes, was coming slowly through the central arch. Behind it were four carriages, again drawn by black horses. As the last carriage cleared the gate, the cortège came to a halt. From the back carriage, four mutes emerged. They were clad from head to foot in black. Across the breast of their black overcoats, black crape was swathed. Their top-hats were hung with it. Each carried a staff in his hand, heavily draped in black. They walked with grave solemnity to the head of the cortège, forming two pairs. Then they began a measured walk, the carriages following after. They were still a hundred yards from the chapel when they halted. From the third carriage four undertaker's men emerged. They approached the hearse with heads bent. One of them opened the glass door at the rear, and the coffin was taken on their shoulders. The mourners got down from the other two carriages and formed a group behind. Morton noticed that Alice Harvey had joined the widow and her two sons. There was a couple, arm in arm, that he did not recognise. The woman was in her late thirties, the man somewhat older. Colley had obviously been allowed to close his establishment; for he too was there, head gravely bowed. But the man who dominated the little group was Sir John Newby; offering Elizabeth his arm; doffing his hat and seeing that the other men did likewise; setting a stately pace as the coffin was borne into the chapel.

Bragg and Morton crept into the back pew. There was no choir; no anthems to waft Newby's soul through the golden gates. A white-haired cleric was mumbling his way through the service. The mourners huddled at the front, as if seeking solace. The gleaming black coffin rested on trestles before the altar. It alone asserted the importance of the deceased in this world, and his determination to count in the next. It was a shoddy send-off, Bragg thought. It was almost as if the City was turning its back on him; did not want to be associated with anyone who had been so inconsiderate as to get himself murdered.

The undertaker's men moved quietly up the aisle, to take up the coffin. Bragg nudged Morton.

'Come on, lad,' he muttered. 'I think we have seen enough.'

After lunch Bragg and Morton went to Chancery Lane again. They climbed the stairs to the offices of Parkin Cheesewright & Co. and, after a parley with the young woman in charge of the telephone instrument, they were shown into Fummery's office.

'You didn't go to the funeral, then,' Bragg greeted him.

'Goodness, no! If we attended the obsequies of every client who died, we would never make any money!'

'But you could charge for your time, surely?'

Fummery laughed. 'You are coming close to counselling malfeasance, at the very least, sergeant!'

'You didn't tell us, the other day, that you are a trustee for Nathaniel Pendleton's settlement,' Bragg said reproachfully.

'You did not ask me!'

'All the same, it might have paid you to tell us. After all, one of the trustees has been murdered. Who knows but you might be next?'

Fummery gave a guffaw of laughter. 'You are letting your invention outrun your judgement, sergeant,' he said.

'But what would happen if you were put out of the way – to the Pendleton trust, I mean?'

Fummery's brow furrowed. 'I would have to look at the trust deed – which I must now do anyway! In general terms, however, I can tell you that there will be a clause empowering the appointment of additional or substitute trustees, as events dictate.'

'And is that a power to be used by the trustees?'

'Yes.'

'Suppose all the trustees have been knocked off before you get around to it?'

Fummery cocked his head. 'Why, an approach to the Chancery Court would be necessary, so that new trustees could be appointed.' He smiled. 'That institution is a splendid generator of fees for the legal profession, as Mr Dickens has so felicitously pointed out!'

'Can you give us any information about Nathaniel's will?' Bragg asked.

'I see nothing to prevent it . . . You must understand that Pendleton Vinters is an old-established concern. It goes back almost as far as Newbys. So it was a great disappointment to Nathaniel, that his wife failed to present him with a son. They persevered, goodness knows, even to the lengths of taking the waters at Vichy. But it was all to no avail. They had to settle for two daughters.'

'When did Nathaniel die?' Bragg asked.

'Not until ten years ago. The Pendletons are a long-lived breed.'

'Except that they are now dying out!'

'Indeed. Where was I? Oh, yes; there were no sons to carry on the firm. Now, Nathaniel was very old-fashioned in some ways. He would not entertain the notion that his daughters might be capable of conducting the business satisfactorily. I urged on him my view that either of them was sufficiently able. But he said that, even if he conceded the point, he could not leave his major asset to one only. Moreover, he was convinced that it would be folly to leave it to them jointly, since they could never agree on anything.'

'Is that why he put the business in a trust?'

'Indeed, sergeant. In one sense it was a satisfactory solution. The only man he had ever wholly approved of and trusted, was married to one of his daughters.'

'Rodger Newby?'

'Yes. So he named him as trustee, together with me and my successors. And he added Canon Wilkes and his successors to complete a triumvirate, in case of serious disagreements between us.'

'And you regard that as satisfactory, do you, sir?'

Fummery wrinkled his nose. 'Is such a situation ever satisfactory, I wonder? I have to say that I strongly counselled against it. But Nathaniel had made up his mind, and that perforce was that.'

'In fact, he was relying on Rodger Newby to run the business.'

'You could say that. Although he indicated that Edgar Newby should be brought into it, in due course.'

'Well, Rodger was the only businessman among the three of you . . . The funny thing is that, when we went down to Pendletons, yesterday, it looked as if no one was running it. The office manager, Ward, does his best, but there is no feeling of purpose about the place. And it's not because Rodger has been killed; to me it has been drifting for years.'

Fummery sighed. 'I would not seriously take issue with you. All I can say is that Rodger was aware of it.'

'Then, why did he let it go on?'

'Human affairs are never simple, sergeant. Even to a man like Rodger, there were other imperatives than making money.'

'You wouldn't think it, if Frederick is any yardstick. He even had the shop in Poultry open, the day after the murder. He thought there might be casual purchasers, because people would want to see where it had happened. The bugger of it is, he was right!'

Fummery smiled. 'And yet, I have to say that the ambivalence in Rodger's attitude does not wholly surprise me. After all, the Newby goldsmiths' business has been handed down from father to son for centuries. It has become almost a sacred trust. Rodger could never feel the same about Pendleton Vintners.'

'But you are a trustee, sir. How do you feel about it?'

'I? Well, I would not presume to give a businessman's view of it.'

'But you must know more about it than most . . . What would happen to Elizabeth Newby and Alice Harvey, if it went under?'

Fummery swivelled round in his chair, and gazed out of the window for a space. Then he swung back. 'I can only say that they would be grievously affected. The vintners' business is the only substantial asset of the trust. Its profits are the source of the annuities which are paid to the two ladies. Mrs Newby could reasonably look to her family for support; but as for Mrs Harvey, I suspect that she would be destitute.'

Bragg frowned. 'Then, I don't understand how the trustees let things get as bad as this,' he said. 'Why didn't you do something about it?'

'It would never have been as easy as you appear to think,' Fummery said defensively. 'In the olden days, I gather, wine merchants could rely on keeping their customers, generation after generation. They could buy the same wines, confident that demand for them would be maintained. They invested large sums in fine vintages, certain that in due course they would sell them at a handsome profit. In truth, the prerequisite for a thriving business was not wide experience and a discriminating palate. What you needed was an established connection among the wealthy merchants and landed families. The business would then run itself.'

'Are you saying that has changed?'

'Is changing, certainly . . . Some people put it down to the influence of the Prince of Wales.'

'Everything bad is put down to him,' Bragg said gruffly.

Fummery laughed. 'Mostly without foundation, I am sure. However, fashions are changing in all kinds of ways, there is no doubt about that. And, for the first time, there is beginning to be a fashion in wine-drinking. It is no longer enough to do as your father did. You have to keep up with the trends, particularly among London society. I fear that Pendletons did not realise it, before some of its connection had been eroded.'

Bragg mused for a space, then: 'Are you saying that Rodger Newby did not have his wits about him?' he asked. 'After all, he was the only businessman among the trustees.'

Fummery hesitated. 'Rather, I think, that he was torn between taking control personally, and giving his son time to prove himself.'

'Edgar?'

Fummery nodded.

'And how did you and Canon Wilkes feel about that? You could always have outvoted him. That was what you were there for.'

'The matter never emerged as explicitly as I have expressed it,' Fummery said defensively. 'I only became aware of this apparent conflict in Rodger's mind, in the last few months.'

'And what did you do about it?'

'I mentioned my concern to him. He said that he would take steps to assuage my anxieties. So I left it at that.'

'And now he has been murdered.'

'Yes, sergeant. Though I would be reluctant to believe that the two are in any way connected.'

Back outside, Morton waved down a hansom and directed the driver to take them to Bond Street. For a time there was silence between them, as the cab trotted through the light afternoon traffic. Then Bragg roused himself. 'So, what did you think of our friend Fummery?' he asked.

'I began to feel that he should change his name to Flummery,' Morton said with a smile. 'He was exceedingly uncomfortable, towards the end of the interview.'

'Yes . . . You see it often enough. These professional trustees are only there for the fees. As long as they have a meeting a month to charge for, they don't care what is decided at them.'

'Until things begin to go wrong.'

'He didn't put any flesh on this notion of Edgar being a wrong 'un.'

'No. But there was hardly an obligation on him to do so. He is a servant of the law, after all!'

'Huh! I reckon old Fummery only started to bother, when he could see the business going down the drain . . . I think, tomorrow, we might poke about at Pendletons. With your background, you should be able to tell whether there is anything in Fummery's notion of a fashion in what people drink nowadays.'

Morton hesitated. 'Tomorrow is Saturday, sir,' he said.

'I know that, lad.'

'I am afraid that there is a meeting, at Lord's, of all those involved in the Australian tour. I must be there.'

'God Almighty!' Bragg exclaimed. 'It's bad enough, you being off for three months! What is this meeting for?'

'I do not know. It may be that there will be a discussion of the strengths and weaknesses of our probable opponents. After all, some members of our side have not toured Australia before.'

'But you have. Why need you be there?'

'They are trying to weld a team together – some members will have travelled from as far away as Lancashire . . . The Commissioner has given me express permission to take off whatever time is called for.'

'Buggeration! It's a fine state of things, when catching murderers has to take second place to knocking a little red ball about!'

The cab came to a halt in Bond Street, outside Newby's shop. Bragg clambered down and flung open the door. The shop was devoid of customers. The grey-haired assistant was polishing the glass door of a display cabinet. He looked up with alarm. 'Oh, it's you!' he exclaimed.

'That's right. Is Frederick Newby in?' Bragg snapped.

'No. He has gone to his father's funeral.'

'Of course.' Bragg paused, then: 'Where did he go on the afternoon of Monday the fifteenth?' he asked.

'The day Mr Rodger was . . .'

'That's right.'

A hunted look spread over the man's face. 'He went out at noon . . . He said he was taking some pearls back to Lady Brassingham. They had been brought in for repair.'

'And where does she live?'

'In Berkeley Square.'

'That's only spitting distance! What time did he get back?'

The man looked away. 'That's just it,' he said uncomfortably. 'He never came back that day.'

Next morning, Bragg went to the office early. He determined he would gather his fragmented jottings into some order; get the Newby case into focus. He put the name of each suspect at the top of a separate piece of paper, then began to list beneath it the facts that had been established in relation to each. Frederick had been away from the Bond Street shop, Edgar had allegedly been with a crony in the West End. That could hardly count for much as an alibi – indeed, he had almost been challenging them to disprove it . . . Then there was Colley. He had claimed that he came back from lunch to find Rodger Newby dead. But what if that was all invention? What if they had quarrelled . . . and they would never do that unless the shop was empty. Suppose Colley had demanded a rise, and Newby refused out of hand. Colley could easily have followed him into the office . . . argued perhaps. A contemptuous refusal and bang! The statue was nice and handy. Colley saw it every day; might have thought it would be a useful weapon against a burglar. He might even wipe it after . . .

Blast it! The trouble was, he had got too used to having Morton around. And not only to toss ideas to and fro. Morton had got insights into the nobs that he could never have; could see inside their heads, at times . . . Not that he had come up with any flashes of inspiration in this case; but you never knew. That was what made their partnership special. Two people with totally different backgrounds and experience; not even sharing the same assumptions of what people might do in a situation . . . And he was going to be in Australia for three months, playing cricket!

Disgruntled, Bragg took a cab to Bond Street. This time Frederick was in. Bragg went through to the office.

'Good morning, sir,' he said cheerfully. 'Did everything go well yesterday?'

Frederick looked at him resentfully. 'Since you were so inconsiderate as to go to the cemetery, you must know that it did,' he said icily.

Bragg sat down on the chair opposite him. 'Not many people there,' he remarked. 'But next Wednesday will be the time for public show, I expect. When is the memorial service?'

'At three o'clock, in St Lawrence's.'

'Just across from the Guildhall?'

'Yes.'

'Then there will be a good turn-out of City folk; should be worth seeing . . . I can't think when a Lord Mayor was last murdered.'

'My father was not Lord Mayor,' Frederick said irritably.

'But as good as . . . Anyway, I came in to see if you could clear up one or two points.'

'What is it that you wish to ask?'

Bragg leaned back in his chair. 'There is a little thing that has been nagging at me. People are always talking about goldsmiths. It's painted over the shop in Poultry; the livery company is the Goldsmiths'. Yet the shop sells mainly silver, from the looks of it.'

'It is merely historical,' Frederick said in a flat voice. 'A goldsmith has always been understood to mean a worker in gold and silver.'

'I see – and a seller of both, nowadays.'

'Yes.'

'Good . . . Now, your father was an expert on silver. And he got very excited about the Malpas bowl. What was that about?'

'The Malpas bowl? I have never heard of it!'

Bragg gazed at him in disbelief. 'Nobody would think you

lived in the same house,' he said roughly. 'Did you never speak to each other?'

'Of course we did! We were very close. And, as is evident from the fact that I have run this establishment for almost nine years, I enjoyed his complete confidence.'

'Hmm . . . Well, it appears that a man called Malpas brought a silver punch-bowl into the City shop. He left it so that your father could value it.'

'I cannot think that such a happening would be worthy of mention.'

'Ah, but that is where you are wrong. You see, this punch-bowl had been made by Paul de Lamerie.'

Frederick raised his eyebrows. 'I see. That would certainly have been a matter of interest to me.'

'It seems your father got quite excited about it. "Intrigued" was Colley's word. He said he wanted to show it to you.'

'And when was this?'

'A week, to the day, before he was murdered.'

'Well, all I can say, sergeant, is that my father made no mention of it. He did, after all, have other, more important matters on his mind.'

'Yes . . . The interesting thing is that, after the murder, the Malpas bowl was missing.'

Frederick frowned. 'Colley has said nothing to me about this. Strange . . . We did have a telephonic conversation on Tuesday morning – but, in view of the circumstances, I imagine it slipped his mind.'

'No doubt . . . Now, I understand that you are engaged to marry a young lady named Nancy Osborne.'

A flicker of alarm crossed Newby's face. 'That is correct,' he said in a dead tone.

'Did your parents approve of the match?'

'Of course! She is eminently suitable.'

Bragg gazed at him. 'That is not the way we have heard it,' he said.

'Then what you have heard is wrong!'

'We are told that your father would not countenance your marrying, until you reached thirty.'

'Utter rubbish! I have had no inclination to marry, until recently.'

'I see, sir,' Bragg said amiably. 'Now, what can you tell me about the silver salver that was stolen from the shop in Poultry, at the end of April?'

'I know that it was stolen, and that we recovered its cost under our insurance policy.'

'You didn't flog it yourself, to make a bit of pocket-money, then?'

A contemptuous smile crossed Frederick's face. 'No, sergeant, I did not.'

'Right.' Bragg got to his feet. 'Now, sir, if you can find a quiet corner for me, I want to go through the business books.'

'Whatever for?'

'Just routine. If they had been two separate businesses, I don't suppose we would have bothered. But the coroner is a stickler for procedure. Comes from being a lawyer, I expect.'

'I see . . . But I have to go out. It will not be convenient at the moment.'

'Don't you worry, sir,' Bragg said amiably. 'I expect I can find my way around them. If I get lost, I expect your assistant will be able to set me right.'

Frederick hesitated, frowning. 'Very well,' he said. 'What is it that you wish to examine?'

'Why, the stock book, the sales ledger, the cash book . . . That should be enough.'

'Are you sure you do not want the petty cash book also?' Frederick said disagreeably. 'You would have everything then.'

'If you feel it would be helpful, sir . . . Would you object if I were to smoke my pipe in here? It helps me to concentrate, you know. Looking at business records is not the easiest of jobs, when you are not trained to it.'

'If you must.'

Frederick went to a massive safe in the corner and unlocked it. As he swung the heavy door open, Bragg could see that it contained several shelves, arranged relatively close together. On them were stacked cardboard boxes with labels on their end. He had expected to see the shimmer of pearls in profusion, the soft gleam of gold bangles, the glitter of diamond tiaras. It was not much different from a shoe shop! But this was the business side of social pretension. The jewellery which would signal the status of the wearer – perhaps render a plain girl marriageable – was here no more than a commodity. From the bottom shelf Frederick took several account books, and brought them over to his desk.

'All the transactions for the past seven years are there,' he said curtly. 'If you wish to go back further, I shall have to get the earlier ledgers from home.'

'Goodness me, no, sir!' Bragg said expansively. 'I am not interested in ancient history. These will do me very well.' He sat at the desk and pulled out his tobacco pouch. 'Is there anything in there that you think I should know about?' he asked.

Frederick looked at him woodenly. 'No. Nothing at all.'

'Right. Then you can leave me to get on with it, and go about your business.'

Frederick hesitated, then turned on his heel and strode out.

When Bragg had got his pipe going well, he glanced through the books. The system was exactly the same as that employed at the City branch. That being so, the stock book ought to point to the answer. It was clear that Frederick was working for a pittance – pocket-money that would no more than cover the incidental costs of socialising. So, where had the engagement ring come from? It hadn't been borrowed from stock, to be popped back after the ball was over. Yet there was no way that Frederick could have paid for it. Some fiddle then – a fiddle that would not be discovered at a glance . . . The supplier of the ring must have been paid. And if not by Frederick, then it must be the business. Which meant that it must have gone through the business books.

Bragg leafed through the stock book till he came to the section devoted to rings. The engagement had taken place in September, so he need not consider any entry after that. According to Miss Marsden, the ring was a brilliant-cut solitaire diamond set in platinum . . . If only Newbys had followed their practice with silver plate, and scratched the stock book reference on the inside of their rings, it would have been easy. Miss Marsden might have been persuaded to ask if she might examine it; have made a note of the reference number. Bragg chuckled to himself at the picture of her producing a lens from her handbag, and scrutinising her friend's engagement ring as if she thought it might be glass! No, she would never have agreed to that . . .

But, by the look of things, it would not have been necessary anyway. He was already back as far as June, and there had been only one sale of a ring matching that description. That was on Friday the twenty-fourth of August. The cost was shown as one hundred and sixty pounds. A profit margin of twenty-five per cent would be normal in this class of business. But where had Frederick got the two hundred pounds from? Bragg looked down the cash book entries for August the twenty-fourth. The two hundred pounds was in the takings for that day; had presumably been duly banked. So Frederick had found the cash from somewhere.

Bragg knocked out his pipe in the waste-paper basket, then turned back to the sales ledger. August the twenty-fourth had been a busy day. Perhaps socialites had been buying presents for acquaintances, to mark the end of the Season . . . A silver cigarette case at fifteen pounds; a diamond pendant at sixty pounds, discounted to fifty . . . Discounted? Since when did Bond Street jewellers need to discount their wares? Bragg went slowly through the day's entries . . . Another discount! A silver tray reduced from a hundred and ninety to a hundred and forty pounds. That would have more than wiped out the profit on the sale. It looked as if Frederick was milking the takings from these items, to cover the cost of the engagement ring. Bearing in mind Rodger's reputation, it was thoroughly reckless! Yet on these two items alone, he had covered sixty pounds of the ring's cost. So where was the balance?

Bragg began to compare the cash recieved for every item sold that day, with the stock book and the sales ledger. After half an hour he was beginning to doubt his theory. He had gone through the rings and pendants, the bracelets and brooches; no further discounts had appeared. His theory had broken down. He had been barking up the wrong tree after all . . . Then he found it! It was either breath-taking audacity or desperation. A large silver-gilt epergne, which was in the stock book at a cost of £3200, had been sold for a mere £3860. The normal sale price would have been four thousand pounds. A massive reduction! But together these three discounts totalled two hundred pounds. Bragg would stake his pension that the articles had all been sold at the full price, and the records manipulated so that Frederick's theft of the ring would be concealed. It was a foolhardy act. It might deceive an auditor, but Rodger Newby would have seen through it at a glance.

Bragg had lunch in a pub, then took a cab to Blackfriars Bridge. He crossed the embankment to the Royal Hotel, and went to the porter's desk.

'Police,' he said. 'Sir John Newby is staying here, I understand.'

The porter looked at him mistrustfully. 'And who told you that?' he asked gruffly.

'He did.'

'I see. All right, he is.'

'Do you know if he is in?' Bragg asked.

'It's not my job to watch when people go in and out,' he said defiantly.

'It's important.'

The man shrugged and turned away.

Bragg lunged across, grabbed him by the collar and hauled him backwards on to the counter. 'If you want to be in clink for obstructing the police,' he snarled, 'you are going the right way about it.'

'Let go! You are choking me,' the porter gasped.

'Is he in?'

The man's face was puce. 'See if the key's there . . . Three three seven.'

Bragg released his grip and went behind the counter. 'Why, there's no key here,' he said genially. 'I expect he's at home! Thank you for your help, sir.'

He turned and made for the hydraulic lift. To him this was the most useful of modern inventions. Electric light was right enough, but you could read just as well by gaslight. And as for horseless carriages, you might as well walk! But the lift . . . all that effort, climbing flight after flight of stairs . . . He smiled contentedly as the attendant pushed the polished brass handle that sent them soaring upwards.

In answer to his knock, there came footsteps within; the door opened and Sir John Newby looked at him quizzically.

'City Police. Sergeant Bragg.'

'Ah, sergeant. Do come in! I am sorry if I appeared not to

recognise you. In truth, I have seen so many unfamiliar faces in the last few days. Please forgive me.' He ushered Bragg into a spacious sitting-room. To the right of the door was a pile of baggage, bearing labels printed *SS Clan Macnab*.

'I am sorry to trouble you, sir,' Bragg said. 'But I am loath to bother the family, at this time. And I am sure you can tell me all I want to know.'

'Of course! Take off your overcoat, and sit by the fire. I can tell you, I feel the cold myself, after India.'

Bragg stretched his hands towards the flames. 'I am trying to get a picture of your brother's background,' he said. 'I don't like investigating a case in a vacuum.'

Sir John nodded. 'Of course; very commendable,' he said. 'I will, naturally, do all in my power to assist you. As I think I said, I have spent the whole of my career in the administration of justice.'

'If I am honest,' Bragg said earnestly, 'I am a bit out of my depth. My education finished when I was nine. And most of the time, we are dealing with footpaddings, and men knocking their wives about. I need all the help I can get.'

'It will be both my duty and my pleasure, sergeant.'

'Usually, I would want to ask you if your brother had any enemies,' Bragg said. 'But I doubt if you would know.'

Sir John smiled tolerantly. 'I am not aware of any, but your surmise is correct.'

'Very good. Now, I gather from Mr Frederick Newby that your family have always been well up – in society, I mean. After all, you are a baronet.'

'That, at least, is indisputable!'

'Your father was Sir Thomas Newby. How far back in the family do the baronets go?'

'The Newbys have been members of the Order since its inception,' Sir John said proudly.

'I see. And you inherited the title as the eldest son.'

'Indeed, sergeant.'

'And your son will inherit it from you.'

A cloud crossed Sir John's face. 'Alas no. My son died as he was born . . . I lost my wife also.'

'I am sorry to hear that,' Bragg said in a concerned voice. 'The very same happened to me . . . Did you remarry?'

'No.'

'Or me. Life can be hard . . . Tell me,' he asked, with a change of tone. 'Was anyone in your family Lord Mayor in the past?'

'No, sergeant.'

'So your brother Rodger would have been the first.'

Sir John smiled indulgently. 'That seems to follow,' he said.

'But the Newbys would have been influential in the Goldsmiths' Company. After all, you have been trading in the City since seventeen twenty-five.'

'That is certainly true. Indeed, my father was at one time Prime Warden of the Goldsmiths, as was Rodger.'

'Is the Prime Warden the top man?'

'Yes . . . yes, he is.'

'But your father never wanted to be Lord Mayor?'

'So far as I am aware, no.'

'I see . . . And have you always kept in touch with things?'

'Yes, sergeant. I am, after all, head of the family. In fact, I was home on furlough two years ago.'

'I am sure Mrs Newby is very glad to have you here. When do you go back?'

'Go back? No, sergeant, you misunderstand! I have now retired from the Indian Civil Service. It was my intention to find a house by the sea, at Eastbourne; to spend some time on my hobbies. But, in view of the present situation, I begin to feel I should take lodgings, here in the City. It is clearly my duty to give my sister-in-law all the support I can.'

'That is very generous of you, sir . . . You know, I envy you your life. That sounds presumptuous, and I don't mean it to. But I always longed to see India – all the elephants and palaces.'

Sir John laughed. 'There is a good deal more to India than that! I spent most of my time in Calcutta – a teeming, somewhat squalid city.' He stood up. 'I have some photographs in one of these trunks, though I'm dashed if I can remember which. I managed to get a box-camera sent out from England. I spent every moment of my final leave, touring the great monuments – places like Fatehpur, Agra, Jaipur. So now, when I get homesick for India, I shall be able to take out my photographs and relive it all.'

Bragg got to his feet. 'I would very much like to see them, sir,' he said. 'If you ever find them!'

The next day being Sunday, Bragg slept late. He was awakened by the insistent chirping of sparrows on the gutter above his window. He looked at his watch. Ten o'clock; half the day gone! Mrs Jenks should have wakened him before now, he thought. He put on his threadbare dressing-gown and went down to the basement kitchen, for some hot water.

Once washed and shaved, he felt more like his usual self. Not that it was much help. There was no point in feeling alert, if all your mind did was pick over the same old heap of facts. After breakfast he went out into the garden. He cleared away the dead vegetable plants, and dug over the patch. He ought to have enjoyed it, he told himself. He was a countryman, after all. His soul ought to have been calmed at the sight of the crumbling brown soil. But no. All he could think about was Rodger Newby, and the people who had been involved with him.

Once lunch was over, he got into his Sunday suit, and set off to St Olave's church. It was almost next to the police station, in Old Jewry. He was on nodding terms with the vicar. He told himself he was stupid, wasting his day off when he could have popped in any time. But he felt he had to do something to give the case a push.

He walked past the Mansion House – which should have been Rodger Newby's official residence for the coming year. In its classical grandeur, it seemed totally aloof from the machinations of the people who looked on it as their ultimate goal. Bragg crossed a deserted Poultry, and turned into Old Jewry.

The vicarage was behind St Olave's church. He rang the bell and stood gazing at the churchyard, which had not seen a burial since the Great Plague, three hundred years ago. He heard the door open behind him, and turned.

'Good afternoon, Canon Wilkes,' he said, doffing his hat.

'Ah, I believe I know you. Are you not one of the City Police?'

'Yes, sir. Sergeant Bragg. Sorry to disturb you, but I hoped I might have a word with you.'

'Come in, sergeant. Sunday may be your day of rest, but it is certainly not mine!'

He led the way to a study at the back of the house. 'I am sure the sun must be well over the yardarm,' he said genially. 'May I offer you a sherry? Or would you prefer whisky?'

'Neither, thank you, sir . . . I have come about the Newby murder.'

'Ah.' The vicar seated himself by the window, his white fluffy hair forming a halo round his pink face. 'I shall, of course, be happy to assist you,' he said. 'Though he was not a parishioner of mine.'

'No. But I understand that you were made a trustee, with him, of the Pendleton settlement.'

'That is true.'

'I went to see the servant of the law, on Friday, and didn't get very far. So I have come to the servant of the truth.'

Wilkes smiled broadly. 'Religious truth is often more elusive than fact, sergeant,' he said.

'I don't think religion has much to do with this case, sir . . . Mr Fummery gave me the impression that, as a trustee, he was prepared to let Rodger Newby make all the running. Would you say the same of yourself, sir?'

Wilkes considered for a moment. 'I suppose that must be true. He was, after all, a businessman. Moreover, he was married to one of the beneficiaries of the trust. Neither Fummery nor I ever had the slightest doubt of his probity.'

'Of course not, sir . . . Did you know Nathaniel Pendleton well?'

'Yes, very well. Although he did not live in this parish, his family had once owned a house where the insurance office now is. Ancestors of his are buried in the graveyard, apparently. So he had a historical attachment to St Olave's.'

'Can you tell me why you consented to become a trustee?'

Canon Wilkes frowned. 'I honestly cannot say . . . We were on warm personal terms; he explained the difficulty the trust was created to overcome . . . It seemed a Christian thing to do, I suppose. I made it clear to Nathaniel that I was blessedly ignorant of business and the law. But he seemed to think this an advantage.'

'So, what was your role to be?' Bragg asked quietly.

'To be an honourable outsider, I suppose. Perhaps to dampen any excess of ambition or zeal on the part of my co-trustees . . . perhaps to see that Rodger dealt even-handedly with both of the beneficiaries. I cannot really say. But Nathaniel seemed considerably relieved, when I consented.'

'Right. When was the trust set up, sir?'

'Let me see . . . Nathaniel died in 'eighty-four . . . and it was after his first seizure. That was only slight, but he said it was time to put his affairs in order. Yes . . . I would say that he set up the trust in eighteen eighty-two.'

'Twelve years ago.'

'Yes.'

'And did the trustees meet regularly?'

Wilkes gave a puckish smile. 'We did not meet at all, until well after his death. There were no assets in the settlement, until his will had been proved. Once the vintners' business had been transferred to the trust, we had one or two meetings to decide the policy to be adopted. After that, we would meet annually, so that the auditor could explain the figures to us.'

'And how were the funds to be applied?'

'It was simple enough. Once provision had been made to meet the future needs of the vintners' business, the surplus was to be divided equally between his two daughters. On the death of either of them, their share was to be distributed equally among his grandchildren.'

'His daughters are Elizabeth Newby and Alice Harvey.'

'That is so.'

'Am I right in thinking that the Harveys do not have any children, sir?'

'You are. And, indeed, Mr Harvey himself died some years ago.'

'Hmm . . . So, when Alice dies, it will all end up with the Newbys. No wonder she is so concerned she gets her proper share.'

'Is she? I had no idea.'

Bragg paused for a moment, then: 'Mr Fummery told us about the trouble with Edgar Newby,' he said.

Wilkes gave a relieved smile. 'I am so glad,' he said. 'It would have been more difficult for me – such a betrayal of Christian charity.'

'Yes . . . I wonder why he went off the rails.'

'I have pondered the matter, sergeant; agonised over it, indeed. The other boy, I gather, is dutiful and obedient. Why Edgar should be so wilful, I cannot imagine . . . Of course, he has got into bad company. I understand that he has become involved with a fast set – people who have far more money than he will ever have. I fear that they go in for gambling on horse races, cards and so on.'

'And how did Rodger take this?' Bragg asked.

'Why, very badly. He felt that it reflected on himself; that his own standing might suffer.'

'And Rodger let him stay on at Pendletons, in the hope that he would improve. Was that it?'

Wilkes hesitated. 'I think the latest episode overcame even Rodger's restraint. When I last saw him, a fortnight ago, he was adamant that he would turn him out of doors.'

6

'What makes people kill, in your class, lad?' Bragg asked, as they strolled along Lothbury. The wind had shifted round to the south, the sky was cloudless. Were it not for the yellowing leaves on the plane trees, it could have been a spring morning.

'In my class?'

'Yes, the nobs. People who aren't short of a crust.'

Morton laughed. 'Much the same as in any other part of society, I expect.'

'But I don't see that,' Bragg said musingly. 'Apart from their social code, which I imagine discourages knocking off their own kind, they have so much more to lose.'

'Those in possession have, I agree. Equally, those kept out of possession – or simply waiting around to succeed – may have much to gain from giving nature a helping hand.'

'All right, so we have greed. What else?'

Morton thought for a moment. 'I suppose that amongst the nobs, as you call them, there are relatively few deaths from unreasoning violence. The social situation, of large houses crammed with family and servants, discourages a brutal response to a problem. There must be few murders done under pressure of immediate events.'

'That's nothing to boast about, if you are saying that nobs only commit premeditated murders.'

'Am I saying that? I suppose I am.'

'So what, in their eyes, would justify murder?' Bragg asked.

'I imagine greed must romp home first, followed by jealousy and a sense of injustice. All horses out of the same stable. Then there must be revenge as an also-ran, once the race has been decided.'

'Yes . . . in a situation where somebody can't get what they want under the law.'

'Or by custom, such as inheritance,' Morton added.

'Or election . . . It's interesting that the City fathers are getting into such a muck-sweat about Pascoe.'

Morton laughed. 'You have a crystal ball that no one else possesses!' he said.

'No, lad. They are lumbered with their own history. The way Lord Mayors are elected has been settled for centuries. If they altered that pattern, they would be signalling to the world that Pascoe was not fit to hold the office – as good as telling us that he was Newby's murderer. On the other hand, if they endorse the aldermen's decision, that Pascoe was worthy equally with Newby, they might end up with a murderer as Lord Mayor.'

'Or, what would be even worse, an installed Lord Mayor being arrested for murder,' Morton added.

'Yes. But he is the only suspect we have, outside the family.'

'Except for Colley, Malpas and a postulated unknown robber.'

'Yes. I have a mind to go and see Malpas, this afternoon . . . But, as for Colley, I don't see him knocking Newby off his perch. And, if he had, I doubt if he is brazen enough to keep coming back to the shop, day after day, as if nothing had happened . . . We have not heard anything from Foxy Jock, either. If it was a burglar, he didn't get rid of the loot in the London area, that's for sure.'

'In a way,' Morton said, 'I was surprised that it was a tankard that was missing.'

'Why?'

'It was an article of low value. Someone who was perspicacious enough to take the Malpas bowl, would surely have taken a second article of high value?'

'Of course, it might have gone some time back,' Bragg said musingly. 'It might be of a piece with the salver that was supposedly stolen in April . . . You know, I reckon if Newby had spent more time in his shop, and less in currying favour with City folk, he wouldn't be in his box now . . . Ah! Here we are, Emile Erlanger & Co. You take the lead here, lad. After all, you could almost pass for a gentleman!'

They went into the banking hall, and Morton strode up to the counter.

'I wish to see the manager,' he announced.

The young frock-coated assistant looked up obsequiously. 'I am sure that will be possible,' he murmured. 'Are you a customer, sir?'

'Not yet.'

'I see . . . Very good, sir. What name shall I say?'

'Morton, James Morton.'

A look of incredulous delight spread over the man's face. 'You mean Jim Morton, the cricketer? Good heavens! I saw your century at the Oval, last May. It was sheer artistry! And in so short a time.'

Bragg cleared his throat sourly, and the man's smile faded. 'Yes,' he said. 'If you will wait here a moment.' He hurried away.

Soon they were being ushered into the opulent office of the manager. He waved them to deep armchairs by his desk. 'And what can I do for you, Mr Morton?' he asked with great geniality.

Morton smiled. 'Nothing, sir,' he said. 'But you could well be of assistance to Constable Morton of the City Police.'

A shadow crossed the manager's face. 'Ah, yes . . . I see,' he said doubtfully.

'We are investigating the murder of Rodger Newby. From certain papers in his safe, we understand that he was a client of Erlanger's.'

The manager pursed his lips. 'It would appear pointless to deny it,' he said.

'We gather that you hold a deed box on his behalf.'

The manager opened a drawer in his desk and took out a

small ledger. He opened it and ran his finger down the pages, then stopped. 'Yes, that is indeed so,' he said.

'Good. We believe that certain papers which are material to the case – which may, indeed, have been connected with his murder – are in that box. Consequently we wish to explore that possibility.'

'I see,' the manager said dubiously. 'Of course, we are always anxious to assist the police – especially in such a dreadful and, if I may so describe it, sensational case. But there is a well-defined procedure . . . We ought to have a court order.'

'I quite understand that, sir,' Morton interrupted with a smile. 'But it is a ponderous proceeding. And we are under considerable pressure from the City authorities. As someone of your experience will appreciate, the murder of the Lord Mayor-elect is creating unprecedented problems in many areas. Not least is conjecture about the perpetrator of the crime. It would greatly compound their problems, if Newby's substitute were found to have been . . . shall we say, unsuitable.'

'Hmm . . .' The manager rubbed his nose in perplexity. 'I see . . . Yes, I quite understand. Yet, I am at a loss as to how I can help you.'

'We do not wish to take any documents away. But, if we could examine the contents of the deed box, we could satisfy ourselves in a certain area. I need hardly say that, if production of the documents were deemed necessary, then formal proceedings would be instituted. In that event, you would be, at least, forewarned.'

The manager pondered, frowning. Then he leaned forward and pressed an electric bell on his desk. 'If I am to be caught between Scylla and Charybdis,' he said, 'I would at least prefer to be under full sail.'

A youth appeared in the doorway. 'Yes, sir?' he said.

'Please bring me deposit box number one seven three five,' he said. He leaned back in his chair and gazed at the elaborate plaster cornice. After a short time the young man returned, bearing a steel deed box. He placed it in front of the manager, smiled ingratiatingly and went out.

The manager pushed the box over to Morton, got to his feet and went to stare out of the window. Bragg took Newby's bunch of keys out of his pocket, and began to try them in the lock. Then he gave a grunt of satisfaction. There was a click and he raised the lid. He took out a bundle of documents and untied the green tape that held them. There were four leases of property, and he jotted down their particulars in his notebook. There was, however, no will. He went rapidly through the remaining contents, but there was nothing bearing on the investigation. He placed the contents in the box and relocked it.

The policemen got to their feet. 'Thank you, sir,' Morton said.

The manager swung round anxiously. 'Did you . . .?' he began.

Morton smiled. 'I am sure that you can rest easy,' he said. 'I do not think that formal access will have to be sought.'

Once in the street, he turned to Bragg. 'You obviously found great cause for satisfaction,' he said. 'What was it?'

'Pity you said that about our not taking anything,' Bragg said with a sly grin. 'Still, I got enough for our purpose, I reckon . . . Those leases – there was one for the house in Throgmorton Avenue, and the leases for the two "establishments". But there was also one, in Rodger Newby's name, for an apartment in the West End!' He took out his notebook. 'Apartment four, at thirty-five, Grosvenor Mansions. What about that, lad?'

'It is very near the house of Miss Marsden's parents.'

'A posh area, then?'

'Oh, yes. I think those apartments are relatively new.'

Bragg's moustache twitched in pleasure. 'I find that very interesting,' he said.

The trap took Bragg and Morton down the winding pot-holed drive leading to Great Melford Hall. The centre of the building was a black and white Elizabethan block – probably the original hall, Morton decided. From either end jutted Jacobean wings built of warm brick. It seemed a pleasing amalgam of styles; the whole still small enough to be domestic. Telling the driver to wait, they walked through the courtyard to a door in the central block. Weeds were growing through the gravel, the plaster of the building looked as if it had not been whitened for years. Morton pulled the bell. They heard the jangle, but no one came. Bragg battered on the door with his fist, in irritation. Still no one appeared. He marched out of the courtyard, and round to the back of the house. As they turned the corner, a man could be seen walking towards them. A shotgun drooped in the crook of his arm. He was carrying a couple of rabbits.

'Are the family at home?' Bragg shouted.

The man raised his hand in acknowledgement, and quickened his pace.

'We have come to see Mr Henry Malpas,' Bragg called, as he neared them.

'I am Henry Malpas!' He was in his early sixties. His Norfolk jacket and tweed breeches were well-worn and shapeless; his face was weather-beaten.

'We are officers of the City of London Police; Sergeant Bragg and Constable Morton. We would like to have a word, if you don't mind.'

'City Police? A bit off your beat, aren't you?' His voice was light and colourless. 'Just a minute, while I get rid of these.' He disappeared into an outhouse, and returned empty-handed.

'We will go into the estate office,' Malpas said tentatively. 'I am afraid I cannot offer you tea. The servants are at liberty in the afternoons, and my wife is at some church meeting or other.'

He led them down a stone-flagged corridor, to a room in one of the Jacobean wings. The leaded windows gave on to a geometric rose garden, enclosed within high hedges. The beds were overgrown with weeds; dead leaves had drifted on the pathways. A large desk occupied the centre of the room, its top littered with papers. Malpas gestured towards a couple of bentwood chairs.

'I am afraid there is a bit of a mess in here,' he said apologetically, scooping the papers into an untidy pile. 'If I had known you were coming, I could have . . .' His voice tailed off inconclusively.

'We only want a quick word, sir,' Bragg said indulgently. 'You will have heard about the death of Rodger Newby, I imagine.'

'Yes . . . yes. I read about it in *The Times*.'

'You had some dealings with him recently.'

Malpas looked up guardedly. 'That is true. I took a punchbowl to be valued.'

'When was that, sir?' Bragg asked gently.

'A fortnight ago today.'

'Why did you take it to Newbys? Wouldn't somebody in Ipswich have been as good?'

'Hardly. The piece is supposed to be rather special . . . And, if I am honest, I thought he might do it for me as a kind of favour. His brother, now Sir John, used to fag for me at Eton.'

'You mean, Rodger might have valued it for free?'

Malpas nodded.

'And is that all you wanted him to do? To value it?'

'At that stage, yes. I always understood that it is valuable. It has been in the family for generations.'

'In that case, surely it was insured separately. You would have got a good idea from the insured value.'

'No. It was just lumped in with the rest of the contents of the house.'

'Which insurance company?'

'The Hand-in-Hand, of Bridge Street in London.'

'I know it . . . So, they never asked you to specify individual items?'

Malpas shifted in his chair uncomfortably. 'When my wife still had her jewellery, that was mentioned separately.'

'I see. So, why this sudden interest in what the punch-bowl is worth?'

Malpas sighed. 'Well, if I am to be perfectly honest, I am getting to the end of my tether, one way and another. The fact is that estates like this are an anachronism. In the old days – even up to my grandfather's time – it was reasonably prosperous. It was at the centre of a stable community; every skill needed for it to thrive was available in the village. In our own terms, we flourished . . . But we are in a very different world now.' He stared gloomily out of the window.

'The soil does seem a bit thin, hereabouts,' Bragg remarked.

Malpas nodded. 'No more than sandy gravel, in most of my fields. Good only for corn. But, in the past, you could get a good price for your grain. We are near to London, the biggest concentration of people in the country. We could do well . . . until they opened up the American West. Now they can ship grain to millers in this country, for less than it costs us to grow it! And, with the Canadian prairies being opened up, things can only get worse.'

'I see. That sounds bad.'

'It is catastrophic, sergeant! And here am I, saddled with this mouldering pile of bricks and plaster. It has been in the family for four hundred years. What am I to do? Do I leave it to rot? Do I pull it down, and sell the rubble to make roads? How much difference would that make financially? And, if I did, what would happen to the people who still depend on me for their livelihoods?' He glared down angrily at his clenched hands.

'It's a problem, I can see that.'

'And an immediate one. The surveyor says that the lead on the roof of the east wing needs replacing. He was not telling me anything I did not know. It should have been done two years ago, when I did the rest. But my wife's jewellery would not stretch to it.'

'So you thought you might sell the punch-bowl, and get the money that way?'

Malpas looked up irritably. 'I don't know what I thought! I was casting about for ways of finding money . . . I had no idea what the bowl was worth, but I thought I should find out.'

'But, according to Newby's assistant, it is a de Lamerie,' Morton interposed.

Malpas looked round blankly. 'What significance has that?' he asked.

'Well, it would be around two hundred and fifty years old. And, in his day, de Lamerie was the pre-eminent English silversmith.'

'Really? All I know is that I have to rip off the old lead, replace all the roof beams and relead it. That is going to run into . . . maybe thousands of pounds. It is not as if I can employ my own people. I have to use specialists – people from London. And they are so busy building churches all over the place, they are not looking to come to an out-of-the-way area like this.'

Bragg let a pause develop, while Malpas's anger evaporated, then: 'You took the punch-bowl to Newbys on Monday the eighth of October,' he said.

'Yes.'

'Was it on spec?'

'What? . . . Ah no. I had written to him, saying that I might pop in.'

'Did he look at it while you were there?'

'He said he was on the verge of going out. He had been elected to be the next Lord Mayor, you know. So he was very busy. He had a cursory glance at it. He remarked that it looked interesting, then put it in one of his display cabinets, and we both left together.'

'You knew him, did you?'

'Only slightly. We met briefly at a garden party in our twenties. As I said, it was his brother that I was acquainted with.'

'So, what will you do now? Sue Newbys for negligence?'

Malpas frowned. 'Why on earth would I do that?' he asked.

'Oh, did I not say? It's missing! It was one of the pieces taken at the time he was killed.'

'No, it was not! I have it in the butler's pantry, at this very moment.'

'You have it?' Bragg exclaimed incredulously. 'Then how the bloody hell did it get back here? According to Colley, the shop assistant, it vanished at the time of Rodger Newby's murder.'

'I can assure you, sergeant, that Rodger was very much alive, when I left him.'

'What do you mean, "left him",' Bragg demanded roughly.

'I mean what I say. It is convenient for me to go up to town on a Monday. I took the bowl on Monday the eighth, and arranged to pick it up on Monday the fifteenth.'

'What time was that to be?'

'I did not give a more specific time than during the lunch hour. My train got into Liverpool Street station at twenty minutes to one. I walked to Poultry. I must have been there by quarter-past one.'

'Who was in the shop?'

'Rodger Newby only.'

'Are you sure that no one was in the office at the back?'

'Yes I am, in fact. The bowl was on his desk; he had been examining it there.'

'What did he say about it?'

'He said that he would write to me, giving a formal valuation. That seemed eminently reasonable.'

Bragg frowned. 'You see, he told Colley that he wanted his son Frederick to see it.'

'Perhaps he had done so.'

'No, we know that he hadn't.'

Malpas shrugged. 'Well, I can hardly be held responsible for that.'

'Hmm . . . And you didn't tell him you would be there at two o'clock on the fifteenth?'

Malpas shrugged. 'There was some discussion . . . I think that, when I took the bowl in, I might well have arrived at two o'clock. I remember that I had my hair cut in the barber's shop at the station.'

'So, you think he might have assumed the same time for the following week?'

'I do not understand why you are harping on about two o'clock,' Malpas said irritably. 'I have told you, he was alive when I left the premises.'

'And you didn't see anyone approaching the shop, as you left?'

'No.'

Bragg pondered for a moment, then: 'May we see the punch-bowl?' he asked.

'I see no reason why not,' Malpas said with an attempt at geniality.

They followed him back into the Elizabethan part of the building, and round to the other Jacobean wing. He stopped at a stout oak door, and retrieved a key from the architrave above it. He unlocked the door and led the way into a spacious butler's pantry. There was a range of glass-fronted cupboards, containing cut-glass goblets, decanters, pewter tankards. A flight of steps in the corner led down to what was presumably the cellar. Malpas picked up a leather hat-box, which was resting on a stool, and carried it over to a table. He opened the lid and took out a silver bowl. Its proportions were admirable, Morton thought. The foot was smaller than any of those at his family home. It conveyed elegance rather than solidity. A pattern of leaves and grapes was embossed in the rim; a similar band encircled the body of the bowl. It gleamed softly in the light. Morton picked it up. It was satisfyingly solid.

'Do you have the ladle also?' he asked.

'Alas, no. I fear I shall have to accept a diminished price because of that.'

Bragg took the bowl from him. 'You mean, sir, that you carried this valuable piece around London, in that hat-box?' he said.

Malpas smiled. 'Why not? No one would think twice about it.'

Bragg crossed to the table and gently lowered the bowl into it. 'You are right, sir,' he said. 'And it fits a treat.' He picked up the hat-box and swung round to Malpas. 'I am temporarily taking charge of this punch-bowl,' he said pompously. 'It may be needed as evidence in the trial.'

Malpas looked up in alarm. 'You cannot do that!' he exclaimed.

'Oh? Why can't I?'

'Because it is my property!'

'I will give you a receipt for it, if you like.'

'You have no possible reason for taking it,' Malpas said angrily. 'It can have no bearing whatever on the murder! I tell you, I took it away from the shop while Newby was still alive!'

'That's what you said, yes. No doubt you will have the chance to prove it, in due course. But I'm still taking possession of the bowl.' He pushed past Malpas, then marched triumphantly down the corridor and out to the trap.

It was late in the afternoon when they got back to Old Jewry.

'The Commissioner has been looking for you, Joe,' the desk sergeant said. 'Been hanging around like a broody hen.'

'Trouble, is there?'

'Not for me, anyway!'

Bragg put the hat-box on the desk. 'Look after this for me, will you, mate?'

'What's in it?' the desk sergeant asked suspiciously. 'Somebody's head?'

'It's only a little one,' Bragg said, straight-faced. 'It hardly counts, really.'

The desk sergeant hesitantly undid the buckle and raised the lid. 'Blimey!' he exclaimed. 'I know you like a drink, Joe. But you could have a bath in this! What is it?'

'A silver punch-bowl; very valuable.'

The grin faded from the desk sergeant's face. 'Silver, eh? I don't know that you should leave it with me,' he said. 'It might get pinched!'

'It is evidence, in the Newby murder case. But I want it kept quiet. So forget you have it, will you?'

Bragg went up the curving Georgian staircase, into the gracious ante-room with its bentwood chairs, and tapped on the Commissioner's door. He heard a strangled bark, and went in.

'Ah, Bragg, there you are!' Sir William's tone was almost petulant. 'I was wondering how you are getting on with the Newby case,' he said.

'Morton and I have just come back from Suffolk, sir. We were interviewing the last person to see him alive.'

'The murderer, then,' the Commissioner said with a foxy smile.

'It might turn out that way. He certainly admits to being in the shop from a quarter past one, that day. But, naturally enough, he says that Rodger Newby was alive and well when he left.'

'Are you getting near to finding your man?' Sir William asked testily.

Bragg pursed his lips and gazed out of the window. 'I cannot truthfully say that I am, sir. You have made it plain that we must be sure, before we make an arrest. That has got to be the right way. It is not as if any of our suspects are likely to do a runner.'

Sir William looked pained. 'How many suspects do you have?' he asked.

'At the moment, five – if we exclude the possibility of a casual robber having done it.'

'Five?'

'Yes, sir. Mainly family.'

'I see . . . Talking of which, I have received a message from one of the family – Sir John Newby.'

'Oh, yes,' Bragg said guardedly.

'He says he is very anxious that progress should be made. He offered any assistance that he could provide. He seems to be a sound man, Bragg. Wrote that he has been a magistrate in India, for most of his career. The family seem to be relying on him somewhat.'

'And well they might. He is the only one of them safely out of the way, at the time of the murder.'

'Are you saying that you suspect Newby's widow?' Sir William asked, aghast.

'She cannot be ruled out. I doubt if things were as smooth between them as she would have everybody believe.'

'But surely a gentlewoman, such as she, could never bludgeon her husband to death?'

'It has been known,' Bragg said drily. 'But more likely she got help from one of the sons.'

'That would be a scandal indeed.'

'Yes, sir . . . Perhaps you will be able to help me on one point, you being closer to these things than I am.'

The Commissioner gave a gratified smile. 'You only have to ask,' he said.

'It's to do with tradition, sir. This Newby goldsmiths' business has been in the family since seventeen twenty-five. It has been handed down to the eldest son in every generation, it seems, until the last one. But, in the mid eighteen-fifties, old Thomas Newby did something different. He sent his elder son off to rule the empire. It was his younger son, Rodger, that he brought into the business.'

'Why should that concern you?'

Bragg sighed. 'I have to confess that I don't know. There must have been a reason. After all, the goldsmiths' business was the major family asset. Those who didn't inherit that, have had to shift for themselves, it seems . . . Is it just that tradition didn't matter any more, by eighteen fifty? Or was it that the status of a tradesman had declined by then?'

'But am I not right in thinking that Rodger Newby himself reverted to the earlier pattern?' Sir William asked.

'Yes, indeed,' Bragg said warmly. 'I was forgetting that. So, why did his father put Rodger in?'

'Well, it cannot have been incapacity on the part of the elder boy. He must have done very well, in India, to be knighted.'

'No, sir,' Bragg said earnestly. 'It's not like that. He didn't earn his title, like you did. He inherited it.'

'Ah!' Sir William preened himself. 'Then it must be a baronetcy,' he said.

'Yes, sir. Sir John said his family had been in the Order since its inception. Which means, according to Morton, that they bought the title for four hundred quid!'

'I see!' Sir William gave a smug smile. 'Yes, that does rather put a different perspective on it.'

7

Next morning, Bragg and Morton went down to the Pendleton Vintners office in Crutched Friars. This time Ward was at his desk. He acknowledged them with a raised hand, but went on checking a column of figures. He placed a tick at the bottom of the page, then looked up.

'You lot again?' he asked disagreeably.

'Got out of the wrong side of the bed, this morning?' Bragg asked.

'Huh! You are nothing but trouble; I can guess that.'

'Do you not want to know who killed Rodger Newby?' Bragg said mildly.

Ward glowered at him. 'The likes of me have to sort out the mess, when you lot have cleared off!'

'It sounds as if you have a good idea who we should be looking for.'

'I didn't say that.'

Bragg gazed at him in silence for a time. 'Very well, sir,' he said. 'Now, let us go back to what we were talking about, when we came in last time.'

'How do you expect me to remember?' Ward exclaimed truculently. 'I have other things to think about, if you haven't.'

'It seems to us that, whatever was supposed to happen, it was you that was really in charge.'

'Huh! I bet I don't get paid half as much as . . . as him! But then, he's family.'

'You are talking about Edgar Newby?'

'Who else?'

'But I thought the financial records were in your parish. You said his area is selling.'

'I do keep the trading books, yes. But not the private

ledger. He is paid from old Fummery's office, so no one will know!'

'You have never got a chance to glance at the accountant's working papers?' Bragg asked.

'No. They are very close about him.'

'It must be very difficult for you,' Bragg said soothingly. 'What part did old Rodger play in Pendletons?'

Ward sat back in his chair, his brow still furrowed with indignation. 'I could never tell what he did behind the scenes. Edgar would come in some mornings, and say that his father wanted us to do such and such. We could never tell if it was true. And we daren't challenge it. That's the trouble with family businesses.'

'Where is Edgar now?'

'I don't know,' Ward said peevishly. 'If there's horse racing on within twenty miles of London, he'll be there – flat or over the sticks . . . And his father barely cold in his grave. There'll be no holding him now.'

'We understand that Edgar came to work here as a youth,' Bragg said.

'That's right. He started when he was eighteen; straight from the City of London School . . . He was wild there, too, they tell me. Old Mr Nathaniel knew as much. He would take me on one side; confide in me. "Ward," he would say, "I shall have to bring Master Edgar in. But I will make it that he can't ruin everything." Huh! What use are lawyers and trustees? They are not here all the time. "Look after him," he would tell me. "Keep him under control. He is a decent lad, really." I tell you, sergeant, he couldn't have been more wrong. But what could I do?'

'Did Rodger Newby not control his son?' Bragg asked.

'If you ask me, he didn't even try, till it was too late.'

'He has been on the fiddle, we gather.'

Ward looked at him suspiciously. 'Who told you that?' he asked.

'Fummery, the lawyer.'

Ward's face relaxed. 'Funny old codger, but he's all right really. I think he knew what was going on, but he left it to Rodger.'

'And to Canon Wilkes?'

'Huh! What good is a parson? Edgar has only to say, "I'm sorry; I won't do it again," and Wilkes has got to believe him. I can't understand what Mr Nathaniel thought he was doing, making that lot trustees.'

'According to Canon Wilkes, his aim was to keep the business profitable, to provide for his two daughters – Mrs Newby and Mrs Harvey.'

'She's all right, that Mrs Harvey.' Ward nodded approvingly. 'She'll come in sometimes, as large as life. "Find me a good bottle of claret," she will say. "I am entertaining tonight". Who she's entertaining, it doesn't do to ask, her being a widow and all.'

'Let's get back to Edgar Newby, shall we?' Bragg said gruffly.

'All right. I was going to say that his grandfather meant him to be employed in this business, to make up for Frederick taking over Newbys. But they are as different as chalk and cheese, those boys. If you ask me, Edgar is a wastrel, and always will be.'

'It seems that he was not paid enough by Pendletons to meet his expenses,' Bragg prompted him.

'That's right. But it took me some time to cotton on. We began to have deliveries of wine going astray. By then, Edgar was in the warehouse – I'd had enough of him in here. I told his father, either he goes to the warehouse, or I leave!'

'I can't imagine Rodger Newby taking kindly to that,' Bragg said with a smile.

'Oh, he didn't! He looked as black as thunder, when I told him his son had been pinching petty cash from the day he came. But he was a fair man, and he heard me out. When I'd finished, he said never a word. But he went straight up to French Horn Yard, and ordered the cellarman to find Edgar a job.'

'And then wine started going astray.'

'Yes . . . In those days, they weren't all that strict about getting delivery notes signed by the customer. You know, if there was nobody at home, they might leave the wine with a neighbour, or down by the area door. I would get my copy of the delivery note from the warehouse, and I would send out my invoice. And, like I said, sometimes the customer would tell us he'd never got the wine . . . Well, it's easy enough to say. And, for a start, we didn't believe them. But you can't call a man a liar, and expect him to trade with you again. We lost a good few customers, before we realised it was us at fault.'

'And it was down to Edgar, was it?'

'Well, he was in the despatch department at the time. I didn't accuse him of it. How could I? But Mr Rodger could see what was happening, all right. He insisted that we should never invoice a customer, until we had a signed delivery note – which is as it should be, in this class of business.'

'When did this new system begin?'

'Well, the trading year ended last thirtieth of June. When the accountants came down, they told us what we should be doing . . . I suppose it would be at the end of August.'

'Still in the flat-racing season,' Bragg remarked with a grin. 'What did Edgar do for pocket-money then?'

Ward hesitated. 'I don't know as how I should tell you,' he said. 'Nothing has been said about it. Mr Rodger made me promise.'

'Rodger Newby is dead,' Bragg said drily. 'You never know, you could be next.'

Ward's face blanched. 'Here! It's not my fault! I did all I could. They knew what was going on. If they chose to ignore it, they can't blame me!'

'They are not blaming you; no one is. But, until this matter is out in the open, you could be at risk.'

'Yes, well . . . All right, I'll tell you what I know. We have a long-standing connection with the army at Aldershot. We supply several of the officers' messes with wines and spirits. We sent a big consignment, by railway, on the tenth of September. Edgar was looking after our end of it. He made out the delivery note. The copy I got was perfect . . . He went with the van to Waterloo station, and filled out the railway consignment forms there. It should have been straightforward. But the delivery never got to Aldershot. It just vanished.'

'So, what happened then?'

'Why, the consignee wouldn't accept my invoice. I asked Edgar for our copy of the consignment note, but he said he'd lost it . . . Well, things couldn't rest like that. There were hundreds of pounds involved. I had to tell Mr Rodger.'

'Did he shrug it off, as usual?'

'Not this time. There was a big row. Mr Rodger sent me to

call Edgar, then told me to stay outside. I've never seen him so angry. I thought he would have an apoplexy! I could hear them shouting at each other; though I couldn't make out what they were saying. Then Edgar came flinging out. All I can say is, he looked vicious. Then Mr Rodger called me in. He said there were going to be changes. From then on, Edgar was not to be involved in the stock side at all. He would just be going out, getting orders. I was to see to it, he said.'

'Which put you in a difficult position . . . And when did this latest quarrel take place?'

'It was the second of October – Tuesday the second.'

'And, on the fifteenth, Rodger Newby was battered to death . . . So, what is happening now?'

'Well, Edgar is doing as he pleases, isn't he? I mean, no complaint has been made to the police, so they can do nothing.'

'I wouldn't be too sure about that,' Bragg said grimly. 'I wouldn't be too sure.'

Sending Morton to make enquiries of Malpas's insurers, Bragg himself walked towards Whitechapel Market. Once over the City's boundary, the streets were rutted and dirty. The mean terraces huddled together, their cheap bricks flaking on to the uneven pavement. In a hundred yards you could make the transition from cosseted wealth to near destitution . . . Yet, surely they could help themselves a bit? A lick of paint on the door, some new curtains, would brighten it up. Needn't cost the earth. They spent as much every Saturday, he'd bet, on beer and the music hall. Somebody should take them in hand . . . No, he thought. They knew best what they wanted from life. His censoriousness was born of his own guilt; for belonging to the City force; for spending his life keeping rich folk secure, people who didn't give a toss about what went on out here, as long as their skivvies got to work on time.

He turned a corner and came upon the market. The stalls were set up on the roadway, facing the pavement. That meant the stallholders would be standing well out in the street. A runaway horse could create mayhem. Bragg strolled along the pavement. It seemed to be a purely local market. Here was a stall selling muffins and bread. Next to it was a costermonger's barrow – carrots, potatoes, apples, and a pile of tired, yellowing cabbages. Back in Dorset, they would have thought twice about feeding them to the pigs! But this was London, the wealthiest city in the world, the heart of empire, the mother of parliaments . . . Here was a second-hand clothes stall. Women were picking through the jumble of garments; squabbling fiercely over a skirt or a feather boa; disdainfully spurning a light cotton dress. Some of the pampered City matrons ought to come and see this, Bragg thought. It might shake them out of their complacency. But, like as not, it would only confirm their sense of God-given superiority.

He went over to a woman selling gaudy cotton materials. 'Where is Albert Smith's stall?' he asked.

The woman looked up in surprise. 'He ain't here,' she said. 'He got hurt, didn't he?'

'Ah, I did not know that. When did it happen?'

She considered for a moment. 'Last Saturday week,' she said. 'A bleedin' great van come out of the side-street. Knocked him for six, it did. He was hurt bad.'

'Where was his stall?'

'Four along from me – on the corner.'

Bragg strolled to the space where Smith's stall had been. It should never have happened, that was certain; yet it was clear how it could. The side-street was narrow, the left turn tight. It only needed a spirited horse, the driver behind time. It was easy enough for a wheel to catch the stall. The momentum of a loaded van would turn it over as easy as wink.

Bragg walked to Stutfield Street. The Spotted Dog seemed a pleasant enough pub. Through the window he could see a roaring fire, polished brass beer pumps. He felt a dryness in his throat; a pint would go down a treat. But he resisted the urge, and went on to the house next to it. His knock was answered by a middle-aged woman in a spotless white apron.

'Mrs Smith?' Bragg asked, raising his hat.

She looked at him uncertainly. 'Yes,' she said.

'Police.' He waved his warrant-card at her. 'I have come about your husband's accident.'

'Have you caught him, then?' she asked sharply.

'Who is that?'

'The man what done it.'

'We need a bit more information. Is your husband at home?'

'Course he is! Got a bad leg, hasn't he?'

'Do you think I could have a word with him?' Bragg asked ingratiatingly.

'How many more times? . . . Oh, all right. Come in.'

Smith was sitting in the parlour, before a blazing fire. His right leg was propped on a stool. His trouser leg had been cut, so that it could accommodate the bulky bandaging.

'Police again, Albert,' Mrs Smith said sharply. 'Don't you go getting up!' She glared at Bragg, then whisked out of the room.

'Sorry to disturb you, Mr Smith,' Bragg said. 'We are not finding it all that easy. I wonder if you can give us a better description of the van that overturned your stall.'

'Sit down, mate,' Smith said chirpily. 'Don't you mind the wife. She's a bit of a worrier, that's all.'

Bragg pulled out his notebook, and flipped over the pages. 'The accident happened on Saturday the thirteenth of October, didn't it?'

'I don't know about accident, mate. It was just bleedin' carelessness.'

'Would you say it amounted to criminal negligence?' Bragg asked solemnly.

Smith looked startled. 'Here! I don't know about that . . . I'm not sure as how I'd want to give evidence.'

Bragg smiled reassuringly. 'It might help you to get compensation, even so.'

Smith raised his eyebrows. 'Compensation? I hadn't thought about that . . . Yer, I reckon I'm due some.'

'Did anyone recognise the driver?'

'Nah! And I was serving a customer, wasn't I? It's a funny old world, isn't it? I'd just sold a glazed pot to an old lady. I was reaching over to give her the change, when this van knocks us all arse over tip. There was me, with half the bleedin' stall on top of me; pandemonium all round. And this little old dear climbs over the wreckage, and takes her tuppence-ha'penny out of my fist!'

'You sell crockery, do you?'

'Yeah. Pots and pans, china seconds, that sort of thing.'

'I bet a lot of your stock was damaged. You ought to be able to claim for that. Have you got a solicitor?'

Smith snorted. 'Leave off, mate! Go to them, and you end up out of pocket, however much you win. Nah! They're for the nobs, not for the likes of me.'

'But you were injured yourself. You have lost your livelihood – for the time being, at least. You must have a good claim.'

Smith frowned. 'Yeah, I suppose I have. Careless bugger! And he just carried on as if he didn't know. Pity the street was clear, or I'd have caught up with him . . . Then again, I might have done myself more damage.'

'Were you badly hurt?' Bragg asked sympathetically.

'Well, I didn't think so, at first. I even stood around, watching my mates clear up the mess. I did get a lift home . . . My leg felt sore, but that wasn't no surprise. I didn't get much sleep that night. It got all hot, and started to ache. I should have gone to the hospital next morning. But it was Sunday, and you know what women are like. She didn't want to bother the doctors, she said. By Monday morning it was up like a balloon. And talk about hurt! By ten o'clock, even she said I'd got to go to hospital.'

'Where did you go?'

'The London Hospital, on Whitechapel Road . . . Of course, by the time we got there it was eleven o'clock; there was a queue a mile long. And nowhere to sit! Three hours I was waiting; being pushed from bleedin' pillar to post. They decided I'd got a fractured tibia. So there, mate. Sounds as if it should be good for a few quid . . . I'll tell you what, it bloody hurts!'

'I bet! And what time did you get back home?'

'Just after three. I was buggered, I can tell you. And I've got to sit with it up for a fortnight. Then I go back to the hospital again.'

'And you cannot describe the driver?'

'No. But I gave your blokes a description of the horse. I'd know that again, all right.'

When Morton passed through the marble portico of the Hand-in-Hand Insurance Company, he found himself in a somewhat shabby general office. Electric lights dangled over scratched desks; clerks with sleeve-protectors pored over bundles of documents. He stated his business, and was directed to the office of an assistant manager, two floors above. It was perverse, he thought. Any prudent policy holder ought to applaud a strict control of overhead expenditure, rejoice in a studied lack of ostentation. But let him encounter chipped paintwork and worn linoleum, and he worried lest the funds might not be there to pay his claims! He knocked on the door indicated and walked in. A man in his forties looked up in surprise.

'City Police,' Morton said. 'I wonder if you can help me concerning one of your customers.'

The man gave a tentative smile. 'I will do what I can, of course. What is the name?'

'Henry Malpas, of Great Melford Hall, near Sudbury.'

'Hmm . . . I do not recognise the name, but that is hardly surprising.' He went to a file index under the window, and flicked through the cards. 'Ah, yes,' he said. 'I have him . . . A customer of long standing. Just a moment, while I get the file.' He went out.

Morton's eyes drifted guiltily over the files on the desk. He was almost relieved that he recognised none of the names. That was where he differed from Bragg; why he would never make a complete detective. Everything was grist to Bragg's mill. Every stray fact would be garnered, against the day when it might combine with others to make a pattern.

The door opened, and the official reappeared with a large bundle of files. He set them on his desk, and released the canvas strap holding them.

'Goodness!' he said. 'The Malpases seem to have been clients of ours since the early seventeen hundreds.'

'That shows a commendable confidence in your company,' Morton remarked.

'Yes . . .' He was riffling through the files. 'There seems to have been an inordinate number of claims,' he murmured. 'I am surprised that the premium has remained so static.' He began to jot down figures on a piece of paper. After some minutes he looked up.

'I calculate that we have paid out over seven thousand pounds more, in claims, then we have received in premiums,' he said.

'Over what period?'

'Since seventeen twenty-seven.'

'That hardly seems good business!' Morton said. 'Why would you want to maintain the connection?'

'A good question!' The man turned to a correspondence file, and began to browse through it. 'Ah', he said, 'the business comes through one of our agents, in Ipswich. I see that, at one time, there was an intention to invite the Malpas of the day to take his valuable business elsewhere! But the agent protested most strongly. He said that, because of the Malpas connection, we obtained profitable clients from the surrounding area. Our management gave in to his pleas, and we have continued to insure Great Melford Hall and its contents. Perhaps the time has come to review the situation again . . . Here we have a claim that gave rise to a great deal of soul searching at the time. The stable block burned down in seventeen eighty-three. It was alleged in the claim that there had been a lightning strike. But that was in February; not a month when thunderstorms are prevalent. Moreover, our assessor could find no one in the locality who recollected such a storm. However, we paid out. We later learned that a fine new stable block was built; far roomier, to accommodate a modern carriage, and in a more convenient place.'

'We saw it, when we went down,' Morton said with a smile.

'Do you have, er, a professional interest in the present family?' the man asked.

'You have obviously heard of the murder of Rodger Newby, the Lord Mayor-elect.'

His eyes widened. 'Of course! Is Malpas mixed up in that?'

Morton shook his head. 'He happens to have been in Newby's shop, a few minutes before he was killed. One might say that he was the last person to see him alive. He says that he was collecting a valuable item of silver, which he had left at Newbys for valuation. It would be of interest for us to know what silver has been covered in the insurance policy.'

'Yes, yes, of course.' The man turned to another file. 'There is an old list of valuables here . . . We have a silver punch-bowl particularised. Is that the piece you are referring to? I see there is a note that there is no matching ladle.'

'That sounds right.'

'Well, there is little or no information about it; no formal valuation, if that is what you are after.'

'I see. Then how is it dealt with in the policy?'

'It is lumped in with silver cutlery, and so on. The insured value of all of them is currently set at a round four hundred pounds.'

'And if the punch-bowl were lost?'

'Why, the claims assessors would have to agree as to how much of that sum could be reasonably allocated to the bowl.'

'Right . . . May I ask you a rather odd question? Do you think that Henry Malpas is an honest man?'

The man gave a smile. 'All our clients are honest, officer. When they are not, they are no longer our clients.'

'That's a load of balls, lad!' Bragg exclaimed, as they conferred in Bragg's room next morning. 'It sounds to me that the Malpases have been on the fiddle for generations. The Hand-in-Hand have stuck with them till now, because they were gentry; and it doesn't do to call the gentry fraudsters. They have loaded other people's premiums, to make up for what the Malpases have cheated them of. So, by now they think they can get away with anything!'

'Even if that were true,' Morton remarked, 'it is a far cry from establishing a motive for the murder of Rodger Newby.'

'Motive! Why do you need a motive? Murder isn't always rational, you know!'

Morton laughed. 'Mainly because you have taught me always to look for one.'

Bragg frowned. 'Yes . . . Well, so you should. But you shouldn't close your eyes to everything else.'

'Nevertheless, sir, Malpas does seem to be of an equable temperament. He would have to be provoked to a considerable degree, before reacting in so extreme a fashion.'

'Maybe . . . But he's a wrong 'un at bottom. Remember that! Now, tell me, lad, why do you reckon Sir Thomas Newby, baronet, sent Rodger to the City of London School, and his elder brother to Eton?'

Morton thought for a moment. 'I can see why some people might believe that Eton was the pre-eminent school for their sons,' he remarked. 'It has cachet, it has influence, it might even provide a reasonable education for those interested in such matters.'

'But that's not the point. If he thought that, why not send both boys to Eton?'

'Well, if you were set on your son's attaining a position of power and influence in the Civil Service, or public life generally, then Eton would carry more weight than the City of London School. The very title of the latter bespeaks parochialism, money-grubbing in fusty offices. On the other hand, it is probably free of the clannishness and snobbery that seem to rule the lives of those who have been to our great public schools.'

'All right, that explains the elder boy, and Eton.'

'Surely it explains the choice for both? I cannot see an old Etonian being willing to serve in a shop, however prestigious.'

'So, you reckon it was just horses for courses, eh?'

'I imagine so. *Who's Who* does not record that Sir Thomas himself was educated at Eton.'

'I can't sort this family out, lad,' Bragg said with a frown. 'If old Sir Thomas decided it was time to push the family up a notch, why not put his elder son into the British Civil Service, or Foreign Service?'

Morton smiled. 'I doubt if it was anything so deliberate, sir. There must have been considerable interest in India, in the late eighteen-fifties. Robert Clive's victory at Plassey, in 'fifty-seven, consolidated British power there. Plainly, thereafter, an aspiring administrator could look to have a full career in India. And particularly in Bengal, where Sir John Newby served.'

'I suppose so. But it seems a bit hard on Rodger, being left at home to mind the shop. You would know all about that, being a younger son yourself.'

'It is true that the elder son tradition ruled in my family also. Although my mother's American libertarian instincts could not prevent Edwin from following my father into the army, at least I was shielded from sharing his ghastly fate.'

There came a knock on the door. The desk sergeant poked his head in. 'A visitor to see you, Joe,' he said. He opened the door wide, and Sir John Newby strode in.

'Good morning, sergeant,' he said affably. 'I thought I should inform you of my intentions. I have decided that, from tomorrow, I shall spend much of my time in the Poultry office. I have considerable experience in poring over account books and documents. It is just possible that I might find some clue, in the business records, which could point you in the right direction.'

'I see, sir,' Bragg said cautiously. 'You have the permission of the executors, I suppose.'

'I have spoken to Elizabeth, Rodger's widow,' Sir John said confidently. 'As you can imagine, she is grateful to have an experienced person to lean on at this juncture. The two boys do not exactly have an easy relationship, I gather. As to Rodger's legal representatives, I have spoken to Fummery. It seems that Rodger may have died intestate. I do not know the circumstances. I would have thought it rather reprehensible. However, I have offered to act in any capacity which will mitigate the effects of this terrible tragedy.'

'That is very good of you,' Bragg said drily.

'Yes . . . And I must say, sergeant, that I deplore your visit to Pendleton Vintners yesterday. As you must know, it is the family business of my sister-in-law, and has never had any connection with Newbys. My brother even went to some lengths to dissociate himself from the running of it.'

'But he was the principal trustee,' Bragg said mildly. 'That might not amount to ownership, but it was a close association with Pendletons. And, as you are well aware, we are not limited as to where we poke about.'

Sir John nodded. 'Of course. And I am in no way seeking to hinder your investigations, sergeant. Indeed, I will do all I can to assist. To that end, I have enjoined full co-operation with the police, on my late brother's family. I have not even pressed them to take the elementary precaution of having a solicitor present, when you question them. Nothing but good can come from their full and willing co-operation in your investigations. All I would ask, is that you inform me in advance, if you wish to interview any of them. So that, should they wish it, I can be present.'

Bragg nodded. 'I have taken note of what you say, sir. As you will appreciate, any decision on that is out of my hands.'

There was a knock at the door, and the Commissioner came in. He gave an apologetic glance towards Bragg, then advanced on Sir John.

'I gather you have spent your working life in India,' he said, hand outstretched.

Sir John rose to his feet and shook hands. 'Indeed, sir. Whom do I have the pleasure of addressing?'

The Commissioner looked slightly confused. 'Sir William Sumner. I am in charge of the City force. I heard you were in.'

Sir John gave a complacent smile. 'I am gratified to meet someone so distinguished,' he said.

The Commissioner seemed taken aback at this attribution. 'I was in India, also, for some of my career,' he said tentatively.

Sir John beamed at him. 'Were you really, sir?'

'Yes. I served in the British army. But I did a spell in Bombay, on the general staff . . . Enjoyed it immensely. Among the best experiences of my life. And the sun! A bit different from London in October, eh?'

'Indeed, Sir William. Did you go via the Suez Canal, or round the Cape?'

'The Cape. They had barely started the canal, when I made my trip.'

Sir John smiled reflectively. 'It shortens the journey very considerably, of course. But I missed the leisurely journey; the interesting ports we called at – Mombasa, Durban, Cape Town . . . Do you remember the old Clan Line steamers? Marvellous little ships. Out of sheer sentimentality, I came back this time via the Cape. On the *Clan Macnab*. Getting a little shabby now, but it was marvellous to potter along the coast of Africa again.'

Bragg cleared his throat noisily, and Newby gave him an apologetic glance. 'I have just been offering my services to your sergeant, Sir William, in the matter of my brother's death,' he said.

'Ah, yes . . . A bad business, that. You have my deep sympathy.'

Sir John gave a grateful smile. 'Thank you. I will convey your condolences to my sister-in-law and her family. And now I must be off. The memorial service takes place this afternoon.'

He made a half-bow to the Commissioner, glanced briefly at Bragg and Morton, then strode purposefully out.

As Bragg and Morton approached St Lawrence Jewry, they could see Catherine Marsden talking animatedly with a man in a fur-trimmed scarlet gown. Then he shook his head, made some final observation and escaped into the church. Catherine saw them and beckoned.

'You noticed me speaking to Alderman Levitt?' she said. 'I am sure that they have made a decision as to what will happen about electing the candidates for Lord Mayor, but no one is prepared to say as much.'

'Is it a matter of such moment?' Morton asked in amusement. 'You have missed today's edition, anyway. You will probably get to know before Saturday.'

'But this secrecy is so stupid!' Catherine said crossly. 'I am sure that, if I were a man, someone would have been prepared to disclose it.'

'I doubt that,' Bragg said stolidly. 'These City folk like to make lesser mortals wait . . . I didn't think this memorial service was going to be a fancy-dress affair.'

'Nor I, sergeant. Had Newby died in his bed, I suspect it would not have been. Perhaps they think that a dash of pageantry will mask the taste of murder.' She smiled. 'I must make a note of that! Though I doubt if Mr Tranter would let me use it!'

'Is your editor here, then?' Morton asked.

'Oh, yes. All the great and the good have been summoned. It is being turned into a formal City occasion. The church will be packed.'

'Then we had better be going in, miss,' Bragg said. 'If you get any interesting snippets, you will let us know?'

Catherine cocked her head. 'If you are prepared to pay my price,' she said, and turned away as another alderman approached.

Bragg and Morton pushed their way through the doors of the organ screen, and into the interior of the small church. An usher directed them to places on the north aisle. From there they could see a solid block of scarlet, in the middle section of pews. The first two rows, however, remained empty. The organ was playing solemn music; there was an undercurrent of whispered conversation. Glancing back, Morton saw Catherine sidling into a place by the organ. He looked around him. This must be one of Sir Christopher Wren's smallest churches, he thought. It was a pity that, with so much scope after the Great Fire, the principal architect should have had such an earth-bound imagination. With its coffered ceiling and plaster coving, the building could just as easily have been a municipal library. It had elegance and serenity, but it did not uplift the spirit. Yet perhaps that was apt, in the church of the Corporation of London. Asked to choose between prosperity on earth and heavenly bliss, most of its members would have settled for the former.

The organ faded away in a whisper. There was a stir at the back of the church. A carefully modulated clerical voice announced the hymn, and the congregation stood. The organ played the first phrase on a quiet reed stop, then began in a firm diapason.

> *O God our help in ages past . . .*

There was no choir, no soaring treble line. A few women's voices could be heard, but they were overwhelmed by the assertive baritone of the men.

> *Under the shadow of thy throne*
> *Thy saints have dwelt secure . . .*

Rodger Newby was one of Mammon's saints that had notably failed to be secure, Morton thought. Were the hearty singers there to celebrate his life, or to protect their own by some magical ritual?

> *Be thou our guard while troubles last*
> *And our eternal home.*

During the last verse of the hymn, Morton had been aware of a procession making its way towards the east end. The vicar of St Lawrence led the way, head reverentially bowed. He was followed by a liveried figure in knee-breeches, bearing the mace of the City of London. Behind him came the incumbent Lord Mayor, his black robe richly adorned with gold embroidery. Across a white lace jabot rested his gold chain of office. His angular face was composed in a mask of great solemnity. A yard behind him came George Pascoe, in his scarlet alderman's robe, his eyes fixed on the east window. Following the civic procession, almost as an afterthought, came Newby's family. His widow, red-eyed, was supported on the arm of Sir John Newby. After them walked Frederick Newby, with a pretty young woman on his arm. She looked about her self-consciously. Bragg nudged Morton. 'Nancy Osborne,' he whispered. Behind them came the woman they had seen at the funeral. This time the man was not with her. The rear was brought up by Alice Harvey with Edgar Newby.

The Lord Mayor stepped into the front pew, followed by Pascoe. The family mourners filed into the second. The vicar paced solemnly onwards to the sanctuary, the mace-bearer following. At the communion rail the vicar turned, took the mace and laid it on the altar. Then they all knelt, and there followed a series of prayers. Their import seemed to combine a mild chastisement of God, for not having looked after Newby better, with a plea that He should support the City by ensuring that the next candidate got a trouble-free run. After a resounding 'Amen' from the congregation, the vicar mounted the steps of the pulpit.

He began his oration with a celebration of Rodger Newby's life. He had belonged, he said, to a distinguished City family; inherited a centuries-old tradition of service to the community and his fellow men. To Morton, the sermon was an exercise in reinforcing the corporate loyalty of the City. Newby had fallen by the wayside, but the baton would be picked up by others; the City and its institutions would endure. God's purpose would be fulfilled. Then the vicar referred to Newby's family, so evidently overwhelmed by their tragedy. He saw God's hand in the fact that his brother, Sir John Newby, had recently come home from India, to be their support and succour. He enjoined the congregation to remember them in their prayers, and to live upright and fruitful lives themselves. Then he brought his oration to a close.

There was a final prayer of thanks for Newby's life, and its example to others. Then the organ began to play Handel's Largo. The vicar went to the altar and took up the mace. He presented it to the mace-bearer, who solemnly bore it down the sanctuary steps and along the aisle. The Lord Mayor and Pascoe stepped out behind him, then the aldermen joined the procession. They moved slowly down the nave, through the organ screen and out into the street.

The organist had now embarked on a Bach fugue, the phrases entwining playfully. The appropriate genuflection towards death had been made; man's frailty had been acknowledged. Now it was time to turn again to the family gods of the City – power and profit.

8

Catherine woke at seven o'clock, next morning. Daylight was beginning to seep round the edges of the curtain, the tip of her nose felt cold. She wondered whether to get up; she was wide awake. Surely there was something useful she could do, before she left for the office at nine? But the servants would only just have lit the fires. There would be no hot water yet. She would merely get in the way. And her father might well be prowling around in his dressing-gown. He had been dropping heavy hints, of late, that time was rushing by; that, within a year, he looked to have her safely and satisfactorily married. Thus far she had been able to fob him off. After all, it was he who had encouraged her to go to a boarding school. He had said it would give her independence of mind and spirit. She smiled to herself. He had not always been pleased to discover how fully his predictions had been fulfilled!

Yet he had been unreservedly proud of her. He had manifestly wallowed in the celebrity that her scoops had brought her; had seemed to welcome the resultant relationship she had formed with James. But he had been showing signs of restiveness for some months. At the beginning of the Season he had even tried to manoeuvre her into a marriage with the cretinous

Lord Wheatley. There had been a family row; a real shouting-match. The first she could ever remember. In the end, she had pretended to capitulate. Of course, she had been able to outwit him. She had only needed to assert that she was a rampant feminist, for Wheatley to back off. Poor Lavinia Deveraux! She was welcome to him, title and all!

Yet, she had to admit that her attempts to defend a false position must some day end. It was perfectly true that her salary from the *City Press* paid for little more than out-of-pocket expenses and clothes – and not even all her clothes. She was as delighted to accept presents of rich ball-gowns and jewellery from her father, as he was to bestow them. But were a complete breach to occur between them, were she really compelled to live on what she could earn, she would be in the most straitened of circumstances . . . She was being foolish, she told herself. They were all three of them civilised adults. Her father had actively encouraged her desire to have a career, to be more than a simpering wallflower. Yet, to him, it had never been an end in itself. He had wished her to become a self-reliant woman, with a wider experience of life than the average socialite. But he had never envisaged that she would break away from the society she had been brought up in.

Nor had she. If she were honest, she would admit that she had seized on her father's wish to indulge her. In truth, her position was little better than that of the vapid girls who clustered near the dance-floor, fluttering their eyes at the men. Her independence, at her own level in society, was illusory. As with her chastity, it was something to cherish; only to lose it at the right moment. Finding this conclusion thoroughly disagreeable, she got out of bed and went in search of some hot water.

Cook made her some toast, which she ate in the warmth of the kitchen. She knew full well what had brought on this fit of self-flagellation. It was seeing Nancy Osborne on the arm of her fiancé, at the memorial service. Although they were good friends, Catherine had secretly disdained Nancy's unquestioning acceptance of the conventions of her class. She had made no attempt to be at least independent in spirit. She had not sought to be anything but the chattel that she had bewailed being . . . And yet, she had now got what she wanted. She had walked down the aisle, at the memorial service, with confidence

– with almost a suppressed radiance. Soon she would be married, have a house of her own, children . . .

Immediately after breakfast, Catherine hurried out of the house and took a cab to the City. She was in no state of mind to bear her mother's vague chatter about acquaintances, or the latest novel of Thomas Hardy. She felt she had to do something to work off this self-critical mood . . . It was James, of course. She might as well admit it. Or rather, his blithely going off to Australia for three months – and without any thought of how she felt about it . . . She was behaving stupidly, she told herself. Having rejected his proposal of marriage, she could have no possible claim on him. And yet, they were still good friends. He might at least have expressed to her his hopes of being selected for the team.

She paid off the cab in Cheapside, and walked up King Street towards St Lawrence Jewry. She realised it was a course totally devoid of logic. But she had a vague feeling that, if she were to see that church again, the niggling feeling of dissatisfaction and failure might be exorcised. The church was open, and a communion service was in progress. A few worshippers were kneeling in the front pews, murmuring the responses. Far from assuaging her unease, the mechanical gabble merely irritated her. She squatted down in a pew, perhaps to pray about her dilemma. But it would not work. If answer there were, it lay within herself. She went back into the street . . . Perhaps there was no answer. She could hardly ask James to abandon the tour for her sake; plead that she would be lonely, that she would miss the attentions she had come to take for granted. By such a course she would merely lose his respect.

Suddenly she realised that her feet had taken her to the north end of Old Jewry; that the City Police headquarters was a mere hundred yards away. She glanced at her fob-watch. It was almost nine o'clock. She could reasonably call on Sergeant Bragg, to see if they were making any progress. And if James happened to be there . . . She glanced at her reflection in a window, then began to walk.

Bragg looked up scowling, as she entered his room.

'Good morning, sergeant,' she said brightly, glancing around her.

'It's no use, miss,' Bragg said grumpily. 'He's not here.

Would you believe it, he's gone to Savile Row, to be measured for cricket flannels! I've heard some stupid things in my time, but that takes the biscuit! Half the side will be miners and blacksmiths, from the north. I can't see them playing any the worse because their trouser-leg is an inch shorter than London fashion would have it!'

Catherine conjured up a sweet smile. 'But I came to see you, sergeant,' she said. 'I was wondering if your investigations had been advanced, by attending the memorial service yesterday.'

'Huh! A farce that was; just going through the motions. If you ask me, they didn't give tuppence for Rodger Newby and his memory.'

'But surely a good number of your suspects were there?'

'That's true enough. Interesting that Pascoe was in with the Lord Mayor. They must be putting him forward, after all . . . Perhaps they had no option; he was the surviving elected candidate, after all.'

'I will try to find out,' Catherine said helpfully.

'Have you made any progress with the silver auctions?' Bragg asked.

'I am sorry,' Catherine said contritely. 'I have not had time to contact Stanley Rainham again. But he is making enquiries for me.'

Bragg looked at her quizzically, then: 'I saw that Miss Osborne at the memorial service,' he said. 'Whatever she may have been prepared to accept while Rodger was alive, it seems she's been laying the law down since his death!'

'I hope that her husband-to-be is not a suspect!'

'Oh, but he is, miss. Together with half-a-dozen others – nearly all of them at the service . . . Which reminds me. Do you know who the woman on her own was? The one walking after Frederick and Nancy.'

'No, I am afraid not. But I expect that I could find out from Nancy, if you like.'

'Would you do that, miss? As you realise, I'm a bit short-handed.'

Catherine cocked her head. 'I am sure that I could never make up for Constable Morton's absence,' she said lightly. 'But I will at least try!'

*

Bragg took a hansom to Bond Street. Sleet had begun to fall, and the streets were empty. He was glad to push his way into the comparative warmth of Newby's shop. The elderly assistant looked at him warily.

'Is Mr Newby in?' Bragg asked gruffly.

'If you would just wait one moment . . .' He disappeared into the office behind. There was a brief conversation, then the man came back. 'You may go in now, sir,' he said.

Bragg pushed past him. Frederick Newby was sitting at his desk, with the stock book open in front of him. He did not get up.

'It was a nice service for your father, yesterday,' Bragg observed mildly, taking the seat opposite Newby.

'If such things can ever be so,' Frederick said shortly.

'A good turn-out. It must be a comfort to you all, to know that he was thought so well of in the City.'

'Perhaps. But that will not bring him back.'

'No . . . It's a funny thing. You won't want me to tell you this, I know. But we haven't found many folk that would want to bring him back.'

Newby's eyes narrowed. He said nothing.

Bragg leaned back in the chair. 'I see your young lady was at the service,' he said. 'Very nice she is, if I may say so, sir . . . Could she not get to London for the funeral?'

Newby's lip curled. 'She lives here, as you very well know,' he said contemptuously.

'Do we? If you say so . . . It's difficult to keep track of every remark you hear, in an investigation like this. Of course! Miss Nancy Osborne. I remember now. Lives with her parents, in Belgrave Square . . . A good family, are they?'

'Of course.'

'Yes . . . I expect her parents are pleased, to be marrying their daughter into the Newby dynasty. There aren't many traders as prosperous, I'll be bound . . . And quite relieved, too.'

'What do you mean by that?' Newby asked angrily.

'By what? . . . Oh, I see. No, I wasn't insinuating that she is in the family way! I'm sure you are too much of a gentleman for that. No, I meant that there had been trouble over your engagement.'

'Mr Osborne has expressed himself as more than content to have me as a son-in-law,' Newby said curtly.

'I'm sure . . . I was talking to your uncle, the other day. The one who is a baronet.'

'Sir John is my only uncle.'

'Yes. From the way he explained it, you will be a baronet one day; succeed to his title, as his brother's elder son. So Nancy is like to become Lady Newby.'

'In due course, yes. Though not, I hope, for many years yet.'

'Indeed, sir. Do you know, I did not realise, at first, that he and your father were twins. Funny thing, that. Two sons born the same day. One becomes an aristocrat, the other stays a commoner. One goes off to rule the empire, the other stays at home and sells necklaces.'

'If you think you can rile me into making some injudicious remark,' Newby said angrily, 'you are making a great mistake!'

'Ah, I see. Well in control of yourself, are you?'

Newby merely glared at him.

'Well, your uncle wasn't so sure. He asked me to arrange for him to be present, when next I saw you.'

'I have no need of any third party to hold my hand, sergeant. I have done nothing for which I might remotely feel ashamed.'

Bragg cocked his head and stared at him. 'Well, from what I understand, you and your father didn't always see eye to eye. Even about the business.'

Newby snorted in exasperation. 'You really do scrape the gutters, don't you?' he said contemptuously.

'If we have to, sir. Not that we put more weight on gossip than it will bear. And I gather that your father was not an easy man to have dealings with.'

'I cannot think where you got that idea!' Newby said. 'He was exceedingly well regarded, in trade circles and the City – as yesterday's memorial service demonstrates.'

'Oh, it was certainly a demonstration of something. For instance, I think that you and your fiancée were demonstrating that, from now on, you are going to do what you want. Otherwise, it would have been plain bad taste, to parade your relationship for the first time at your father's memorial service.'

Frederick frowned. 'Very well,' he said. 'My father did oppose my desire to marry Miss Osborne.'

'Did he not like her?'

'It was not a matter of that. He had the notion that thirty was the time for a man to marry. He said that I should not settle down, until I had made my way in the world.'

'That's a bit of an old-fashioned idea, isn't it, sir? Anyway, you were working in his shop, not sailing to America to seek your fortune. And I would have thought that running a Bond Street jewellery establishment was making your way in the world.'

'This shop is merely a branch,' Newby said irritably. 'To date, I have been no more than a manager.'

'But you are . . . how old?'

'Twenty-nine.'

'So close?' Bragg said musingly. 'It was hardly worth killing him, was it?'

'I am glad you agree that I am innocent of my father's death.'

'Did I say that? I hardly think so . . . Here you are, a man of straw, with a beautiful young lady in tow. If you don't make good your intentions, she'll cast off and drift over to somebody else. You go as far as you dare. You get engaged to her secretly. But that is not satisfactory for either of you – and these things leak out. You decide to have it out with your father, once and for all. You go to the shop in Poultry, at lunch-time on Monday the fifteenth. You tell him you are engaged, and are intent on getting married. He says you are not yet thirty; that you have to wait another year. This time, you are man enough to tell him to shove his job up his arse . . . That puts him in a spot. He is only paying you a pittance. If you go, he will have to pay out real money for a manager. He blusters and threatens, as usual. You get furious, and clock him one with the statue. You didn't actually intend to murder him, but you killed him nevertheless.'

Frederick blinked his eyes, and shook his head woodenly. 'There was never any reason why I should bear my father ill will,' he said. 'It was his stated intention that I should acquire ownership of this branch on my thirtieth birthday.'

'So, why should he make everybody miserable, for the sake of a year?'

Frederick stared down at his clenched hands. 'My father was a man of fixed ideas,' he said. 'And he was not amenable to reason. He would never bend to circumstances. Rather, he would seek to compel circumstances to conform with his preconceptions.'

'So, he was prepared to chuck you on the rubbish heap, for the sake of one year?' Bragg asked.

'As I have said, he was utterly inflexible. But we would have managed to co-exist for another year.'

'Until your young lady gave you her ultimatum, you would. But then things changed . . . Tell me, sir. Where were you over the lunch-time of Monday the fifteenth?'

Frederick frowned in an effort of recollection. 'Ah, yes. I went to the home of Lady Bressingham, to return some pearls we had repaired.'

'What time did you leave the shop?'

'Well . . . it would have been a little after half-past twelve.'

'But Lady Bressingham lives in Berkeley Square. You could walk there in ten minutes. Blast it! You were only delivering them . . . Or is she young and frisky? Did she invite you up to her bedroom, to try them on her?'

Newby flushed. 'There was nothing like that! I merely handed to the housemaid an envelope, containing the jewel-case with the pearls in it, and the bill for our work.'

'So you are your father's son, so far as chasing the money goes,' Bragg said contemptuously. 'And what did you do after that?'

'Why, I came back here. I did not learn of my father's death, until I returned home in the evening.'

'No . . . That won't do, sir. We know, from your assistant here, that you did not come back to the shop that day.'

Newby frowned. 'I have to admit that my memory is very hazy. Perhaps I just walked . . . The shock of my father's death, and the manner of it, has obliterated everything else.'

'You don't remember killing him?'

'I know very well that I did not! How on earth would I remotely profit from doing so?'

'I would have thought it was obvious. But it might have been not so much to profit, as to avoid loss . . . Shall I tell you what I think started it?'

'No doubt you will, whatever my wishes.'

'Thank you, sir . . . Well, as I said, it all goes back to your young lady, and her pressing you to make your intentions clear to the whole world. So, you feel you have to placate her and her family; to go through with the engagement. Now, this puts you into all kinds of difficulties. In a few short months, you will be a prosperous tradesman in your own right. You might reasonably expect to inherit the business in Poultry, as well, when your father dies. And you have expectations under Nathaniel Pendleton's will, when your mother and her sister are gone. You will be very wealthy; have an important position in society to keep up. Being a jeweller, you would be expected to have given your fiancée a handsome engagement ring, not diamond chippings set in white gold. So you have to find a way of giving Nancy a decent ring. The only option you have is to pinch it from your father.'

'That is absurd,' Frederick said with a sneer. 'You have seen our books. You know full well that every item is accounted for individually. I could not delete an item from the stock ledger, without having a sales docket to correspond.'

'That's true,' Bragg said good-humouredly. 'It puzzled me for a time. Then it clicked. You see, in a place like Bond Street, you are amongst the wealthiest people in the world. If they want something, they will pay for it – no haggling. Never any question of taking a bit off the price, to get a sale . . . I tracked down the ring you gave to your young lady easily enough – a brilliant-cut solitaire diamond, set in platinum. Two hundred pounds might be small beer to an Indian maharajah, or a Texas oilman. But, in your world, it was a ring you would never need to feel ashamed of, however wealthy you became.'

'This is pure fantasy!'

'Oh, no. I could prove it easily enough, by comparing Miss Osborne's ring with the stock records . . . As I said, your problem was how to pay for it. You dare not approach your father; you had no money of your own – and I reckon your mother was too scared of her husband to give you any of hers. Then I put myself in your shoes. I worked in an office for a good few years, and it comes back easily enough. What you had to do was get the ring out of the stock records, in a way that would look perfectly natural. And what more natural than a sale? I don't think your father was your first concern. I bet you thought he would trust you not to defraud him. But if the accountant picked it up, at the year end, you would be in trouble. It's not as if you are selling boiled sweets. Every item here goes through the bookkeeping system individually. Your fiddle must be covered up in some way . . . Then I noticed three items that were out of the usual pattern. As I said, in this area you don't need to give discounts to get your sales. Yet, here were three costly items, on which a discount had been given. And, do you know, those discounts just happened to add up to two hundred pounds! Quite ingenious, really. You sold those items for the full price. The money which was represented in the books as discount, went into the till as coming from the sale of the diamond ring. Am I right?'

Newby was staring at him fixedly. He said nothing.

'The trouble was,' Bragg went on, 'that what I could find out with a great deal of effort, your father could see at a glance. I reckon that, for some reason – perhaps the same rumour about your engagement that we heard – your father decided to look at the books of this branch. Of course, he wouldn't want to have a row with you in front of the assistant here. Nor with your family present – it would undermine his authority even more. So he called you up to the City shop in the lunch hour, and told Colley not to come back till three. Plenty of time to sort you out, he would think. But, instead, you sorted him out. When he charged you with the theft, you saw red. You remembered how you had worked all these years for a pittance; always danced to his tune, like an organ-grinder's monkey. So you picked up the bronze and hit him. Maybe you didn't mean to kill him. But kill him you did . . . Wasn't that the way of it?'

Newby's face was chalk-white. He licked his lips and blinked. 'It is true about the ring,' he said slowly. 'My father's attitude was monstrous. Had I not formed an attachment to Nancy, I supposed it would not have mattered . . . But he allowed me no self-respect. In her eyes, I would have been a subservient weakling. I was not prepared to lose her, to satisfy my father's sense of what was proper. Whether he discovered my stratagem, I do not know. What I do know, is that I did not kill him!'

When Bragg got back to Old Jewry, he found Morton engaged in constructing a family tree of the Newbys. He peered over his shoulder.

'Well, it looks pretty, anyway,' he said grumpily. 'And how did you get on with your tailor? Are you going to Australia as a conservative English gentleman, or as a masher?'

Morton grinned. 'I am sure that, if I were to go as a masher, the accepted style would have changed before I got there!'

Bragg sat at his desk and stared out of the window at the tower of St Olave's church. 'Frederick Newby admitted the ring fiddle,' he said thoughtfully. 'But he would have none of my very persuasive suggestion, that he killed his father over it.'

'That was wise of him.'

'You know, lad, I can't get this family clear in my mind. They seem to live in a never-never land; not mere traders, and not quite nobs.'

'You are excluding Sir John from that comment, I presume.'

'Huh! For somebody who has to be outside what happened, he tries his damnedest to be in on everything. I don't mind telling you, he gets my goat.'

Morton smiled. 'In my researches, I discovered something that might resolve your difficulty, sir. To some extent this has to be hypothetical, so we should not build too much on it.'

'Get on with it!' Bragg said crossly.

'Despite the investment in the baronetcy, back in sixteen eleven, I suspect that the Newby family did not thrive. It may be that they became disaffected from the Royalist cause. If they were trading in the City during the Civil War, they would have had to be on the side of the Parliamentarians.'

'But the business was only set up in seventeen twenty-five,' Bragg objected.

'The existing business, yes. But I suspect that one could not open a shop in the heart of one of the dominant communities of goldsmiths in Europe, without extensive experience. However, the theory I am propounding is that, despite the title, the Newby family was of limited consequence until eighteen thirty-seven.'

'So, what happened then?'

'Sir Thomas Newby, later the father of John and Rodger, had the foresight to marry a certain Gertrude Allen. She was the daughter of a veritable merchant prince. Her dowry must have transformed the family's fortunes; have given them a social cachet they had never achieved before. It could, for instance, explain the decision to send the future Sir John to Eton. To plan a career for him, that would open up a world beyond selling silver plate to livery companies.'

'I see . . . While still doing as they always had with Rodger. It makes a sort of sense, I suppose.'

'And perhaps we have been assuming that the goldsmiths' business has been more profitable than it was in fact.'

'Hmm . . . Maybe that explains why Rodger was keeping a tight hold on things, not letting Frederick have his head. As I said, Frederick admitted the fiddle over the ring. It sticks out a mile, that he hated his father's guts, but he swears he didn't kill him.'

'Yet he has no alibi for the time of the murder.'

'In common with Colley, Edgar Newby, Pascoe, Malpas . . . Oh, Miss Marsden was here, first thing.' A look of disappointment flitted across Morton's face. 'I reminded her about the auctioneers' catalogues,' Bragg went on. 'She had done nothing about it. Women! Still, she promised to get on with it today.' He cleared his throat censoriously. 'Do you play chess, lad?' he asked.

'I used to play with my father, yes.'

'You will know well that you can spend hours circling round each other, advancing one minute, seeming to retreat the next; always looking for the right moment. But, if you don't judge it exactly right, you can end up where nobody can move – in a stalemate. Nothing to do but shake hands and bugger off home. Both of you have lost . . . Certainly, neither of you have won. I reckon you are bloody near stalemate with that young woman, lad.' He raised his hand to still Morton's protests. 'I know you feel you have nothing to offer her. But that's of a kind with joining the police as a flat-foot. You can see you will inherit a great estate in Kent; in time become Sir James Morton. You don't want to offer her less. But women aren't just men in skirts. They have different needs, different priorities – a home of their own, children . . . If you ask me, lad – which you don't – I would say that you are being selfish and stupid. I begin to wonder how I can trust the judgement of somebody who is, at bottom, so bloody idiotic!'

Morton's face was stony. 'You may be sure,' he said coldly, 'that I will give your remarks the respect they deserve.'

'Right.' Bragg stood up briskly, 'Then let us see if we can find out a bit more about Edgar Newby, and his fiddles, shall we? Which is the railway station for Aldershot?'

'Waterloo, sir.'

'Right. Did you make a note of the officers' mess, where the wine went missing?'

'The Royal Artillery.'

'Then find us a cab, will you?'

They drove in silence to Waterloo station; stood mute on the freezing platform; journeyed almost to Aldershot without exchanging a word.

'You know where the mess is, do you?' Bragg asked, as the train slowed for the station.

'Yes, sir,' Morton said distantly.

As the train stopped he leapt out in search of a trap. It took them through an area of low, sandy hills clothed with heather and pine trees. Bragg wanted to comment on it; compare it with the lush pastures of Dorest; but he held back. He had gone too far; broken the cardinal rule of not interfering in a fellow policeman's private life. He ought to have known better – certainly should apologise. But not yet. In Morton's present state of mind, an apology might only provoke a self-righteous explosion. Better to leave it. To Bragg's way of thinking, it had needed saying. Best now to pretend it had never been said.

The trap drove up a narrow road, and stopped at a barrier. A non-commissioned officer in a red tunic marched briskly towards them.

'Could you direct us to the officers' mess?' Morton asked.

The man took in the confident air, the authoritative tones. 'Yes, sir,' he said crisply. 'Follow the road to the right; over the crest of the hill. The officers' mess is the brick building on the right-hand side.'

'Thank you, bombardier.'

The man smiled, stepped back and saluted.

'What was that bombardier bit about?' Bragg asked, grateful to find a neutral topic to converse about.

'That rank of non-commissioned officer is called a bombardier, in the artillery. Elsewhere in the army he would be a corporal.'

'Good thing you knew that. Always helps.'

'I ought to know it,' Morton said brusquely. 'My father was a general, after all.'

'But not a gunner?'

'No. Cavalry.'

The conversation wilted, and nothing more was said until the trap had dropped them at the pillared portico of the officers' mess. Morton strode into the entrance hall, where a soldier was leaning against the wall. Seeing Morton, he sprang erect, concealing a cigarette behind his back.

'We wish to see the officer in charge of messing arrangements,' Morton said crisply.

'Yes, sir! That will be Captain Parkes. I saw him come in, not a half-hour ago. His room is down the corridor to the right; second on the left.'

'Thank you.' Morton marched off down the corridor and rapped on the door. There was a shout from within. He opened the door and stood back for Bragg to precede him.

Bragg took out his warrant-card, and gave it to the captain. 'We would like a brief word, if we may, sir,' he said.

The captain scrutinised the oblong of paste-board. 'Very well, Sergeant Bragg. What is it about?'

'The consignment of wine that never reached you.'

'Ah! Glad that someone is taking the matter seriously! Been made to look a damn fool! Came as near as damn it to authorising payment. Always been trustworthy before.'

'This is Pendleton Vintners, you are referring to?'

'Yes, sergeant. Supplied our wines since time immemorial. Totally reliable.'

'Can you tell us what went wrong this time?' Bragg asked quietly.

'Dashed if I know! At the beginning of September we take stock of the cellar. Usually been run down over the summer, with garden parties and various junketings. So it's a big order.'

'Do you remember what you ordered on this occasion?'

'I have a copy of it somewhere.' He started to rummage through the contents of a drawer. 'I know we were low on clarets; and the ladies had seen off most of the champagne . . . Here we are.' He glanced down a closely written sheet of paper. 'Everything is out of their catalogue, of course. Nothing fancy.'

Morton took the sheet and glanced through it. 'You do not

stint yourselves,' he remarked with a smile. 'First-growth clarets, vintage ports, fine cognacs.'

Captain Parkes shrugged. 'There must be compensations . . .' he said. 'But what I want to know is, what has happened to the damn stuff. We cannot wait for ever! Good thing we have this rule about not paying an invoice till delivery, or we would be out of pocket. Pendletons said they were looking into it, a good three weeks ago.'

'Do you have their invoice here?' Morton asked.

'No! Sent it back, after we had waited a week. Can't deal with people who are inefficient.'

'What was the date of the invoice?'

'Wouldn't know precisely. Over four weeks ago, obviously.'

'May we keep this list?'

Parkes frowned. 'I suppose so. The underlying information must be in the cellar book.'

'Can you remember,' Bragg asked, 'what exactly happened in relation to this consignment, so far as you are aware?'

'I have told you. We sent off the order. A week or so later we got an invoice – payable on demand. As the wine had not been delivered, I returned the invoice, asking what the hell they were playing at!'

'And you have heard nothing since?'

'Not a word.'

'I expect they are in a bit of a turmoil,' Bragg said in a placatory voice. 'One of the people running the business was murdered last week.'

'Ah. Too bad. Well, if you see them, tell them we will not wait for ever.'

When Catherine entered the Osbornes' sitting-room, she found Nancy leafing through the pages of *The Lady*. She scrambled to her feet, and gave Catherine a warm hug.

'What a difference ten days can make!' Catherine said teasingly.

Nancy gave a wry smile. 'The wedding cannot take place for ages yet,' she said. 'But I thought I could be looking for some ideas.'

Catherine settled herself on the sofa. 'When will it be?' she asked.

'Of course, Frederick wishes it to be as soon as possible, and with little or no fuss.'

'How like a man! Let protocol go hang!'

Nancy frowned. 'He is so impatient! He feels that thirty is ten years too long to wait. I tell him that, if he had married at twenty, he would have been marrying someone other than me!'

'I suppose that Mrs Newby will wish to observe the customary year's mourning,' Catherine said.

'I am sure she will. I must confess that Frederick and I have not discussed our marriage with her . . . It might have been easier if Frederick had been closer to his father.'

'But, at least, you are now accepted as a future daughter-in-law.'

'Yes! I keep telling Frederick that we must not rush matters; that, for the moment, it is enough to be regarded as being one of the family. But he has lived in his father's shadow for so long, he feels compelled to assert himself.'

'I suppose that he is head of the family now,' Catherine said musingly.

'There will be a tussle between him and his mother, before anyone else thinks so! Perhaps that is why he is so anxious to have a family of his own.'

'Not, I trust, until the expiry of the natural period after your marriage!'

Nancy blushed. 'Of course not!' She paused, then: 'I sometimes think that to hurry our wedding is the last thing we ought to do,' she said.

'Why is that?'

'Perhaps I ought not to say this to you. I know that James Morton is one of the police officers investigating Rodger's murder. And you and James are very close.'

Catherine forced a smile. 'Even so,' she said, 'I would not pass on any information which you wanted to be withheld from him.'

Nancy frowned. 'It is not that. Frederick said he had not killed his father, and that is enough for me . . . But it is what other people will think. I am sure that, if we marry with indecent haste, some people will draw the conclusion that Frederick was impatient with his subordinate status. After all, he has gained greatly from Rodger's death.'

'Nonsense!' Catherine said firmly. 'No one would kill a parent, to gain independence a year earlier than was promised.'

Nancy looked down at her hands. 'I tell myself that, of course. But Frederick has been getting more immoderate, when talking of his father. And, as it now is, he will control the whole business.'

'I am not sure about that,' Catherine said slowly. 'I wish I had paid more attention now . . . From what James was saying, Rodger might have died intestate.'

'Yes, he did! The family solicitor, Mr Fummery, said as much. There was a solemn conclave after the memorial service. Frederick insisted that I should be there. Anyway, Fummery said that there could not be the normal reading of the will, because the original could not be found, and the status of his copy was a matter of doubt.'

'I see. Oh, dear!'

'No, I think it is a good thing,' Nancy said spiritedly. 'No one would say that Frederick killed his father, in order to get less than was due to him!'

Catherine allowed a pause to develop, then: 'Who was the lady in the procession at the service?' she asked.

'Immediately behind Frederick and me? That is Rodger's sister, Mary Wilshire.'

'Really? She seemed very much younger. In her late thirties, I would guess.'

'I believe that Rodger's mother, Gertrude, had . . .' She hesitated and blushed. 'Had a bad time, when the twins were born. It seems that Mary was an unexpected afterthought.'

'Ah! And why has she not appeared before?'

Nancy shrugged. 'She is married to a landowner, in the West Country – near Chippenham, I think. They never come up to town.' She gave a malicious smile. 'So far as those spiteful society dames are concerned, she could hardly be said to exist, could she?'

*

When Bragg and Morton got back to London, darkness had fallen. Bragg left Morton to make enquiries of the Waterloo goods department, and went in search of a cab. The sleet of the morning had turned to wet snow, and was driven into his face, as the hansom crossed Waterloo Bridge. Bragg could feel it settling in a soggy, cold crust on his moustache. He longed for a hot cup of tea; to thaw in front of the fire, in his room at Old Jewry; to mull over the case for an hour, then off home.

'Ah, Joe,' the desk sergeant greeted him. 'Sir Rufus Stone has sent for you! His clerk wasn't too pleased that you were out. Said you was to go to Sir Rufus's chambers, the minute you got in.'

'Oh, hell! Why doesn't he go home at a decent hour, like other people?' Bragg said irritably, going out into the cold once more.

By now the evening traffic was building up. The steel tyres of the lorries were sliding on the slushy streets, the horses scrabbling to get a footing. The Bank crossing was jammed solid, the streets leading to it were congealed with vehicles. His coat collar turned up, Bragg walked cautiously past St Paul's cathedral and along the Strand to the Temple. In the olden days, this place had been occupied by the Knights Templar. Now the defenders of the faith had been replaced by jousters with words. Men who fought for their beliefs had given way to a lesser breed of mortals: men who scrupulously avoided believing in the cases they argued, lest it should cloud their judgement and restrict their tactical freedom. Bragg turned into Pump Court, and went up the staircase leading to Sir Rufus Stone's chambers.

The coroner's clerk looked up, as he entered. 'Ah, sergeant,' he said. 'Thank goodness you are here! Sir Rufus is not in the best of moods, this evening. He has been in court most of the day, and I have a feeling the case may be going against him.'

'What? Do you mean he can actually lose a case?' Bragg said jocularly. 'I cannot say I have ever heard him admit as much!'

A door opened, and Sir Rufus strode towards him. 'Have you cause for mirth, Bragg?' he demanded. 'Do you dally with my minions, while I await your presence?'

'I've just come through the door, sir,' Bragg said meekly.

'Hah! It is now three hours since I sent for you. I am not

accustomed to kicking my heels in my chambers, while my officers gallivant around no one knows where.'

'Constable Morton and I were down in Aldershot, sir,' Bragg said quietly.

'Aldershot? Well, you would hardly go there for pleasure, I'll allow. Come in, out of the cold. I cannot understand why the clerk to these chambers refuses to heat the place adequately. Goodness knows, he filches enough of the pitifully small fees which the cases he accepts bring in!' Sir Rufus turned and stamped back into his room.

Bragg closed the door quietly behind them. 'We went down to Aldershot, to follow one of the strands in the Newby case,' he said.

'Then you are deigning to apply at least some effort to its solving,' the coroner said disagreeably.

'Indeed, sir. Pendleton Vintners are long-standing suppliers of wines and spirits to several officers' messes. A particular consignment, worth a great deal of money, has gone astray.'

'Pendletons? Is not that where the younger Newby son is employed?'

'Yes, sir. He has been on the fiddle a good while, if you ask me. But, this time, he seems to have tried something big.'

'How big?'

'Over three hundred pounds, according to the invoice.'

'Hmm . . . And why are you expending valuable time pursuing bottles of *vin ordinaire* in the depths of the Home Counties? Surely this could be dealt with by some country flat-foot?'

'I felt it best to investigate myself, sir. This ties in with the murder of Rodger Newby, to my mind.'

'Pah! You seem to be floundering, Bragg!' the coroner exclaimed. 'How can the failure to deliver some cases of military wine be linked with the death of a goldsmith?'

'As I said, sir, we think that Edgar Newby, the younger son, has been defrauding Pendletons. Up to recently, it has been in a smallish way – just enough to pay his gambling debts. But he is now in with a fast crowd; probably needs more and more. Rodger was the principal trustee of the Pendleton trust. So he had prime responsibility for the business. He knew what was going on, all right, but turned a blind eye.'

'Foolish of him, Bragg.'

'Yes, sir. But we reckon this time the fraud was so blatant, even he could not ignore it. So he tells Edgar to come to the shop in Poultry, during the lunch hour. That way, they can have it out with no Pendleton staff and none of the family there.'

'That, in your view, is the reason for Newby's telling his assistant not to come back from luncheon until three o'clock?'

'Yes, sir.'

'Hmm . . . A possibility – but the evidence is somewhat tenuous. You will have to put more flesh on it.'

'Very good, sir.'

The coroner went over, and warmed his back at the fire. 'You will know that Pascoe is to be Lord Mayor?' he said.

'Is he? Now, that is interesting!'

'Yes. And rather surprising in the circumstances.'

'Why do you say that, sir?'

Sir Rufus frowned. 'He had made some injudicious comments, when Newby was preferred to him.'

'You mean, he didn't lose like a gentleman?'

'If you must express yourself like a groundling at the music hall, it might be an apposite remark.'

'What sort of comments?'

'As you can imagine, Bragg, Newby's financial resources were infinitely greater than Pascoe's. The former had, I believe, a fine house in the City, was prepared to entertain lavishly . . . Pascoe is said to have commented that Newby bought his way to the Lord Mayoralty.'

'So, he could have taken his revenge with a bronze pipeman?'

'Pipe-man?' the coroner exclaimed. 'What on earth are you talking about?'

'The bronze statuette. It is of an Old English Pipeman. The Prince of Wales has one like it in Sandringham House,' Bragg said, straight-faced.

Sir Rufus looked at him suspiciously, contemplating a crushing remark, then thought better of it. 'Well, it is not beyond the bounds of possibility that Pascoe could have gone to the shop, that lunch-time,' he said.

'Particularly as he lied to us about where he was.'

'Lied to you? In what way?'

'He said he was with a sick friend, at his home in Whitechapel. We know that the friend was in hospital then.'

'Good God, Bragg! Then, if you are going to arrest him, it would be better if it were done before the public announcement . . . Perhaps I can delay that for a few days. It is not as if they need a name. Everyone knows they have to make somebody Lord Mayor on the eleventh of November.'

'But he will be expecting his nomination to be publicised.'

'Then the delay will put pressure on him, stretch his nerves. One should always put one's adversary on the rack, Bragg. Remember that.'

Next morning, Bragg and Morton went to Pendleton Vintners' premises in Crutched Friars. On asking for Edgar Newby, they were directed to French Horn Yard. As before, the warehouse was deserted, except for Edgar, who was checking cases of wine against the stock book. He looked up irritably as they entered.

'We would like a chat, sir,' Bragg said amiably.

'Cannot you see that I am busy?' he said.

'It won't take long, I assure you. We wanted to have a word about the wine for the officers' mess in Aldershot.'

'What about it?' Edgar snapped.

'You mean, you don't know it went missing?'

'Of course I know!'

'We went down to Aldershot,' Bragg said evenly. 'Saw the messing officer. He wasn't best pleased. It seems the order has still not been delivered.'

'If it is any concern of yours, sergeant, we are waiting for delivery of certain items from our shippers. Then the matter will be dealt with.'

'Oh, I think it is a concern of ours, all right,' Bragg said evenly. 'It was a big consignment that disappeared. I should think you will lose a valuable customer over it.'

'It is not a criminal offence to lose a customer,' Edgar said sharply.

'No, that's true, sir . . . I gather that you went to Waterloo station, and made out the railway consignment forms.'

Newby frowned. 'Yes. It is part of my duties.'

'Of course. But you made a mistake! Constable Morton went

to the goods depot at Waterloo, to see how it could have gone astray. What was it you found, constable?'

Newby's face was tense, as Morton took out his notebook and flicked through the pages.

'On the evening of Thursday the twenty-fifth of October,' he said solemnly, 'I proceeded to the goods office at Waterloo station. I made enquiries about a consignment of wines and spirits, despatched by Pendleton Vintners to the officers' mess of the Royal Regiment of Artillery at Aldershot.' He was savouring this, he thought. In his head, it sounded like the sergeant of police in *The Pirates of Penzance*! 'According to our information, the consignment had been taken to the goods depot for despatch, on the tenth of September. I examined the railway company's records, but could find no entry for such a consignment. There was, however, a consignment sent by Pendleton Vintners, on that date, to a Mr Edward Palliser at Walton Old Hall, Dorking, Surrey.'

'That's your friend from the Moulin Rouge club, isn't it?' Bragg said sarcastically. 'Did he give you the price of the wines? Or was it for something else?'

'I do not see that I have to answer questions on matters that are of no concern to the police,' Newby said sharply.

'Oh, we are concerned all right.'

'Then tell me this, sergeant. Has any information been laid before the authorities, by any person at Pendleton Vintners?'

'No, sir. I can't say that it has.'

'You must know that, until it has, you are not empowered to make any enquiries whatever into the matter.'

Bragg frowned. 'So you are up with the law, then?' he said sardonically. 'But our enquiries arise out of the murder of your father.'

'Which has nothing to do with consignments of wine from Pendletons.'

'Ah, but you see, sir, it could have. This is how we read it. We know that there was a big row between you and your father, on the second of October. We reckon it was over this diversion of the Artillery wines. We are told that your father was furious over it; that he thought you needed reining in. As we see it, he told you to come to the shop in Poultry, during lunch-time on the fifteenth of October. He told Colley not to

145

come back till three, because he wanted it to be between the two of you . . . When you got there, he told you what a useless wastrel you are; and what he was going to do to clip your wings. I expect you had your say, and it all got to such a pitch that you got hold of the statuette and hit him with it. I'm not saying you meant to kill him; perhaps he needled you so much, you didn't know what you were doing. but that was the way of it.'

Edgar's lip curled in contempt. 'I have already told you where I was,' he said.

'Maybe. But Edward Palliser doesn't sound such a good bet, now we know about the wine.'

When they got back to Old Jewry, they found Catherine Marsden sitting demurely in Bragg's chair.

'I am tasting the sensation of real power,' she said gaily. 'Power of life or death, no less!' She got to her feet and went to the window. 'Actually, I was wondering if you have any information on the Newby case, that you wish to share with our breathless readers! Tomorrow's edition is not yet put to bed.'

Bragg hung up his coat, and sat down. 'You know, miss,' he said despondently, 'any one of six or seven people could be said to have a motive. But we can't get half-decent evidence against any of them. Have you any ideas?'

Catherine looked startled. 'I am a reporter,' she said. 'I do not make the news!'

'No. But you are an intelligent young woman. You know most of the people involved – at least by repute.'

'I am sure that I could never achieve the necessary emotional detachment,' Catherine said with a smile.

'What I can tell you, in the strictest confidence, is that George Pascoe is to be the next Lord Mayor.'

'Oh, yes! Everybody is talking about it,' Catherine said, with an amused smile.

'Are they? Blast it! I thought we had a few days . . . Sorry, miss!'

'Is he still under suspicion?' Catherine asked.

'Oh, yes. His alibi didn't stand up . . . But we haven't told him yet. I expect he thinks he has got away with it.'

'Then please hold your hand until Tuesday. It would give me something sensational for Wednesday's edition!' Catherine said lightly.

'I'm not sure I know what sensational means, miss. If I did, I reckon it would not be our business to provide you with it.'

'Not even in exchange for valuable information?'

Bragg picked up his pipe. 'That would depend, miss,' he said cautiously.

Catherine smiled at Morton. 'As to the value, I am quite content that James should be my assessor! I have two items of interest for you. Firstly, I have discovered that the lady in the procession at the memorial service is Mary Wilshire, the sister of Rodger Newby.'

'Sister, eh? She looked a good bit younger.'

'Yes. She is eighteen years younger than her brothers.'

'Hmm . . . That must have been a shaker! I expect it was her husband with her, at the funeral.'

'Appropriately enough, he is a landowner in Wiltshire! They do not seem to have a close association with the members of the family in London.'

'Oh, well. I expect that is another strand we shall have to unravel. And what is this second bit of news?'

'You asked me to contact Stanley Rainham.' She glanced at Morton, and saw an irritated look come over his face. 'He was very apologetic,' she went on. 'It seems to have been a monumental task! He has examined not only the catalogues of Phillisp, Son & Neale for the past three years, but those of every other firm involved in fine art. Only yesterday, he came up with the answer!'

'Come on, miss,' Bragg said testily. 'Don't string it out.'

'Would you deny me my moment of triumph, sergeant?' Catherine said gaily. 'It appears that a de Lamerie sauce-boat was sold, by Phillips themselves, in an auction at Norwich this July. It was the usual three-footed design, but one of the feet had broken off and was lost.'

'Not much use then, was it?'

'Exacty. Which no doubt explains the very modest sale price

of twenty pounds . . . But who do you think the purchaser was? None other than Henry Malpas!'

9

Bragg and Morton made their way in feeble sunshine to Throgmorton Avenue. This time, the Newbys' pert young maid was glum.

'Is your mistress in?' Bragg asked.

'She is. But I don't know if she'll see you,' the girl said crossly.

Bragg smiled. 'Getting you down, is it?'

'I don't know as how I can stand it . . . the curtains half-drawn still, his picture draped in black, everybody whispering – when they aren't shouting at each other. I'll be looking for another position, if this goes on.'

'Well, it's not as if it was a natural death,' Bragg said consolingly. 'It will take a bit of time to get over.'

'But I'm not having her telling me off, if I start to sing to myself when I'm dusting!'

'That is going a bit far . . . Anyway, will you tell her we are here?'

The maid half-closed the front door. They could hear her footsteps going up the stairs. They waited for a good five minutes, Bragg showing increasing impatience, before she returned. She showed them into the sitting-room overlooking the Drapers' gardens. Bragg beckoned to Morton, and they sat on the window seat. Morton gently eased the curtains open a little more. They heard the click of the door catch, and stood as Mrs Newby entered. If anything, she seemed less self-controlled than when they had told her of her husband's murder. She looked tired and strained; her eyes were puffy.

'We really dropped in for a chat, ma'am,' Bragg said earnestly. 'To see how you are getting on.'

Elizabeth dropped into a chair opposite them, the daylight showing clearly the lines on her face. 'I suppose I ought to ask what progress you are making in catching the person who murdered my husband,' she said in a fretful voice.

'Our enquiries are proceeding, ma'am. These things have to take their time.'

'Time was precisely what was taken from Rodger.'

'Time to do what?'

She gestured with her hand. 'Who knows? To achieve his heart's desire . . .'

'You mean, the position of Lord Mayor?'

'That was part of it, certainly.'

'And the rest?'

She gazed past them at the orange foliage of a plane tree. 'To order his own little world as he would have it, I suppose.'

'And those in it?'

Reluctantly she dragged her eyes from the window and looked at Bragg. 'Yes,' she said. 'One of his less endearing traits was a desire to dominate all around him. In a sense, it was once part of his attraction. I took it for moral strength, a sense of certitude. It was only when we had married, that I realised how it stifled everyone around him.'

'Including you, ma'am?' Bragg asked quietly.

'To an extent,' she said listlessly. 'Of course, while my father was alive he was generous to me. I had no need to depend on Rodger for my personal needs.'

'And, after his death, you had the income from the Pendleton trust.'

'Yes. But financial independence was not the whole remedy. Even in the household, which would normally be my sphere, he would give me the benefit of his opinions. If he did not care for a member of the staff, that servant had to go . . . When we moved to this house, he insisted that a firm of furnishers should be consulted. Everything had to conform to modern tenets of taste; be moulded to further his ambition.'

'I can see this would be a fine place to entertain in,' Bragg said amiably. 'I expect you did a fair bit of that.'

'Yes . . . I regret that most of all, in his death.'

'How do you mean?'

'That he was fated never to become Lord Mayor. He strove so hard for it, and it was snatched from his grasp.'

'I see . . . And what will happen now?' Bragg asked quietly.

'Happen? Why, nothing. That is the strange thing, sergeant. Except for those nearest to him, he will not be missed at all.'

'Frederick will take over the goldsmiths' business, then?'

'Yes. He is well experienced. He ought to have been given more scope years ago. But Rodger would have none of it.'

'I have the feeling,' Bragg said mildly, 'that he did not get on well with his sons.'

'It was not always so. When they were young they worshipped him. Anything which would advance their education, broaden their horizons, he would gladly provide. And, since they attended the City of London day-school, they had a very close relationship with him . . . He was a good parent then,' she said musingly. 'It was as they entered adulthood that strains developed between them.'

'I gathered that Edgar and his father didn't get on.'

Elizabeth sighed. 'It seems almost like betraying his memory to say this, but it was Rodger's own fault. As he was employed at Pendletons, Edgar was less under his father's control than was Frederick. And he is an impulsive boy, more independent. He was able to display his resentment more openly. So there was constant friction in the house . . . And it could have been so different . . .'

'At least, you now have a prospective daughter-in-law,' Bragg said consolingly.

'Yes!' Her face brightened. 'Nancy is a charming girl. She is everything we could have wished for. Such a pity that Rodger's death should blight their happiness.'

'I expect they will get over it . . . And, in the meantime, you have Sir John to lean on.'

Elizabeth twisted her lips. 'I must confess that I find his presence both comforting and irksome,' she said. 'It is ungrateful, I know, for he is a man of wide experience and integrity . . . but my sons plainly resent him.'

'I am sure he means well, ma'am . . . I hadn't realised, until recently, that he and your late husband were twins. I expect that leads him to do all he can for you.'

'Yes. Twins seem to be in a special category of their own . . . I was looking through some photographs, the other night.

There was one taken when Sir John was over on leave, with his wife. The four of us look very wooden and self-conscious! But, do you know, it was scarcely possible to decide which twin was which!'

Bragg smiled. 'Well, they both had the Newby nose, I suppose!. . . Sir John is married, then?' he said blandly.

The faint flush of pleasure faded from her face. 'No longer,' she said. 'Adela died of cholera, eight years ago. It was a great shame. She really brought him out of himself.'

'He seems forthcoming enough to me!' Bragg said with a rueful smile.

'Well, he has the public school veneer, but beneath it he is a rather reserved man. I suspect that he has always found it difficult to make friends.'

'You surprise me, ma'am. So, what was it she saw in him?'

Elizabeth gave a faint smile. 'Why, his title, of course! Surely you have heard of the fishing fleets?'

'Only on the Dogger Bank.'

'Well, sergeant, the Suez Canal solved more than navigational difficulties! Until eighteen sixty-nine we had the situation where hundreds of eligible bachelors were serving officers in the East. Often they did not come back to Britain until their career was ended. At the same time, there were hundreds of well-born maidens for whom no husband could be found. When the canal opened, the journey to India was reduced by half. It became tolerable for European ladies to travel there. And with the wives travelled these well-connected spinsters, in search of a husband!'

'And was this Adela one of them?' Bragg asked in surprise.

'Indeed she was! She was already twenty-eight when she went out – ostensibly to visit her uncle, General Graham, who was the commander of the British forces in Bengal. John was then thirty-five, and apparently a confirmed bachelor. But he had recently succeeded to the baronetcy, which made him quite a prize.'

'So they got married?'

'Yes. And, as I said, she was very good for him. She gave him twelve years of contentment. Took him into the upper levels of society, whereas before he had been looked on as a dull minor functionary . . . I am really very sorry for him. He must have missed her dreadfully. When they used to come over on furlough, it was obvious that he doted on her.'

'Life isn't easy, ma'am, even for the well-off.' Bragg got to his feet. 'I am sorry we bothered you like this,' he said.

'Not at all! I enjoyed our chat. I fear that I have been dwelling on my own problems far too much, of late.'

The young maid intercepted them as they left the sitting-room. She gave Morton a provocative smile, as she showed them to the door.

'What did you make of Mrs Newby, today?' Bragg asked, when they gained the street.

'She was very much in control of herself,' Morton said thoughtfully. 'She was content to talk about Sir John, but she seemed very tense when you mentioned her sons.'

'Natural enough, I suppose. But how about her as the killer?'

'Elizabeth? Kill her husband? I doubt it!'

'Why? She strikes me as a resolute woman. I reckon, if she had to choose between husband and sons, it would be the husband that would get the chop . . . I wonder if he was playing fast and loose.'

Morton laughed. 'Your imagination is running wild, sir,' he said. 'There is not the remotest indication that he was being unfaithful to his wife.'

'But why shouldn't he be? These pushful men often have a piece on the side. It's another way of dominating everybody around them . . . Suppose she found out? She would know he was always on his own, in the shop, from one o'clock till two. She might have popped in, that Monday lunch-time, on the off-chance as it were. Found he was alone, clocked him one, burnt the will and off again.'

'Why should she burn the will?'

'She might have thought it was the new one. She wouldn't have time to read it. But she would know it was going to leave Edgar skint.'

'You have missed your vocation, sir!' Morton chaffed him. 'You ought to be writing stage-plays.'

'All right,' Bragg said huffily, 'who do you reckon did it?'

Morton shrugged his shoulders. 'I confess that I do not know.'

'Well, try and contribute something! Your job is not just to knock other people's ideas down, you know. It's your turn now.'

Morton pulled out his watch. 'It is half-past ten,' he said. 'If we hurry, we might catch George Pascoe before he goes home.'

'Right, lad, Stop that cab.'

By the time they reached Gracechurch Street, the traffic had clogged up completely. Bragg hammered on the roof of the hansom, and called to the driver to let them off. He gave him a sixpence, and they began to pick their way through the stationary vehicles. Five minutes later, they were striding down St Mary at Hill towards Billingsgate Market. They were relieved to see Pascoe's shirt-sleeved figure bustling importantly round his stalls. He saw them and frowned.

'Good morning, sir,' Bragg called.

'Go in the cabin,' Pascoe growled. 'I'll be with you in a minute.'

By the time he joined them, Pascoe had recovered his composure. 'Right, gentlemen,' he said. 'What can I do for you?'

'First of all,' Bragg said genially, 'may we congratulate you! We gather you are to be Lord Mayor.'

There was no answering smile. 'It's not supposed to be common knowledge yet,' Pascoe said grumpily.

'Well, you know how these things get out, sir. For my part, you getting the top job would be a good thing. These nobs have had things their own way for too long.'

'How do you mean, "would be"?' Pascoe said edgily.

'Well, nothing is certain in this world, is it? I mean, less than a fortnight ago, Rodger Newby would have said he was going to be Lord Mayor.'

Pascoe passed his tongue over his lips. 'I see.'

'And, after your being given pride of place at the memorial service, I would have put my money on you. Now I am foxed. I don't know who the other runners might be.'

'What do you bloody mean?' Pascoe blustered. 'It's all cut and dried! There is nothing can stop it now!'

'I would have agreed with you,' Bragg said equably, 'until I found out that you had lied to me.'

'Lied to you? I've done no such thing!'

'There you are, you see. Once you start, there is no stopping.

If you remember, you told me you couldn't have murdered Rodger Newby because, at the time, you were with your old friend Albert Smith, in Whitechapel. We have found out that he was in hospital, when you said you were visiting him at home.'

Pascoe dropped his head. 'Christ!' he muttered. 'All right. It's my own bloody fault. I should have told the truth first off . . . I was with a young woman.'

'Oh, yes?' Bragg asked in disbelief.

'Why shouldn't I be? I'm not knackered yet awhile!'

'Because you are married, for one thing.'

'Lay off,' Pascoe said roughly. 'Are you a bloody Salvationist, or something?'

'You went so far as to tell us that you took one of your wife's eel pies to Albert Smith. Your wife confirmed it.'

'Yeah. I heard you'd been snooping round.'

'So, what is the truth?'

Pascoe sighed irritably. 'I met this young woman, six months ago. She took a shine to me, and we got chatting. She's a seamstress, name of Dora Gittings. She lives in the rooms over a fish shop I own in Whitechapel – retail. We've been good friends ever since.'

'So, when you knock off here, you go over to Whitechapel, and stuff your little bit of fluff. Is that what you are telling us?' Bragg demanded.

'Not every day, I don't.'

'So, how do you remember that you did on that particular day?'

'Because on the way home, at five o'clock, I saw the posters about Newby's murder.'

'What is the address of this young lady?' Bragg asked coldly.

'Five, Leman Street.'

'And what happened to your wife's eel pie?'

Pascoe grinned. 'Why, we ate it, didn't we?'

When they got back to Old Jewry, Bragg found a note on his desk, telling him to go to the Commissioner's office as soon as possible. When he entered, Sir William bounced out of his chair in irritation.

'You must have passed him in the street!' he exclaimed.

'Jumped-up nincompoop! These Members of Parliament go on as if they were God Almighty, decreeing what must be done. I will not be spoken to as if I were a raw recruit!'

'Who was he?' Bragg asked cautiously.

'Why, he was the MP for the Sudbury constituency. Partington-Fane, he said he was. They all seem to have outlandish names out there . . . Said one of his constituents, called Malpas, had complained about the conduct of my force. Mentioned you in particular. Alleged that you had stolen a valuable piece of silver from Malpas's house.'

'Now, that is interesting,' Bragg said slowly.

'What do you mean, man? That is not the word I would apply to larceny by one of my officers! Is there any truth in this accusation?'

'I mean, it is interesting that Malpas should create this fuss now. It was Monday we went down. Why leave it till now to complain?'

'Are you admitting that you did take it?' Sir William demanded.

'Take it? Oh, yes, we took it. The article in question is a silver punch-bowl, of the rococo period . . . That's early eighteenth century, sir.' He glanced out of the corner of his eye, but the Commissioner did not rise to the bait. 'This particular bowl was taken by Malpas to Newby's shop, a week before he was murdered. It was in the shop on the morning of the crime. After the murder, it was gone.'

'Stolen, you mean?'

Bragg nodded gravely. 'That had to be our first inference, sir; the person who took the bowl killed Newby for it. So, of course, we put the word about. But, from what we could discover, no known cracksman was trying to sell such a bowl. Then we learned that it had been made by Paul de Lamerie; which, as I am sure you know, makes it a very important piece. Your ordinary burglar would never know it from all the other pieces of plate in the shop. So we got to wondering if the thief was in the know, if he already had a buyer for this particular bowl.'

The Commissioner looked at him suspiciously. 'I hope this recital is getting somewhere,' he said.

'Indeed it is, sir. At that point we decided to go down to

Malpas's house. It was at the back of my mind that he might have an idea whom this buyer was . . . somebody who had admired it, perhaps. You can imagine our surprise, sir, when Malpas said he had taken it back! He showed it to us. It was in an old hat-box, in the butler's pantry. It seems that he had been in Newby's shop, between one and three o'clock on the day when Rodger Newby was murdered. In fact, he was the only person we could pin-point as having been there. So he had to be a suspect.'

'But why did you steal the bowl?' the Commissioner asked testily.

'Steal? Oh, we didn't steal it, sir. It was evidence! I informed Mr Malpas that I was taking it as such. And he did not demur. He had a shotgun. If he had wished to do so, he could easily have prevented us from taking it.'

'Hmm . . . Then why did he send his MP to me, to complain?'

Bragg looked earnest. 'That is what I would like to find out, sir,' he said. 'It is a bit of a change of tack.'

'Well, one thing I am clear on, Bragg; we must not keep the thing.'

'Very good, sir. I will send a wire to Mr Malpas, saying he can collect it.'

'Do that, will you?' The Commissioner cleared his throat diffidently. 'As you know, I go to great lengths to back up my officers . . . But *force majeure*, Bragg; *force majeure*.'

Bragg made his way back to his room.

'You appear somewhat disconsolate, sir,' Morton said cheerfully, as he slumped in his chair.

'Huh! He's afraid of his own shadow, that man. How he ever commanded an infantry regiment, I shall never know. Well, we have our marching orders. "Get rid of the Malpas bowl; it has become an embarrassment to efficient policing!" Where is the sodding thing?'

'You left it in the care of the desk sergeant.'

'So we did. Let's see if we can find it.'

They retrieved the hat-box and set off along Gresham Street.

'What is the object of this exercise, sir?' Morton asked.

'We have got our orders to give it back to Malpas. But what I want to know is, why it took him so long to complain. And why he sent his MP along, instead of coming himself. I think it's time we saw the new top man on silver. Come on, lad, hurry up!'

They turned down Foster Lane, and went through heavy iron gates into the vestibule of the Goldsmiths' Hall. A commissionaire was sitting in a leather-covered porter's chair, his hands clasped across his paunch.

Bragg marched over to him. 'Police,' he said. 'We want to see somebody on the plate committee.'

The man lifted a bushy eyebrow. 'And what would that be about?' he asked stolidly.

'It's none of your business,' Bragg said curtly.

'Ah, but the members of the plate committee are very important gentlemen,' the man said complacently. 'They can't be expected to waste their time with every Tom, Dick and Harry.'

'If you don't get your finger out of your bloody arsehole, I'll have you in the cells for obstruction!' Bragg growled.

The man looked up, startled. 'Here! There's no call for that,' he exclaimed self-righteously. 'I'm only doing my job!'

'Then get hold of one of them for me!'

'It's not as easy as you make out,' the commissionaire complained. 'They all have their own business to attend to. It's not as if they work here . . . But I think I saw Mr Benson come in . . . Wait here.' He levered himself to his feet and walked stiffly up the great staircase.

It was an impressive building, Morton thought; the dome giving height and grandeur, the coloured marble richness. There was a short flight of stairs on the rear wall, which divided and ascended to the next floor. On the newel posts stood statues of the four seasons, their whiteness contrasting with the burgundy and fawn of the marble behind them. Above them was a great gilded chandelier. It all spoke of solidarity, of probity, of continuity. One could readily accept that mortals inhabiting such palatial surroundings could indeed be entrusted with maintaining the purity of the British currency; that their fiat, stamped on silverware, should be accepted as an irrefutable guarantee of its quality.

A spare, bearded man was coming down the staircase, the commissionaire labouring behind him. He crossed over to them.

'You were asking to see a member of the plate committee,' he said.

'That's right, sir.'

'My name is Charles Benson. I am on the committee. Is it to do with the death of poor Rodger Newby?'

'It could be, sir.'

Benson looked speculatively at the hat-box in Morton's hand. 'Very well,' he said. 'Come this way.'

They followed him through an archway on the left of the staircase, and along a corridor considerably less grand than the hallway. He opened a door and ushered them into a perfectly ordinary office. He gestured towards some chairs.

'How can I help you?' he asked.

'It's a bit of a long shot, sir,' Bragg said confidingly. 'We are out of our depth on this case, I don't mind telling you. I can't understand, for instance, why people still bother with silver dishes and the like. I mean, china and pot are just as serviceable – and a damn sight cheaper. Young Frederick Newby said it was a good way of keeping your wealth and using it too. He reckoned that, if you ran short, you could always melt your silverware down. But, surely, you would lose a good deal of its value?'

Benson smiled. 'Undoubtedly . . . I suppose one could say that the South Sea Bubble started it all. That was a wildcat scheme, which promised investors instant fortunes. The financial markets were in their infancy, in the seventeen twenties. When the South Sea Company failed, all the people who had clamoured to put their money in it lost everything. Sentiment in general turned away from financial investments, towards something more tangible. The crash gave rise to the attitude which Frederick Newby expressed.'

'I see. That makes sense now.' Bragg took the hat-box from Morton and placed it on Benson's desk. 'If you are interested, sir, I would like to play a sort of parlour game. We know that Rodger Newby examined the piece in this box. We also know that he was interested in it, because he said that he would like to show it to Frederick. But we don't know why. What I would like you to do, if you will, is to look at it and tell us what you think of it.'

Benson smiled. 'The proposition sounds intriguing. And

since Rodger's reaction is unknown, I shall lose nothing in the comparison!' He stood up, opened the hat-box, and placed the bowl on the desk. Then, taking a lens, he peered at the hallmark.

'Aha!' he exclaimed. 'A script P and L surmounted by a crown. Undoubtedly the punch of Paul de Lamerie . . . The lion passant for sterling silver, the leopard's head for London . . . I shall have to look up the date-letter,' he said with an apologetic smile. 'I cannot trust my memory nowadays.'

He took a slim booklet from a drawer and turned the pages. 'Here we are . . . yes, it was made in seventeen forty-one.' He slowly turned the bowl round, gazing at it from every angle. He peered at the decoration through his lens. Then he sat back with a frown.

'I am not entirely happy with it,' he said finally. 'It has not got the feel of a de Lamerie. The Goldsmiths' Company commissioned several pieces from him, two of them made in the same period as this one. They are much more flamboyant, more florid in their decoration.'

'Are you saying it's not genuine?' Bragg asked.

'Perhaps.'

Benson took a small bottle of silver polish from a cupboard and, with a soft cloth, applied it to the area around the hallmark. He let it dry, then polished it off briskly. Then he took the dish over to the window, where the light was strong. He breathed heavily on the hallmark through his mouth, and looked again. He turned round with an amused smile on his face.

'Clearly Newby felt, as I now do, that the piece as it stands is not genuine,' he said.

'How do you mean, sir, as it stands?'

'The hallmark does not belong to this piece, it has been lifted from elsewhere.'

'Lifted?'

'Yes. The area bearing the original hallmark has been cut away, and the de Lamerie hallmark substituted. A practice that is not merely dubious, but criminal.'

'How can you tell all that, sir?' Bragg asked. 'I have gazed at it for hours, it seems, but I've seen nothing.'

'If you knew what to look for, you would have no difficulty. You must understand that the piece of silver bearing what we might call the preferred hallmark has to be soldered into position. Now, plate silver is pure metal; but the silver solder contains a percentage of lead. When I breathed on the area, just now, the solder showed up as a fine line.'

'I see,' Bragg said slowly.

'You sound doubtful, sergeant. Very well, let us confirm my diagnosis with another test. Would you be so good as to bring over that candlestick? . . . Right. Now, I will light the candle . . . If you would support the bowl, so that the flame is inside it and under the hallmark . . . Good! Now watch closely. As the metal warms, the solder will show up as a fine grey line at the join.'

There was a pause, then: 'I see it!' Morton cried.

Bragg screwed up his eyes. 'Yes, so do I! It's quite clear, isn't it?' He put the bowl down on the desk. 'So that was what Rodger Newby wanted to show his son. Thank you, sir. Things are a lot clearer now.'

'I suppose you cannot, at this juncture, tell me the name of the owner of this piece,' Benson said.

'No, sir.'

'Because it is highly undesirable that a piece such as this should be left in circulation.'

'It's evidence, sir. You understand that.'

'You mean that Rodger Newby might have been murdered, because he identified this piece as a forgery?'

'I would say it is more than possible, sir. What would have been the worth of this piece, if it were a genuine de Lamerie?'

Benson knitted his brows. 'Of course, de Lameries do not come on the market very often, and they are greatly sought after by collectors . . . If the right buyers were present, I could see the price going up to two . . . three thousand pounds. Perhaps more.'

'And as it is?'

'Well, it must have some curiosity value, I suppose. But essentially, it is now worth no more than the value of the silver it is made of.'

That evening, Morton waited for Catherine outside the offices of the *City Press*. Her face lit up as she saw him.

'James! How marvellous! Are you going to escort me home?' she asked teasingly.

'I have a possibly more interesting idea, if you have an hour to spare.'

'We shall not be dining formally tonight,' Catherine said. 'Papa is in Gloucestershire, painting a duchess! I imagine, Mamma and I will have supper around nine. Anyway, it does not matter. What is this fascinating project?'

'I would like you to come with me to a block of apartments near your home. It would be more authentic, if you were with me . . . if they thought we were looking for an apartment to live in ourselves.'

Catherine's face clouded. 'That is asking too much, James,' she said sharply. 'If I were seen by some acquaintance, my reputation would be in tatters! Much as I trust you, I will not take such a risk.'

'But I cannot see that there is any risk,' Morton protested.

'Men never can! Anyway, why is it a matter of such moment?'

'It is the Newby case, of course.'

'Of course!' she echoed.

'We discovered that Rodger Newby held the lease of an apartment in thirty-five, Grosvenor Mansions.'

'Did he? I wonder why.'

'So do we. There is just a possibility that I might find out, if you were with me. It would look more natural.'

'That is precisely what concerns me! Oh, well, it is not exactly round the corner from Park Lane. But, if I am recognised, you will have to make an honest woman of me!'

They took a cab to Grosvenor Square, and walked the hundred yards to Grosvenor Mansions. Number thirty-five was a large block, built of garish red brick, and five storeys high. As they pushed through the doors into the hall, a concierge looked up from her knitting.

'Good evening,' Morton said cheerfully. 'We are about to be married, and we are looking for an apartment in this area. We gather that the gentleman who rents apartment number four has died.'

'Been murdered, so they tell me,' the woman said with relish. 'Not that I've seen much of him.'

'Murdered? Good heavens! Not here, I hope.'

'No.'

'Good!' Morton took out a pound note, folded it and pressed it into her hand. 'Do you think that we might look around it?' he asked. 'It would be very helpful to my fiancée.'

Catherine summoned up a sweet smile.

'I don't see why not.' The concierge got up, and unhooked a key from a board on the wall. 'Don't you go making any mess there,' she warned as she handed it to Morton.

Catherine blushed scarlet, and hurried to the lift. She looked fixedly at the floor, as the cage soared up to the third floor. Morton pushed open the door and she stalked out on to the landing. Apartment four was directly opposite. He unlocked the door, and stood back as she hurried in.

'Never humiliate me like that again!' Catherine said furiously. 'She clearly thought that I was your strumpet!'

'Nonsense! You look precisely what you are, a virtuous, beautiful, self-possessed young woman . . . cultured, amiable, possessing impeccable taste –'

'And utterly stupid! I cannot think what possessed me, to allow you to drag me here.'

'Well, since we are here, let us at least see what we can find.'

The apartment consisted of a large living-room, two bedrooms, a kitchen and a bathroom. There was a sponge and a tablet of soap on the bath; two towels hung by the wash-basin. There were no foodstuffs in the kitchen cupboards. A scarcely used kettle stood on the gas stove. There were cups and saucers on the table, but no other crockery. The living-room held a settee and chairs; they seemed brand new. One of the bedrooms was empty. The other held a double bed, which was made up with sheets, blankets and pillows. There was a wardrobe in the corner, but it was empty.

'It seems that the concierge is all too well aware of the use to which this apartment is put,' Catherine said crossly. 'I feel soiled simply by being here!' She stooped and picked up a crumpled ball of paper from the fireplace. She pulled it apart. There was an envelope addressed merely to the apartment. There was no stamp on it, so it must have been brought by a street messenger. The note with it was brief.

Alice,
I may be late.
Longing for you!
Rodger.

10

'So the two sisters did agree on one thing – Rodger Newby!' Bragg laid a match over the bowl of his pipe, and puffed clouds of smoke about his head.

'That would appear to be the case, sir,' Morton said with a smile. 'I must confess that I find Mrs Harvey infinitely more appealing than Mrs Newby; though my acquaintance with her is indeed slight!'

'You want to watch that,' Bragg said censoriously. 'It's too easy for a pretty woman to warp a man's judgement – particularly if he is unmarried.' He gave Morton a meaningful look.

'However that be, we have surely another candidate for the killer of Rodger Newby.'

'His wife, you mean?'

'Why not? When we saw the two ladies together, there was a definite current of hostility between them. If you remember, Elizabeth rather pointedly remarked on the fact that Alice had no children.'

'So that, even if they were sharing the same man, Elizabeth was one up on her? Yes . . . But what we have to decide is whether she would kill her husband over it.'

'That might well depend on when she discovered his infidelity, sir. Let us assume that she discovered it that very morning. In the heat of her anger, she might march to the shop; confront him, full of righteous indignation; and, when he made light of the matter, kill him with the bronze.'

Bragg pondered. 'Yes, it could have been like that . . . But, when we saw the two sisters, it seemed more like picking at an old sore than the pain of a fresh wound. Anyway, these people belong to your class. Once an heir has been born, a woman can play fast and loose as much as she pleases – as long as she is discreet. And surely it works the other way round?'

'I am not convinced that your premise is sound,' Morton said. 'These are dyed-in-the-wool City people, with a different idea of propriety from the people who surround the Prince of Wales. Yes, Elizabeth might have accepted, even tolerated, Rodger's occasional fling with another woman. But for the woman to be her own sister, would be a betrayal of a very different order.'

'Then why not murder her sister? That would have put a shot across his bows too.'

'Because it would not be in character. I see Elizabeth as a self-contained, calculating person – someone who finds it possible to go on seeing her sister after Rodger's death, even knowing that Alice was his mistress.'

'But can we assume that Elizabeth knew about them?' Bragg asked musingly.

'I think we must. Only that could have occasioned the unseemly sniping between them, at that interview.'

'Hmm . . . Yet you have no difficulty in believing that this self-contained, calculating person could beat her husband's head in.'

'A sudden quarrel; a violent, overwhelming moment of hatred.'

'Over what?'

Morton shrugged. 'Over Alice, over his treatment of Edgar or Frederick – that was your original theory, after all!'

There was a commotion in the corridor. The desk sergeant appeared, holding Ward by the neck of his jacket. 'This gentleman has something to tell you, Joe,' he said sarcastically. 'Only you will do, it seems.'

Bragg gazed at Ward's dishevelled figure. 'Right. Speak up, man!' he ordered.

Ward swallowed hard. 'It's Mr Edgar!' he cried. 'He's dead! We found him, this morning, at the warehouse.'

'In French Horn Yard?'

'Yes.'

'What time was that?'

'Not half an hour ago . . . He hadn't come in on time – but that was nothing new . . . The cellarman was making up an order, and he found him. Blood all over his jacket, there is.'

Bragg got to his feet. 'Right, constable, get the pathologist over there. I'll go and have a look.'

During the walk to French Horn Yard, Ward was completely silent. As they went through the *porte-cochère* he dropped back, a look of apprehension on his face. Bragg pushed into the warehouse. It looked much as it had done on his previous visit. Ward reluctantly led him down a passage between piles of wooden cases. The body of Edgar Newby lay sprawled by the wall, his eyes staring up at the girders of the roof.

'Have you moved him?' Bragg asked curtly.

'No, sergeant.'

'What time do you start work?'

Ward looked perplexed. 'Why, half-past eight.'

'Then why did you not find him sooner?'

'Well, you know how it is . . . We like to have a brew of tea, in Crutched Friars, these cold mornings.'

Bragg bent over and touched Edgar's hand. It felt quite cold. 'When did you go home last night?' he asked.

'Half-past six. We had been here, sorting out an order for the Merchant Taylors' Company. All bits and pieces, it was. So we were late.'

'Was Edgar Newby here, when you left?'

'No. We locked up, just as usual.'

'Had he got a key to this warehouse?'

'He had a key to everywhere,' Ward said, with bitterness in his voice.

'Hmm . . . Have you noticed anything unusual recently? Anybody hanging around?'

Ward thought for a moment. 'Well, no . . . not really. He would often have friends up here, open a bottle. They were tasting, he would tell me; but I never saw any orders come from it. All we got, was a lot of part-cases. I've even known them nail a case up again . . . have valued customers complaining, because there was a bottle missing!'

'Hmm . . . Edgar was a bit of a scoundrel,' Bragg said musingly. 'I pity you, having to deal with him . . . I don't suppose you knocked him off yourself, did you? Couldn't keep your temper this time.'

'No, I never!' Ward said querulously. 'Anyway, he was shot! You look.'

'Does that mean you couldn't have done it?' Bragg asked, squatting down. He pulled aside Newby's coat. There was a bullet hole in his waistcoat. Blood had seeped downwards, over the yellow and blue check. Above the stain was clear evidence of powder-burn. So, he had been shot from close range. That argued someone who knew him.

The outer door banged, and Professor Burney came bustling in, followed by Morton.

'Another Newby, I gather,' the pathologist remarked, his mouth grinning with anticipation.

'Yes, sir. Younger son of the last one.'

'Goodness me! There will soon be none of them left, sergeant, unless you catch this miscreant.'

'I'll do that,' Bragg said curtly. 'What can you tell me about this one?'

'Well, for a start, he was not killed at this precise spot. And, from the bloodstain on his waistcoat, he was propped up for some time before he was dragged here. Do you see the traces of blood on the floor?'

'I confess I hadn't noticed that,' Bragg said contritely. 'But he was killed in this building, I'll be bound.'

Burney squatted down and unbuttoned the waistcoat. 'You will have noticed the residues of gunpowder, I assume.'

'Yes, sir.'

'He was shot through the heart,' Burney murmured. 'Rigor is well established . . . a cold night, no heating here . . . I would say that he was killed about twelve hours ago.'

'Nine to ten o'clock last night.'

'As a rough guide, sergeant . . . It seems distinctly unhealthy to be a Newby, at the moment. Get the body over to the mortuary, will you?' Burney picked up his bag and sauntered out.

Bragg turned to Ward. 'Wait here, till the van comes to take him away; then I want this place locked up. Where are the other staff?'

'I sent them down to Crutched Friars, sergeant.'

'Well done . . . It looks as if you have what you wanted, sir.'

Ward frowned. 'What do you mean?'

'Why, you are the one in control now; the big boss. All I need to find out, is where you have hidden the gun.' He turned on his heel and strode out of the warehouse.

'That was rather wicked,' Morton said, as they got to the street.

'Well, he's such a moaning, spineless bugger. If he'd had any self-respect, he would have walked out years ago. What a way to run a business! I reckon Rodger Newby must have been a bit of a loony . . . See the body is collected, will you, lad? I suppose I shall have to break the news to the grieving mother.'

Bragg walked slowly through the streets towards Throgmorton Avenue. The plane trees were almost bare of leaves now, their branches stark against the sky. Winter was here; months of biting winds and lowering skies. It could hardly have come at a worse time for Elizabeth Newby, he thought. To lose a husband, and then a son – in the space of twelve days. It was unbelievable . . . unbelievable unless the deaths were connected. But how could they be? Rodger had distanced himself from Pendletons, except for trying to keep a rein on Edgar. Where was the logic behind the two murders? It looked as if it had to be Frederick. He now had the two goldsmiths' shops, after his father's death. And, under Nathaniel Pendleton's will, he alone would eventually inherit the wine business – lock, stock and barrel. Bragg felt the stirrings of compassion for Elizabeth Newby, as he knocked on the door.

The young maid seemed just as perky. 'Oh, it's you again!' she said. 'About time you found out who did it, then we can get some peace!'

'Is your mistress in?' Bragg said sombrely.

'Yes, come in. I'll fetch her.'

Bragg waited in the darkened drawing-room until Mrs Newby entered.

'Please sit down, sergeant,' she said, with a trace of impatience in her tone.

'Thank you, ma'am.' He waited while she went to the window seat. 'What time did your son, Frederick, get home last night?' he asked quietly.

She considered for a moment. 'He had supper at the Osbornes',' she said. 'He arrived home at about ten o'clock, read to me for an hour, then went to bed.'

'And Edgar?'

'He must have been much later. I was asleep when he came in, and he had gone by the time I got up. As I am sure you realise, I have great difficulty in sleeping at the moment. I was awake for hours in the middle of the night, and could not seem to wake up this morning.'

'When was it you last saw him?'

Alarm was growing in her face. 'At breakfast yesterday. Why do you ask?'

'I am very sorry to tell you, ma'am, that his body was found in Pendletons' warehouse, this morning.'

Her face drained of blood. She put her hand to her breast. Bragg started to his feet, to catch her. But she regained control.

'Edgar too?' she whispered. 'How?'

'He had been shot, at close range. He would not have suffered.'

'Who can be doing this to us? Oh, God!' She gave an agonised wail and stumbled from the room.

Bragg let himself out, and began to walk aimlessly. This murder had shaken up his ideas like a kaleidoscope. A totally new pattern had emerged. He had to admit that Edgar would have been his preferred killer. He was such an objectionable man. His murderer was practically doing society a favour. He had been almost a figure from melodrama – the rebellious son having his revenge on the family who scorned him . . . Except that it wasn't quite like that. Elizabeth regarded him as no more than difficult – was convinced that he would grow out of it. Rodger had seen the situation as a reason for restricting Edgar's influence at Pendletons, an excuse to exercise his domination behind the scenes. But that was the nature of the man, his wife had said as much . . . Had it happened the other way round, had Edgar been murdered before his father, it might have made more sense. Rodger had been enough of a martinet to physically impose his will, if need be. Edgar was going off the rails at sixty miles an hour! In no time at all, he would be bringing disgrace to the family. Rodger must have realised it . . . But perhaps Edgar had got in first; realised what might happen, and killed his father. That was in character, sure enough. At their first interview, Elizabeth seemed to have feared it. But, in that case, who had murdered Edgar?

Bragg realised that, during his cogitations, he had walked

beyond the eastern edge of the City; that Whitechapel was a mere hundred yards ahead. He strolled to the High Street, and asked for directions to Leman Street. Pascoe's was a corner shop in one of the better-maintained blocks. Even in this cold, the shutters were rolled up. Shoppers were leaning over the white marble slabs, peering at the fish, pointing out what took their fancy . . . It must be a thriving business, Bragg thought. There were three men serving, in white starched jackets and straw boaters; and a woman in the cash kiosk. The fish looked in prime condition . . . Well, so it should, with Pascoe being so high up in the trade.

Bragg backed to the edge of the pavement. There was only one storey above the ground floor. It seemed prim behind its white net curtains. But only seemed, if what Pascoe said was true. There was a door between the fish shop and the baker's next to it. Presumably that gave access to the rooms above. Bragg pushed at the door and it opened. He was half-way up the stairs when a young woman started down. She was dragging a heavy trunk behind her.

'Steady on, miss!' Bragg cried out. 'If you're not careful, it's going to come down on top of you!'

She stopped and looked down at Bragg. She was in her early twenties; pretty, but with a hard resourceful look about her.

'Well, I got to get out, 'aven't I?' she said. 'Can't wait around for bleedin' Sir Galahad to come and 'elp.'

'You must be Dora Gittings,' Bragg said.

'Wot if I am?'

'Nothing in particular. Why are you off in such a hurry?'

'I told you. I been chucked out.'

'By George Pascoe?'

She bridled at that. 'You a pal of 'is, are you?' she asked peevishly.

'Not really. We were just chatting. He said you were his friend.'

'Not no more! 'E comes last night, and gives me me marchin' orders. Out by noon, 'e said, or else!'

'But why?'

'I dunno . . . 'Cause 'e's bein' made Lord Mayor, I 'spect. A bloody louse, that's wot 'e is!'

'I am sure you can look after yourself,' Bragg said warmly. 'He always said you gave him a good time; particularly a week last Monday . . .'

Her lip curled. 'E was useless! I only went wiv 'im, so's I could 'ave this place. 'E thought I spent my time sewin' nighties – silly old sod!'

'And where will you go?' Bragg asked solicitously.

'I dunno. Back where I come from, I 'spect.'

'Not far, then.'

'Wot you wanna know for?' she demanded.

'Well, you look a nice girl. I thought we might be friends.'

She looked at him sceptically. 'Huh! I reckon you're past it as well,' she said. ''Ere, give me an 'and with this bleedin' trunk!'

When Bragg got back to Old Jewry, he found Morton had returned from the mortuary.

'Any news?' he asked.

Morton shrugged. 'No, sir. He had another subject on his slab, a young woman who had drunk acid.'

'God Almighty! What a way to go! When will he start on Edgar?'

'By the end of the morning, he thought.'

'Right . . . Talking of young women, I had the privilege of meeting Pascoe's doxy this morning. A case-hardened bitch, if ever I saw one! I reckon she was having it off with anybody who had a half-crown in his pocket. And there's Pascoe thinking it was just for him!'

'It is the way of the world, I suppose,' Morton said with a shrug.

'Yes . . . But what was interesting, is that Pascoe had thrown her out! She was in the act of lugging her belongings down the stairs, when I found her.'

'So Pascoe had discovered her extra-curricular activities?'

Bragg considered for a moment. 'No, I don't think it was that way. This was a loud-mouthed slut, if ever I saw one! Told me her whole life history, while I helped her down the stairs with her trunk.'

'Then it must indeed have been brief!'

'Nothing out of the ordinary about her . . . but she said that

Pascoe had told her to be out by noon. And, judging by her haste, there was going to be trouble if she wasn't.'

'When did this conversation take place between them?'

'Last night.'

'So, within hours – perhaps even minutes – of giving us her address, he was trying to ensure that we would not find her.'

There came a tap at the door and Sir John Newby poked his head round.

'The desk sergeant said I might find my own way,' he said apologetically.

'I see,' Bragg said gruffly. 'You'd better sit down.'

'I am here, of course, because of the tragic happening this morning,' Sir John said in a sombre voice. 'I am grateful, sergeant, that you broke the news to my sister-in-law personally . . .'

'She's having a bad time, sir.'

'It is most appalling! You have seen Edgar's body, I presume.'

'Only at the scene, sir. I gather that the post-mortem will be delayed a bit.'

Sir John raised his eyebrows. 'Is there any reason for that? I understood that he had been shot to death.'

'That is so, sir. It's just that there are one or two before him at the mortuary.'

'I see . . . If you have any information to convey to his mother, I would be glad if you would do it through me. She needs a period of seclusion to come to terms with her grievous losses.'

'I will make a note of that, sir.'

Sir John looked down at his hands. 'I fear that this is all attributable to my brother's attitudes,' he said quietly.

'How do you mean, sir?' Bragg asked.

'Even as a child he was aggressive, acquisitive. I then put it down to his being the younger – to jealousy, in fact.'

'I suppose that would be natural enough, sir. Look at Edgar. He was a scallywag, all right, and he was a younger son.'

'Yes. But I do not think that such a situation is common in twins . . . Not that we were identical; we were not created from a single egg, or whatever the latest scientific pronouncements would have us believe. But we were constantly together until we went our separate scholastic ways.'

'You didn't see a lot of each other after that?'

'Oh, we did! There were the vacations; the family holidays in Bournemouth . . . The decisive break came when I entered the Indian Civil Service. I became my own man at that point. Rodger remained under the tutelage of his father until he attained the age of thirty.'

'But your father was married at the age of twenty-six, according to *Who's Who*,' Morton interposed.

Sir John frowned. 'I am not attempting to draw parallels,' he said irritably, 'but to offer an explanation.'

'Go on, sir,' Bragg said.

'What I am trying to express, is that the conflict between his extended subordination in the business, and his aggressive nature, made him the man he was.'

'Domineering, you mean?'

'Yes, sergeant. And I fear that Edgar suffered because of it. To some extent, I believe he inherited his father's faults. And this was exacerbated by the failure to give him any responsibility in what was, after all, not a Newby business. It was a potentially explosive situation.'

'And it did explode. Is that what you are saying?'

'Manifestly so, I would have thought.'

'But why now?'

Sir John looked down at his carefully manicured nails. 'My sister-in-law informed me of a recent quarrel between Edgar and his father. It apparently concerned some wine destined for an army unit at Aldershot. I do not know the details. But, during the quarrel, Rodger informed Edgar that his position in Pendletons was by no means secure. There was apparently some reference in Nathaniel's will that Edgar might take a position in the firm – obviously as a counterbalance to Frederick's involvement with Newbys. Roger said that he had obtained a legal opinion. The effect of it was that this was no more than a facilitating clause. That it neither bound the trustees to offer employment, nor Edgar to accept it.'

'That would be a shaker for Edgar,' Bragg said.

'Indeed, sergeant. And it is my belief that there was no going back for him. He had become involved, I understand, with some very questionable people. Criminals, in fact.'

'So you think Edgar killed his father?' Bragg said.

Sir John sighed. 'I would gladly believe the contrary,' he said. 'But, on the evidence, I can come to no other conclusion.'

'Hmm . . . In that case, who killed Edgar?'

'One should not hypothesize in such situations, I know. And to do so would be to trespass on your field of operations. But we know that Edgar had criminal associates, that some of his activities must have left him open to blackmail, and that he was still not in a position to meet pecuniary demands made on him.'

'It sounds all very neat and tidy,' Bragg said drily. 'So, we can forget Frederick as the murderer?'

Sir John looked at Bragg gravely. 'I feel that Frederick has been so subjected to his father's domination, that he would never have the spirit to assert himself while Rodger lived.'

Bragg pondered. 'It would at least have the merit that there would be nothing further to upset Elizabeth Newby,' he said. 'By the way, sir, do you have your sister Mary's address?'

Sir John looked surprised. 'Yes, of course.' He pulled an address book from his pocket, and flicked through the pages.

'Here we are,' he said. 'She is Mrs John Wilshire, of Benham House, Yatton Langley, near Chippenham.'

'Thank you, sir. And can you, by any chance, give me the address of Alice Harvey?'

Sir John gave a half-smile. 'I ought to have it,' he said. 'We have always exchanged greetings at the festive season . . . Yes, I have her as living at twenty-five, Randolph Avenue, St John's Wood. I cannot vouch for it, sergeant. But it was certainly her address last October.'

After lunch Bragg said that he wanted to do some thinking, so he sent Morton to interview Alice Harvey. Her villa in St John's Wood was spacious, with a lawn in front and newly pruned rose bushes in the borders. Morton's ring was answered by a maid in starched apron and cap.

'Is Mrs Harvey in, please?' he asked.

The girl gave him an arch look. 'What name shall I say?' she asked.

'Constable Morton, of the City Police.'

Her face fell. 'Is it about the . . . goings on?' she asked furtively.

'Naturally.'

She looked at him uncertainly. 'Wait here a minute,' she said, and closed the door on him.

Morton turned and gazed at the traffic in the road. A railway parcels van was attempting to squeeze through the space between a stationary brougham and an oncoming omnibus. The van horse seemed to have more sense than its driver. Despite his whip, it was refusing to go any further. Now the omnibus driver was getting down, whip in hand. Any moment a fight might break out . . . But that was up to the Metropolitan Police to deal with. He had no jurisdiction here, and more important things to occupy him. He heard the door open behind him.

'Constable Morton! Do come in.' Alice Harvey smiled at him warmly. 'I am afraid that my maid is suspicious of strangers.'

He followed her to a comfortable sitting-room at the back of the house.

'It is quieter here,' she said. 'I would take my oath that, when we first came here, there was nothing like the amount of traffic we have now.' She seated herself decorously on a settee, and patted the cushion beside her. 'Do sit down, constable. It is pointless to discharge your onerous duties in discomfort.' Her voice was teasing, provocative.

'You are not of the same mind as your sister,' Morton said inanely, as he sat down.

'Sisters seldom are. But in what particular?'

'This room . . . No curtains drawn, no gloom.'

'Nor am I wearing black. Yet I am mourning Rodger in my own way.'

She seemed to be deliberately contriving an opening for him, Morton thought. But to accept it would be to lose control of the interview. 'How long have you lived here?' he asked lightly.

'Since eighteen sixty-nine, constable. I came to this house as a young bride.'

'I see. Have you been a widow long?'

'Far too long! It is an unenviable situation in our society. Overnight I was transformed from being an intimate of the great families, into a leper. No one wishes to invite a widow. Either they are self-absorbed and uninteresting, or they are dangerous!'

'And which were you?'

She looked at him, mischief in her eyes. 'Oh, I was never self-absorbed,' she said.

Morton could feel the pressure of her knee against his thigh, the stirrings of lust in him. Surely this woman could not be in her forties?

'What did your husband do?' he asked hurriedly.

'Alfred was a tea merchant,' she said. 'We married twenty-five years ago, when I was twenty-one. I think my mother was beginning to despair of me! I was very different from Elizabeth. I was determined to have a good time, before I allowed myself to be sucked into the bog of domesticity.'

'Then Alfred must have been very special.'

She considered for a moment. 'He was vigorous and attentive . . . and he was often abroad.'

There was an inviting smile on her lips. He could smell her fragrance, see the swell of her breasts through the thin silk blouse. 'You do not have any children,' he blurted out.

She lifted an eyebrow teasingly. 'I am unable to have them,' she said in a level voice. 'At first I regretted it deeply . . . But it has had its compensations.'

'I am sorry,' Morton mumbled . . . He need just reach out his hand, perhaps to comfort her – put his arm round her shoulders . . . 'When did your husband die?' he asked, trying to keep his voice steady.

'In eighteen seventy-three He was on a buying trip, in China. He contracted a fever, and was buried out there. So you see, I have not even had a grave to remind me.'

'You were still very young.'

She gazed at him insinuatingly. 'Twenty-five, and a widow. It sounded like a sentence of death – but one learns to be resilient.'

'Did he leave you well provided for?' Morton asked, fighting against his rising concupiscence.

'Barely that. His partners were loath to pay out Alfred's share. Were it not for Rodger Newby, I think I would have got nothing.'

Morton sensed calmer waters ahead. 'Was he able to help you?' he asked.

'Yes. I stayed with my sister for three months, after I was widowed. He was very generous of his time.'

'Surely, your parents were still alive then?'

'Oh, yes. My father died a mere eight years ago. But Elizabeth and I were always very close. Mamma had indifferent health. Elizabeth virtually brought me up. She is six years older than I.'

Morton took a deep breath. 'I would like you to examine this letter,' he said, passing over the creased note that Catherine had discovered.

Alice glanced at it, with an amused smile on her lips. 'I thought it must be something like this,' she said. 'You must be very clever! Rodger swore that no one would ever find our little love-nest.'

'When did you . . . When did it start?'

'Our affair, you mean? While I was staying with them. Rodger was so . . . comforting.'

'Immediately after you were widowed?'

Alice pouted her lips. 'You sound so censorious! I had not seen my husband for six months. His death was more a confirmation of my lonely state, than a tragedy. And Rodger was such a virile person . . . But obviously I could not stay there for ever.'

'You came back to live here?'

'Yes. To lonely widowhood, and our secret assignations. At first he would come here. But, clearly, that was dangerous. So Rodger leased the flat in Grosvenor Mansions.'

'Did your sister never suspect?' Morton asked incredulously.

'Of course she did. She has been making acidulate remarks for years. But she has a cold nature; and it might not have been in her interests to force a quarrel.'

'But surely you are both financially independent, under the terms of the Pendleton trust?'

'Of course. But you have to remember that Rodger was the only active trustee.'

Morton frowned. 'It seems that your father, Nathaniel, was guilty of a grave error of judgement,' he said.

She smiled archly. 'That is a matter of opinion. One might have said that things worked out well for all of us.'

'Except that there was friction – even at the interview when we saw you and Mrs Newby together.'

She wrinkled her brow. 'Was there? It can have been no more than is common between sisters, for I cannot remember it.'

'But the truth might be that Elizabeth resented it so much, she went to the shop and bludgeoned her husband to death.'

'Elizabeth?' she gave a snort of derision. 'She has not the resolve for anything so direct.'

'Whereas you have?'

Alice gave a slow smile. 'Oh, yes . . . But then, I loved the man. He made me feel young!'

Sunday dawned bright and clear. Had it been summer, Bragg thought, it would have been a day for the river. A trip down to Greenwich Park, perhaps, to listen to the band, have a pint or two. By eight o'clock, he was up and dressed – with fifteen hours before bedtime. What on earth was he going to do with them? There would be no church-going, that was for sure. Bragg had barely set foot in a church, since he had buried his young wife and baby. He wasn't for making obeisance to any god who could muck away innocent lives, as if they mattered not a toss. And, as for Sunday, it was a stupid institution. No medical operations on a Sunday, no theatres on a Sunday; everything useful or entertaining had to stop, for a day of sanctimonious gloom. So, how could he enjoy this glorious day, and give the Newby case a push at the same time? He went through its main strands in his mind. That was the trouble with being in the City force; the area was so compact. There was seldom an excuse for a jaunt. In this case, the only far-flung part had been Malpas; and he could stew for a bit longer . . . But there was the sister – Mary Wilshire. She had to be seen sometime. If he were prepared to give up his rest-day for it, nobody ought to complain . . . He thought of the fuss there would be, if he claimed his railway fare and had to admit that she was not at home. But surely to God she would be? What else was there to do in the West Country, on an October Sunday? Deciding to get some breakfast at the station, he put on his heavy coat and his best bowler, and set off for Paddington. Within an hour he was leaning back in a comfortable railway carriage, on his way to Chippenham.

When he went back to his family home, in Dorset, he would travel from Waterloo station. That railway company was really interested only in taking office workers to London and back.

And the line down to Weymouth was more for the ferry to France, than the convenience of locals. But this line from Paddington westward was a different kettle of fish! The Great Western Railway was a title well merited, with its wide gauge and its solid rolling-stock. Even in third class, you felt you were somebody! And the countryside looked good, too; the leaves gone, corn cut – down to its bare bones. But resting, gathering its strength for the spring. On the hillsides he could see pinpricks of light as stubble burned; snaking lines of red on the black, as wind fanned the embers. His heart lifted. That was the life he was born to; the slow pace of a country village, where there was time for a friendly chat, where everybody knew their place. He snorted in self-mockery. It was precisely that which he had rebelled against, which had driven him away. At fourteen he had landed a job in a Weymouth shipping office; from there made his way to London . . . But still a stretch of well-farmed countryside could make him yearn for the old days, wonder if he had chosen aright.

At Chippenham he was lucky enough to find a trap which would take him to Yatton Langley. The wind blew cold, but he turned up the collar of his coat. Nothing was going to spoil his pleasure, his day of playing hookey from London. Benham House was a stone-built manor, with a good range of outbuildings. It sheltered in a fold of the rolling hills. It had been built, centuries ago, as the centre of a working estate. Grown, rather; because there did not seem to be much architectural harmony to it. But it was well cared for. Perhaps a dollop of Sir Thomas Newby's money had followed his daughter down here.

Dogs began barking when the trap turned up the driveway. As Bragg was climbing down from it, a man came out of the front door towards him. He was strongly built, and in his mid-forties. He was wearing a frock coat and striped trousers which would not have disgraced him in Hyde Park.

'Mr Wilshire?' Bragg called.

'Indeed I am.'

'Sergeant Bragg, of the City of London Police. I wondered if I could have a chat about the death of Rodger Newby.'

Wilshire frowned. 'A nasty business, that. Well, since you have come all this way, I do not see how I can refuse. Come in.'

He led Bragg into a large drawing-room overlooking a terrace.

Mrs Wilshire rose as they entered. 'This is Sergeant Bragg, my dear. He wants to talk about Rodger's death.'

A shadow crossed her face. 'I see.' She was dainty beside her husband, her face looked drawn.

'You were at the funeral, ma'am, and at the memorial service,' Bragg said sympathetically.

'Yes . . . I am afraid I did not notice you.'

'Naturally enough. I wondered if I could just talk around a few things with you.'

'Of course.' She sank back into her chair. 'I will do all I can to help you find Rodger's murderer.' The sentiment was unexceptional, Bragg thought, but the tone was hesitant.

Bragg sat by the fire, opposite her. 'In a case like this, it is hard to get everybody into perspective,' he said amiably. 'It's not like somebody robbing the village shop. Your family are distinguished people; Rodger was going to be Lord Mayor of London. So there are lots of layers to it, if you understand me.'

'Yes, I see,' Mary said uncertainly.

'Did you see much of your brother and his family?'

'Rodger?' Mary frowned. 'I would say, very little in recent years. The journey to London becomes more of a hurdle, the older one gets.'

Bragg laughed. 'You are a youngster, compared to most of the people on the train I came down on!'

'That is very gallant; perhaps we have got too set in our ways.'

'There are so many aspects to this case, that I hardly know where to start,' Bragg said musingly. 'It's like a hank of wool the cat's got at. Pull the wrong thread, and you just make it more tangled . . . Of course, we have got to consider the possibility that he wasn't killed in the course of a robbery. And, now that we have Edgar too, it makes it more complicated.'

'What do you mean, Edgar too?' Wilshire demanded.

'Has no one told you? He was shot dead in Pendletons' warehouse. They found him yesterday morning.'

Mary put her hand to her breast. 'Oh, no! Poor Elizabeth!'

'I could see it coming,' Wilshire said roughly. 'There was too much ambition in that family. I've said so, time and time again.'

'You have pointed up the problem precisely, sir,' Bragg said warmly. 'We have to consider if there may be something in the family background, which is leading to these deaths. After all, Edgar may not be the last.'

Mary looked at him uncomprehending. 'But there was nothing very special about us, apart from the title – which seemed rather silly, in my eyes.'

'Why is that, ma'am? It sounds very grand.'

'Perhaps I have spent too much time away from London to believe that, sergeant. Down here we are in touch with the basics of life – sowing and reaping, giving birth and culling. London society is a world away.'

'Do you ever miss it?' Bragg asked warmly.

'No.' She gave a wan smile. 'Well, almost never.'

'Of course, you were born a long time after your brothers.'

'Eighteen years later! Very much an afterthought.'

'You wouldn't remember much about them as young men.'

Mary pursed her lips. 'Almost nothing of John. He was going out to India, when I was a tiny baby. As for Rodger, my earliest real memory is of his wedding – all the flowers and the dresses . . . It is so incomprehensible that he should be murdered!'

'Yes, ma'am. I have to admit that we are scratching around. And, with Edgar gone too, we begin to wonder who will be next.'

'You do not think my wife is in danger, do you?' Wilshire demanded.

'Well, I don't believe so, but it is best to be aware.'

'By God, if anyone comes slinking around here, they'll get some spread-shot up their behinds!'

'You would be better telling the local police to keep an eye open,' Bragg admonished him. 'But I expect you will be safe enough down here . . . Do you know, ma'am, I didn't realise, for a long time, that your brothers were twins.'

'Oh, yes. I think poor Edna was terrified, when our first baby was on the way, in case I might have twins also. It runs in families, you know.'

'Edna?'

'She was my mother's nursemaid, when the twins were born. She was only eighteen then, and totally unprepared for the harrowing experience of a difficult childbirth. She stayed with the family, and in due course was my nurse also. When I married, I brought her with me down here.'

'Is she still alive, then?' Bragg asked.

'Oh, yes, sergeant. Seventy-four, and bright as a button.'

'Is there any chance I could have a word with her?' Bragg asked cautiously.

Mary smiled. 'I see no reason why not. She loves company. After living so long in London, I think she becomes very bored down here. But I think I ought to be with you, to reassure her.'

'That would be excellent, ma'am.'

She led him up a flight of stairs, to a corridor running the length of the building. She stopped at a door half-way along it and tapped. She went into the room and beckoned Bragg to follow. An old lady was sitting by the fire, with a shawl around her shoulders. A canary was in a cage by the window, a cat curled up by the fender.

'A gentleman has come to see you, Nan,' Mrs Wilshire said. 'He is from London. You remember that I told you Rodger had died?'

'Of course I do,' Edna said in a cross, piping voice.

'Well, it is concerning that.'

Bragg pulled up a chair beside her. 'You have been with the family a long time,' he said warmly.

She turned a lined face towards him. 'Fifty-six years. And never a cross word have I had.'

'Of course, you were engaged to look after the boys.'

She gazed into the fire without replying.

'Were you present at their birth?'

'I was!' She glared at Bragg. 'Never should a body have to put up with that! The doctor knew, all right. He said there was twins!'

Her spasm of irritation over, she looked back at the flames.

'She had a bad time, I hear,' Bragg said gently.

'I blame the doctor,' she said querulously. 'He should have cut her to start with, instead of waiting. And her screaming fit to wake the dead . . . Poor love, he put her through it. I tell you, I would never let a man near me, after that.'

'But there was nothing like that, when Mrs Wilshire was born,' Bragg said.

Edna turned eyes full of contempt on him. 'No. But, all the same, madam was a fool to risk it.'

11

At ten o'clock on Monday morning, Bragg and Morton were at the mortuary. As they made their way through to Burney's examination room, they were intercepted by Noakes, his assistant.

'Now, you mustn't keep him long,' he warned them. 'The professor is giving a very important lecture this afternoon, at the Law Society. They are sure to score points, if they can. I don't want him tired and cross!'

Bragg had never seen Burney either tired or cross, but assured Noakes that they would be brief. When they entered his room, Burney was assembling a collection of glass jars, containing gruesome specimens preserved in alcohol. He looked round with his usual sagging smile.

'Ah, sergeant,' he exclaimed. 'I was wondering when I would see you.'

'I take it the autopsy on Edgar Newby is done,' Bragg said.

'Yes, yes! Nothing in the remotest degree complicated. The Newbys are a healthy lot, it would appear.'

'And what will your report say?'

Burney licked his full lips. 'In layman's terms, you mean?'

'Yes, sir.'

'Very well . . . The projectile was a small-calibre bullet – three-sixteenths of an inch diameter; which argues a light, easily concealed pistol. It entered the body between the fifth and sixth ribs, and one and three-quarter inches to the left of the breast bone. The path of the bullet was slightly oblique, and I found it lodged in the spinal vertebrae. No doubt you will need to have it for the trial.'

'If we ever catch the man who did it,' Bragg said gruffly.

'I have every confidence in your abilities, sergeant.'

'Tell me, sir . . . I am sorry if you are busy, but there is something that is niggling away in my brain. Can you tell me what a Caesarean birth is all about? It is to do with this case, in a way.'

Burney smiled. 'Well, as a procedure, it is perfectly straightforward, and of great antiquity. If Pliny is to be believed, Julius Caesar was delivered in that way, hence its name. You are no doubt aware that the normal presentation of a child is head first. But occasionally one has complications, such as a breech presentation. Now, there are limits to the extent one can turn a baby, once labour has commenced. So one perforce has to resort to surgical delivery.'

'The case I am thinking of was twins, sir.'

'I see. Well, in normal labour, one child would be engaged before the other. If there were complications, and a Caesarean section was decided upon, an incision would be made in the wall of the abdomen – that is the belly. Then a corresponding one would be made in the uterus, or womb. The babies would be brought out through the aperture, one after another, and the wounds sutured. It is a perfectly simple procedure, with very little risk of mortality nowadays.'

'And fifty-five years ago?'

'We have learned a great deal about antisepsis since then. But the surgery is still the same.'

'Thank you, sir. I don't know if that helps, but thank you all the same . . . Do I take it that you can release Edgar Newby's body for burial?'

Burney gave his loose smile. 'He is on one of the slabs out there. They may take him as soon as they like.'

Bragg sent Morton to Throgmorton Avenue, then went back to Old Jewry to ponder. He hung up his overcoat and hat, poked the fire into life, and sat down at his desk. The trouble was, he could not see a pattern. There were bits that seemed to come together, but never a clear whole. He took a rope of twist from his tobacco pouch, and cut a fill. He began to rub the slices lovingly between his palms, a soothing circular motion. Then he carefully fed the fragments into his favourite pipe. It was like a ritual, an incantation; trying to lure the flash of inspiration that would clarify everything. Were the Newbys a doomed family? Or just unlucky? Was there a connection between the two deaths? Or were the murders random? He struck a match and laid it across the bowl of his pipe . . . this was the best part of a smoke, the first tang of it at the back of the tongue . . . Perhaps it was to do with the wood the match was made of?

Already the first surge of pleasure was receding, its intensity declining to mere satisfaction. And, to make matters worse, he could hear the bubbling of saliva in the stem. He should have cleaned it out – it would be yellow with nicotine. In irritation he put the pipe in the ashtray, tore up Morton's half-finished family tree of the Newbys, and began another one.

This time he put at the head old Sir Thomas Newby, baronet and husband of an heiress. In the next generation was Sir John, widower and childless. He was a mere custodian of the title, which would pass to his nephew now. Bragg pencilled in Rodger's name, and put a line through it, to indicate that he was dead. The only other one in that generation was Mary Wilshire. She was married, with her own life in the West of England. Presumably, she had got her share of the family fortune when she married, or on the death of Sir Thomas. At any rate, she did not seem likely to benefit from the death of Rodger Newby – and even less so from that of Edgar . . . He heard voices in the corridor and, moments later, Morton was ushering in Sir Rufus Stone.

'Well, Bragg?' the coroner exclaimed in a hostile tone. 'What are you doing to catch this villain at large in the City? Two murders in a week! In the same family! The answer ought to shout at you.' He came round the desk and peered at Bragg's handiwork. 'Huh!' he exclaimed. 'Making pretty charts is no substitute for action, man. This is the City of London! Look where the wealth goes, and you will have your killer.'

'Yes, sir,' Bragg said mildly. 'This chart demonstrates just that.'

'Well, enlighten me!'

Bragg shot a pained look at Morton. 'There are two streams of wealth, if we can describe them as such,' he said. 'The first is the Newbys'. Now, Sir John has been a civil servant, in India, and the stream of Newby wealth has passed him by. But he has no children or dependants, and he seems well set up. He is on the verge of retiring to Eastbourne. Moreover, at the time of Rodger's murder, he was on the high seas . . . We can get rid of their sister, as well. She is married to a West Country landowner, and seems contented with her lot. So that leaves us with Rodger Newby.'

'Rodger Newby deceased,' the coroner said emphatically.

'Yes, sir. He wasn't a ruler of empire, or destined to be a baronet, but he had inherited the goldsmiths' business. He seems to have been a nasty bit of work, for all that he was chosen to be Lord Mayor. There are any number of people who would have wished him dead, if you ask me; from his wife down to his shop assistant.'

'Forget that,' Sir Rufus said impatiently. 'The man is dead. Where does his wealth go? He died intestate, did he not?'

'I gather that is for the courts to decide, sir. But I reckon it won't matter in the end. There were only the two sons, and Edgar has just been murdered. So all the Newby wealth will end up with Frederick, in time.'

'Aha! And what about the second stream of wealth?'

'Well, sir, this is the Pendletons.' Bragg pointed to the chart with his pencil. 'Those are the two daughters of old Nathaniel. Elizabeth is the widow of Rodger Newby, Alice is the long-time widow of a tea merchant called Harvey. Alice Harvey had no children; Elizabeth Newby has had two. But the Pendleton situation isn't straightforward. Nathaniel left the business in a trust. As I understand it, the trust was to pay annuities to Elizabeth and Alice, during their lifetime. Once they were both dead, the trust would come to an end. The Pendleton business would then pass to his grandchildren.'

'And they are?'

'They were Frederick and Edgar Newby.'

'And now there is Frederick only.' Sir Rufus flung out his arm. 'Really, Bragg! I do not understand you. It is as plain as a pikestaff, to any rational person. What alibis has Frederick put forward?'

'He admits he has none for the time of his father's murder. And we have a witness of a sort relating to that . . . A man called Malpas. He was in the shop, the lunch-time that Rodger Newby was murdered. Because of that, he is a suspect. But, in his defence, he claims he saw Rodger later on, in the street. Now, all the Newby men have a prominent, beaky nose. With a coat collar turned up, and a hat pulled down against the wind, he could easily have seen Frederick and mistaken him.'

'And where was Frederick Newby at the time of Edgar's murder?'

'His mother says that he was at home, long before the time that Edgar was shot. But I don't suppose we can rely on that.'

'Indeed, not! So, you see, Bragg, all you need is guidance, and you can arrive at the right result.' Sir Rufus drew himself up to his full height. 'I advise you, Bragg – nay, I order you – to arrest that young man, before he adds to his tally of homicides.'

Bragg nodded. 'Very well, sir. Go and arrest him, constable.'

When Morton got back, an hour later, Bragg barely seemed to have moved. The unfinished family tree still lay on the table; his pipe was untouched in the ashtray. He looked up as Morton entered.

'You got him then?' he asked dully.

'Yes, sir. He is in the charge-room now. Do you wish to see him?'

Bragg hesitated. 'No, lad . . . How did he take it?'

'With equanimity, is how I can best describe it. He said nothing. He seemed to have been expecting it.'

'Oh, well. So that's it?'

'Apparently so. Another triumph for you, sir,' Morton said lightly.

'No, not a triumph. If I'm honest, I did not want it to be him.'

'Why not?'

Bragg shrugged his shoulders. 'I must be getting soft in my old age . . . I suppose it was that young lass – what's her name?'

'Nancy Osborne?'

'That's the one. Just seeing her in the church, among all those fusty, money-grubbing old men, was like a breath of fresh air. It seemed as if there was a promise of spring, a chance to break away, a new start.'

'It will hit her badly,' Morton said quietly. 'She will probably never marry now.'

'Why not? She needn't take it so hard. There are other young men.'

'You misunderstand me, sir. I meant that it is extremely unlikely that she will have the opportunity. She will be for ever tainted, in the minds of society people, with the knowledge that she was once engaged to a murderer – a convicted and executed murderer.'

There came a rap at the door, and the desk sergeant poked his head round. 'A gentleman to see you, Joe,' he said chirpily. 'Come all the way from Sudbury on the off-chance, by the sound of it. Lucky you are in.'

'Lucky for him,' Bragg said resignedly. 'All right, send him in.'

To Morton, Malpas was bursting with feigned indignation. 'I received your wire,' he said abruptly. 'I must tell you that I regard it as very high-handed! Not an iota of an apology. Just a statement that my property is available for collection.'

'There is not a lot of room, on a telegraph form, for apologies,' Bragg said mildly. 'But, if you want apologies, then apologies you shall have.'

'That is not the point,' Malpas said irritably. 'And where is my punch-bowl?'

Bragg gestured to Morton, and he went over to the cupboard. 'By the way, sir,' Bragg said casually. 'Did you drink whisky with Rodger Newby, on the day he was killed?'

'Whisky? Indeed I did not! Why?'

'No real reason, sir.'

Morton brought out the hat-box, and set it on the desk in front of Malpas.

'I shall have to ask you to formally identify the piece, and give me a receipt for it,' Bragg said gravely.

Malpas seemed taken aback. 'Very well,' he said. He sat at the desk and opened the hat-box. He glanced inside. 'Yes, this is it,' he said.

'No, sir. I think you ought to take it out, have a good look at it,' Bragg said. 'I've got to play it by the book now. I'm in enough trouble as it is.'

'I should think so!' Malpas said censoriously. He lifted the bowl out of the hat-box and set it before him. 'Yes, this is it,' he snapped.

'Have a good look at it, sir. Turn it round, look underneath.'

Malpas frowned in puzzlement. But he picked up the bowl, scrutinised it from every angle, then put it down again.

'Is that the Malpas bowl, as we call it?' Bragg said mildly.

'Yes. I accept that it is.'

'Very good.' Bragg took a sheet of paper from his desk. 'How shall I describe it for the receipt, sir?'

'Er . . . A punch-bowl . . . a silver punch-bowl, made by Paul de Lamerie, in seventeen forty-one.'

Bragg wrote it down laboriously, and held the receipt out for Malpas to sign. He read it through quickly, took Bragg's pen and scratched his signature on the bottom. He handed the receipt to Bragg and made to put the bowl back in the hat-box.

'Just a minute, sir,' Bragg said affably. 'There seems to be a mistake.'

'A mistake?' Malpas put his hand out again for the receipt.

'No. I mean that we don't think the bowl was made by de Lamerie.'

'Are you setting yourselves up as experts on silverware?' Malpas said scornfully.

'Oh, we learn all kinds of tricks in this job, sir. And we don't think the hallmark belongs to that piece at all.'

'But you are talking rubbish!' Malpas exclaimed. 'You can see it with your own eyes! It is part of the bowl, man.'

'Ah, but you see, sir, they can do all kinds of clever things with silver. It's a friendly metal, so to speak. Now, I think that hallmark was originally on another piece of silver, and it was transferred to this bowl.'

'Transferred? For God's sake, how can you transfer a hallmark!'

'It's called lifting, sir. In this case, someone cut out the area round the original hallmark and replaced it with a de Lamerie hallmark.'

'But there is not the slightest trace of any such thing!' Malpas blustered.

'I agree, sir. It was very well done. But there are ways of demonstrating it. Get me a candle out of the cupboard, constable.'

Malpas sat fuming as Morton set a candlestick on the desk, put a candle in it and lit the wick.

'I don't mind letting you in on the trick, sir,' Bragg said amiably. 'It's a good one for Christmas parties! You see, the patch with . . . what shall we call it? the preferred hallmark . . . has to be soldered in position. Now, silver itself is pure; but silver solder has to have some lead in it, to make it run. At the temperature of an ordinary room, you can't see the difference. But, if you heat it up a bit, the solder shows as a grey line . . . Hold the bowl over the candle, constable . . . that's it. Now sir, if you will just come round, so that you can see the hallmark . . . Good! Now watch.'

For a moment Bragg thought it was not going to work; that there was something special about the candle in the Goldsmiths'. His heart lurched, he could see retirement looming over him . . . then the faint grey line grew visible.

'You see it, sir? Have a good look.'

Reluctantly Malpas bent over and peered at it. 'Yes,' he said peevishly. 'But I cannot understand what it has to do with me. It could have been done by anyone – long before my family acquired it. All I can say is that I, personally, have had no knowledge of this lifting that you speak of.'

Bragg waited until Malpas had resumed his seat, then he looked up. 'We have been doing some research,' he said quietly. 'A sauce-boat with a de Lamerie hallmark, precisely similar to that now on the punch-bowl, was sold at an auction in Norwich, by Phillips, Son & Neale, in July. It went cheaply, because one of the feet was missing, so it wouldn't stand up . . . Shall I tell you who the buyer was?'

Malpas slumped in his chair, his face drawn. 'It seemed a way out of my difficulties,' he mumbled eventually. 'People in London have no idea of the burden of keeping up a country estate, nowadays. They have more money than they know what to do with. And they would never have found out . . . They would have been just as pleased with the bowl as if it was genuine.' He looked up. 'Very well, sergeant, I admit it. What are you going to do now?'

Bragg pursed his lips in thought. 'There is not much we can do about the bowl,' he said at length. 'For a start, I trapped you into saying it was a de Lamerie; so, if you had a half-decent lawyer, it would not stand up in court. Confession apart, what have we got? You bought the sauce-boat and inherited the bowl. What you have done has ruined them both, where value is concerned. But that is not a crime. As far as we can discover, you have not actually made any misrepresentations concerning the bowl – not to your insurance company, not to anyone in the trade, not even to the police. I would like to get hold of the person who did the lifting for you, but you yourself seem to be in the clear.'

Relief was flooding over Malpas's face.

'I have no doubt,' Bragg went on, 'that you did intend to commit fraud, to pass the bowl off as a de Lamerie. But I don't think we could hang a fraudulent intent charge round your neck, without a complainant. No, you seem to be in the clear, all right. But the Goldsmiths' Company expert said you ought to destroy the piece. He said it wasn't worth more than the weight of the silver, anyway.'

Malpas reached out for the bowl, but Bragg laid his hand on it.

'I said you were safe over the bowl,' he said. 'Now, let me tell you what really happened on Monday the fifteenth. You had left the bowl with Rodger Newby for valuation, as you said. You knew he was on the plate committee of the Goldsmiths' Company. If he accepted it as genuine, you were in clover. But Rodger really was an expert. He felt there was something wrong – maybe it was not as flamboyant as he would have expected a de Lamerie of this date to be. So he did the test on the hallmark, just as we have done. And when you came back the next Monday – the fifteenth – Rodger told you it was a forgery, and he wouldn't touch it with a barge-pole. You tried to argue with him, he became contemptuous, and you hit him . . . time after time, with the statuette.'

'No! No!' Malpas shouted. 'It is not true! I told you, he was alive when I left. Why should I kill him?'

'Because he had your reputation as a worthy country gentleman in the palm of his hand. A word to his cronies, and you would be disgraced. It was what you deserved, after all . . . Henry Malpas, I am arresting you for the wilful murder of Rodger Newby. I am keeping the bowl as evidence.'

Once Malpas had been charged and locked in the cells, Bragg and Morton set off for the West End of London. The hansom set them down in Shaftesbury Avenue, and they walked the hundred yards down Windmill Street to the Moulin Rouge club. They found the street door open, and went inside.

'Shop!' Bragg bellowed. In the dim light from the curtained windows, the club seemed tawdry. At the far end was an apron stage. Tables clustered round it – so that dirty old men could look at the dancing-girls' tits, Bragg thought censoriously. Tables lined the walls of the room also, leaving an area of polished floor in the middle. This modern fashion for waltzing was made for places like this; couples rubbing up against each other in the dimness. No wonder mankind was losing all sense of seemliness.

'Shop!'

This time a plump female figure appeared, bearing a pail and a scrubbing brush. 'What are you shouting for?' she cried in a screechy voice. 'We are not open, anyway!'

'We have come to see Mr Palliser,' Bragg said.

'Oh. Well, he was here a minute ago. Try his office, down the passage.' She gestured towards an opening at the right of the stage, then went off to the foyer.

Bragg led the way down the dim corridor, to the back of the building. At the end, a band of light came from a half-open door. He strode into the room. A burly man in his forties was checking entries in an account book.

'Mr Edward Palliser?' Bragg asked amiably.

He looked up. 'That is so,' he said. He had plainly been handsome in his youth, but his face had a coarse, dissipated look.

Bragg waved his warrant-card at him. 'Sergeant Bragg and Constable Morton, City Police,' he said.

Palliser leaned back in his chair. 'Are you not a little off your beat, sergeant?' he said sharply.

Bragg smiled. 'You would be surprised how many times that is said to us, sir,' he said. 'But we can pursue our enquiries anywhere in the land.'

'So, what brings you to me?'

Bragg sat down with great deliberation. 'The death of Edgar Newby,' he said.

'I see . . . I heard that he had died.'

'He was a great friend of yours, wasn't he?' Bragg asked in a level voice.

'I knew him, certainly.'

'You used to go racing together, didn't you?'

Palliser smiled. 'It is one of the compensations for having to work into the early hours,' he said lightly.

'Edgar didn't have a job with those hours,' Bragg said gruffly. 'He was supposed to be working, when he was following the gee-gees with you.'

Palliser shrugged. 'I am not my brother's keeper, sergeant. In any case, the club is a customer of Pendletons.'

'But not you?'

'It is quixotic, I know, but for my personal wines, I patronise a local supplier in Dorking.'

'I see. Can you tell me where you were on the night of Friday the twenty-sixth of this month?'

Palliser's head jerked up. 'Why do you ask?' he said.

'Answer the question, please, sir.'

He frowned. 'I was here, in the club, from ten o'clock till four the following morning.'

'That is very precise. You have people who will vouch for that, have you, sir?'

'Yes, plenty of them.'

'You see, somebody arranged to meet Edgar Newby in Pendletons' premises in French Horn Yard. You know them, I believe.'

Palliser looked at him uncertainly. 'I have been there, yes. Edgar occasionally had tasting sessions at the cellars.'

'It was there that he was murdered.'

'How?'

'He was shot, through the heart, from close range.'

'Good God!' Palliser's lips twisted in distaste.

'Did you know that Edgar Newby was in trouble, sir?'

'Trouble? No! What kind of trouble?'

'He had been playing fast and loose with the stock. Not just the late-night jamborees you mentioned. It seems his father kept him short of money – and just as well, if he was going to gamble it away.'

Palliser shrugged. 'This is nothing to do with me,' he said.

'Do you know, sir, I have an idea that Edgar Newby liked you – even admired you.'

'I am flattered. But, in all honesty, I scarcely knew him. I went along with Bill Jeffers initially. It was as a result of the tasting that I bought a couple of cases of wine for myself.'

'I see. When was that, sir?'

Palliser's brow creased in thought. 'It would be in July,' he said. 'I remember that I had been at the Ascot races in the afternoon.'

'And did you never buy wine from Pendletons again?'

'Personally, you mean? No, but, as I said, the club buys from them; wines of very modest quality, I might add.'

Bragg leaned back in his chair. 'You know, sir,' he said deliberately, 'I don't think it was like that at all. I think Edgar was a weak character, easily led. And, as I said, he admired you; he wanted to model himself on you. He wanted to go to the races, bet without a care in the world, shrug off his losses, and look to do better in the next race. I expect he was a bit of a nuisance, of late, for he wasn't the most entertaining of men to have around. But you couldn't get rid of him, because he had a hold over you.'

Palliser snorted in derision. 'A hold over me? Don't be absurd, sergeant. I have told you, we were never on intimate terms. He was just one of a crowd, to me.'

'Oh yes, he had a hold over you. Not that he intended it as such. After all, you were helping him out financially.'

'I do not help people out in that way, sergeant. If I ever began, it would never end.'

'Ah,' Bragg said confidingly. 'I wasn't suggesting that you lent him money. Oh, no. It looked like a commercial transaction from both ends. On the tenth of September you took delivery of a consignment of wines – clarets, burgundies, champagnes. And you paid him in cash; probably a fraction of the retail price. Both of you satisfied! The only trouble was that this stock had been diverted from a Pendletons customer, and you knew it.'

'This is total fantasy!'

'No, sir. This consignment, worth hundreds of pounds, was sent to the Royal Artillery in Aldershot – the officers' mess. Do you know where it ended up?'

'No.'

'According to the records of the railway company, it was delivered to Walton Old Hall, near Dorking. That is your address, isn't it, sir? And I bet that, if we were to go along there now, we would find those cases of wine in your cellar.'

Palliser looked up and shrugged. 'Very well, I did buy some

wine from him for personal consumption. He gave me a very good price. I had no idea that it had been intended for another customer.'

Bragg looked at him benignly. 'It won't do, will it, sir? If what you say was true, there would have been no reason for you to deny you had it.'

'I was confused . . . I am buying for the club all the time. It is not a crime to be absent-minded.'

'But you see, sir, once you had gone along with Edgar, become his partner in crime, he had this hold over you. We both know what an unsavoury, untrustworthy man he was. He soon ran through the money you paid him for the wine. But, by then, his father had been killed, and the police were crawling over everything to do with the Newby family. So there was no way he could repeat the fiddle. His only recourse was to blackmail you for money. You couldn't afford to give in to that. So you arranged to go to French Horn Yard on the night of the twenty-sixth; perhaps ostensibly to open a case, try a bottle or two, and talk it over. And you shot him, callously, in cold blood.'

Palliser was shaking his head dazedly. 'It was nothing like that! I have not been near the cellars for weeks. I tell you I was here, in the club till four in the morning. I can prove it!'

'Very good, sir. You shall have the opportunity to do just that. In the meantime, I am arresting you for receiving stolen goods . . . Reach him his overcoat, will you, constable?'

12

After lunch, Bragg went off to ponder, as he expressed it, leaving Morton to do the paperwork. To Morton it seemed a faintly ludicrous proceeding. So far as the murder of Rodger Newby was concerned, he was preparing two separate statements of fact, for two unconnected people, each charged with the one crime. He toyed with absurd scenarios which could have caused Malpas and Frederick to conspire – a chance meeting, the offer of a bribe . . . No. Short of money Frederick might be, but he would not collude in cold blood to murder his father. It would be too risky, and quite unnecessary . . . Yet Frederick himself was under a compulsion. He was in love with Nancy Osborne, secretly engaged. Prepared, to that extent, to challenge his father's edict that he should not marry until he was thirty . . . That too was strange. Why should Rodger impose that age? It was a nice round number, certainly. But, from their various conversations, it seemed that Rodger himself had married when he was twenty-six. Was he unilaterally giving himself another four years of dominance? That would certainly be in character.

Morton brought his mind back to the two accused. Malpas was a self-confessed fraudster, however unsuccessful. Whatever the niceties of the law of evidence might decree, he had deliberately created a counterfeit de Lamerie bowl. Equally he had been scheming to get Newby's endorsement. On the back of that he could have sold the bowl – perhaps to some provincial dealer. There was plenty of money in cities like Manchester and Leeds. Had he pulled off the stroke, he would have been in clover – his mansion restored, perhaps a small surplus to enjoy. No doubt Bragg was correct, about not being able to proceed on a counterfeiting charge; but the circumstantial evidence of murder was strong.

Morton spent an hour writing the Malpas report, breaking it down into sections, giving a concise summary of the evidence. In a right-hand column, he inserted cross-references to various key paragraphs. It looked neat, logical, convincing. He allowed himself a private smirk of satisfaction. Then he took a fresh sheet of paper, and wrote the name of Frederick Newby at the top. The coroner had already sketched out the case against him. Frederick could not, or would not, produce anyone who could prove that he was with him or her, at the time of his father's murder. Moreover, Malpas had seen him, in the City, at the crucial time . . . Morton wondered if Malpas could have been lying. But what would he gain by that? Of course, Malpas thought it was Rodger, or so he said. What if they were conspiring together; obliquely giving each other an alibi? No. That did not make sense. At no time had Frederick admitted that he was in the City . . . Better get back to the bed-rock of motive, means and opportunity. Sir Rufus had stated the motive already: Frederick would inherit the goldsmiths' business, gain his freedom and self-respect. The means and opportunity were there for all to see. Morton had to accept that the case seemed irrefutable. He refused to acknowledge the feeling that Sir Rufus would, just as happily, have argued the opposing case; and with equal conviction.

As he finished the case, there came a tap on the door and Catherine entered. She gave him a delighted smile.

'Sergeant Bragg seems to have put you on the police equivalent of fatigues,' she said lightly. 'Is this a punishment for having the temerity to be selected for England?'

Morton laughed ruefully. 'I have to confess that he has some justification. In two weeks I shall be on the high seas; away for three months. He could, of course, take another constable under his wing. Indeed, he will probably be forced to.'

'And what would happen then, on your return?'

Morton shrugged. 'I honestly have no idea. I would hate the thought of working with anyone else.'

'But you have toured Australia before.'

'Yes. Then it worked out quite fortuitously. The man assigned to take my place was injured. Rather than accept an immediate replacement, Sergeant Bragg elected to wait for my return.'

'No wonder that he feels betrayed now.'

'Betrayed?' Morton balked at the word. 'That is altogether too extreme,' he said.

Catherine smiled. 'Then perhaps, in biblical terms, he thinks it is time you became a man.'

'And put away childish things? Yes, I imagine you are right. Would you agree with him?'

Catherine raised her eyebrows. 'Goodness! I am sure that is much too direct a question for a gloomy autumn day! Let me say that I am sure I would seize the opportunity with both hands, to visit such a fascinating country.'

'But what about your distinguished career?' he asked teasingly.

'There is a time for everything . . . But I did not come here to bandy words. I bear a crumb of information. Sir John Newby has been given a decoration on his retirement.'

'Oh? What is that?'

'He has been made a Companion of the Most Excellent Order

of the Indian Empire. It was gazetted as at the twenty-first of September.'

'It sounds very grand,' Morton said with a smile.

'It is, in fact, the lowest rank of the order. It appears to be conferred on unimportant Indian notables and minor British administrators.'

'So he would hardly be wildly delighted!'

'It is no doubt better than nothing,' Catherine said. 'With his baronetcy, it will probably impress the populace of Eastbourne immensely!'

Morton allowed a pause to grow, then: 'In view of your high spirits,' he said quietly, 'I assume you have not heard the news.'

'News? What news?' she cried. 'You promised that you would tell me everything!'

'I doubt if you will want to put this in your Wednesday edition. We arrested Frederick Newby, this morning, for the murder of his father.'

Catherine sank on to a chair. 'Frederick?' she repeated. 'Oh, no! Poor Nancy!. . . Are you sure?' she asked fiercely.

'The case seems very strong against him.'

'But mistakes have been known to occur!'

'Perhaps. But the arrest was made on the orders of Sir Rufus Stone, after he had personally reviewed the evidence.'

'I cannot believe it!' Catherine cried.

'Frederick is unable, or unwilling, to provide a witness as to where he was at the time of his father's murder. He admits to a hostile relationship with Rodger; we know he was under pressure from Nancy to make public their engagement . . . And now, after Edgar's death, he will inherit both the Newby and Pendleton fortunes.'

Catherine shivered. 'Life is so hideous!' she exclaimed. 'And, this morning, I felt so optimistic . . .'

Bragg entered the lift at the Royal Hotel, and soared upwards to the third floor. He tapped on the door of Sir John Newby's room. After a moment he heard footsteps within, and the door was opened. Sir John seemed taken aback.

'Come in, come in, sergeant,' he said cheerfully. 'I was just looking at some snaps of India.' He gestured to a table which was littered with photographs. 'I will ring for some tea.'

'No. Don't worry about that, sir. I shall not be long.' Bragg sat on a chair by the fire. 'You will know, of course, that we have arrested Frederick Newby,' he said.

'Frederick?' Sir John repeated in consternation. 'No! When was this?'

'The middle of the morning.'

'But why was I not told?' Newby protested.

'It was done on the orders of the coroner. As you are aware, I only have authority because I am the coroner's officer. He ordered the arrest personally.'

Sir John sank into the chair opposite. 'I cannot understand why Elizabeth did not inform me,' he said.

'I expect she is overwhelmed, poor woman. What with Edgar's murder and all.'

'Yes . . . But what I cannot understand is why?'

'Why what?'

'Why you have arrested Frederick?'

'Well, I personally felt there was a lot in what you said, the other day. About Rodger having been killed by Edgar, and Edgar being shot by one of his criminal friends. I said as much to Sir Rufus, but he would have none of it.'

'On what grounds?'

'Well, you, more than anybody, will know how a barrister's mind words. He doesn't like complicated situations. They are difficult to explain convincingly. He tends to ignore side issues, and concentrate on the obvious. Sir Rufus is no different. He brushed aside my views. "Look where the money goes," he said. And, of course, on that basis Frederick has got to be the culprit – to have murdered them both.'

'He has advanced no explanations, no alibi?'

'You have it exactly right, sir. As for the day of his father's death, he went to deliver some pearls to Berkeley Square at half-past twelve. The rest of the afternoon is blank! Not the best of positions from which to defend yourself.'

Sir John looked grave. 'I would never have thought it, sergeant,' he said.

'Nor would I, sir. The coroner's rule of thumb seemed a good bit too simple for me . . . And then I got thinking . . .'

'Excuse me a moment, sergeant,' Sir John said, getting to his feet. 'I find I have no handkerchief.'

He went into the bedroom, and Bragg heard him blowing his nose vigorously. Then he came back.

'I am sorry about that, sergeant,' he said with a smile. 'It will take me some time to become acclimatised to English winters again.' He sat in his chair. 'You were saying that the coroner's views were too simplistic.'

'That's right, sir. Perhaps I should have said that he was taking too narrow a view . . . But then, you yourself must have feared that Frederick would be blamed, when you came in on Saturday morning. You argued very strongly for Edgar as his father's killer. And I went along with it a good way . . .'

There was a pause, both men eyeing each other.

'And then?' Sir John asked.

'Why, I thought I would go to see one of my friends. I was in a shipping office when I was a lad. Came up to London to their branch here . . . It was only by chance that I joined the police.'

There was a silence, then: 'As to Rodger's murder, you were well out of it,' Bragg said. 'I checked up. The *Clan Macnab* only docked in Southampton on the eighteenth of October. Rodger had been dead for three days by then. And yet, I wasn't easy in my mind. And here were you, the head of the family on your own admission, not in line for a penny. It didn't seem fair to me, let alone you. Yet you were out of the country; I'd seen the *Clan Macnab* labels on your luggage . . . It was when you came to plead for Frederick that I got uneasy. It was very earnest, very concerned. Then I remembered you were a magistrate. You had spent your life with clever barristers fencing in front of you; the nuances of language were meat and drink to you. And I got to thinking . . .'

There was a pause, both men staring into the flickering flames.

'It was beautifully done,' Bragg said at length. 'You were arguing that Edgar had killed his father. Quite possible, in itself. Then, when Edgar was found shot, it was believable that he had been murdered by one of his criminal associates. The case was wrapped up in tinsel, a present from you to the hard-working constabulary. But I couldn't get away from the coroner's rule-of-thumb: "Look where the wealth goes." Where were you in all this? There was only one answer: on the outside, trying your damnedest to get in.'

'It is my family's business,' Sir John said mildly.

'Yes, indeed. I have a lot of sympathy for you, sir . . . At first I took you at your face value; I underestimated how clever you are . . . You see, there could have been a different reason for you coming to defend Frederick. If we rejected your argument, then it would make us even more certain that he was our man. Of course, it didn't take us all the way. But I did begin to think about you in a different light. With Rodger and Edgar murdered, Frederick executed, what would happen to the family then? You would be the only male member left. You would have to take over the business, maybe even worm your way into Pendletons as well. It was clearly possible. You were well on the way to making yourself indispensable. On that view, you would have served our purpose very well . . . except that you were on the high seas at the time of the first murder.'

'Indeed!'

'Yes. On the face of it, you couldn't have killed Rodger . . . It's funny, isn't it, that the mind makes connections you aren't conscious of. We accepted that you couldn't have killed Rodger, and we never thought that you could have murdered Edgar. We were looking down a tunnel, as it were.'

'Your conclusions were nevertheless correct.'

Bragg ignored him. 'It was bad police work, sir, I'll admit that. Then I remembered a bit of what I had learned in my youth . . . I still have friends in shipping offices. They made enquiries of the Clan Line in Glasgow, for me. The information they got was that, although you had booked a passage, and had your luggage put on board the *Clan Macnab* on the twelfth of September, you yourself had not boarded the ship . . . That seemed very curious. You had made a point, when speaking to our Commissioner, of saying that you had come home the long way – round the coast of Africa. It was that which established you couldn't be a suspect. I was at a loss, I confess. Then I went back to my shipping friends. It took some finding, I can tell you! Then they had a lucky strike! They found a Sir John Newby, who had boarded the *SS Arcadia* in Calcutta, on the twenty-third of September. I thought it must be a mistake, at first. I went along to the Peninsular and Oriental Company's offices myself. It was you, all right. They could even show me your signed bar bills. Then it clicked! The *Arcadia* came back through the Suez Canal. Although it set off later, it arrived earlier. You got to Tilbury on the thirteenth of October – on a Saturday night. You lay low until the Monday lunch-time. You knew your brother's habits, from visits when you were on home leave. As soon as Colley was out of the way, you went into the shop and killed Rodger.'

There was silence for a space. Then Newby stirred in his chair and, reaching into his pocket, pulled out a small revolver. He rested it on his thigh, the barrel pointing towards Bragg. Then he spoke, in a flat expressionless voice.

'It was so unfair, sergeant,' he said. 'The goldsmiths' business had always passed to the eldest son. Never, in over a hundred and fifty years, had it gone to a younger son . . . My father used to tell me that I had the better part; that I would have a career open to no one of an earlier generation – a way of life more suited to a titled gentleman. And, in a sense, school at Eton reinforced his argument. Service in India sounded interesting, exciting. I went into it with high hopes . . . But I was less than successful, and I began to resent my fate. When I used to come home on leave, I could see Rodger prospering, becoming a man of consequence – and in the heart of the empire, not some teeming Indian city on the periphery.'

He seemed to drift into a reverie, staring deep into the red coals of the fire. Bragg eased himself forward, preparing to leap on him. But Newby sensed the movement. He swung round and levelled the gun at Bragg's heart. There was tension for a space, then he began to speak again.

'It might never have happened, if my wife had not died . . . We had a son, you know, in 'seventy-seven. But he was stillborn . . . That seemed to take all the joy out of our lives. I toyed with the idea of resigning; coming back to live in England. My wife had many relatives over here – though what we would have lived on, I cannot imagine. Then she died, in the cholera epidemic. After that, there seemed no point in leaving. I could bring myself to believe that my work in Calcutta was important, even interesting at times. England became again somewhere to retire to. But, of course, the time came round when I had to face retirement. As I contemplated my future, I became incensed at the disparity of my lot, when compared with that of my brother. And it was in no way fortuitous. My father, Sir Thomas, had decreed it. I was filled with a deep sense of anger and betrayal. And so I planned my revenge . . . It was much as you described it. I knew Rodger's habits from my leave, two years ago. I had arranged for the *Clan Macnab* people to send my luggage to the Royal Hotel; and had booked a reservation there, from the night of the nineteenth of October. I arrived at Tilbury on the *Arcadia*, late on the thirteenth. I had planned the detail over my last weeks of service in India. And all went smoothly. On the Sunday night I went to a small hotel in Bayswater. At noon, on the Monday, I spoke to Rodger on the telephone. I said that I wanted to have a serious talk with him. It was arranged that I would go to the shop in Poultry, at two o'clock. He said he would get rid of Colley, so that we could discuss matters in private.'

He stopped speaking, his eyes staring into the dying embers. Bragg tensed to spring at him, but he swung round and levelled the gun at Bragg's head. 'I would regret having to kill you, before you understand,' he said coldly.

Bragg made himself relax back into his chair, wondering if his last day had come. The man was crazy. By his own account, he had been brooding on the injustice meted out to him for months – years probably. It had coloured his whole existence, soured his life. His retirement had meant coming home to England for revenge. And that, not only to kill his brother, but to take his place. By his own account he was a madman, with perhaps two murders to his credit. Why should he worry about an odd policeman as well?

Newby began speaking again, his eyes on Bragg's face. 'When I went to the shop,' he said, 'Rodger locked the street door, so that we would not be disturbed. I said that, as he knew, I had retired to England. As I was active and healthy, I did not want to live in a mouldering seaside town. I wanted to join him in the family business, as was my right. He became very abusive. He said there was no room for me. He treated me with contempt. He said that he was to be Lord Mayor; that he too would have a title – Sir Rodger Newby. Only he would have earned it, not merely inherited it . . . We were standing in front of the fireplace. He ordered me to leave, to go and rot in

Eastbourne with the rest of my kind. He turned away contemptuously . . . I saw the bronze on the mantlepiece, took hold of it and hit him – and again and again. Then I let myself out of the shop and walked away.'

There was a silence, then: 'Did you take a silver tankard, sir?' Bragg asked quietly.

Sir John looked up with a half-smile. 'Yes. I thought it would make it seem as if there had been a robbery. It is in a drawer in my bedroom.'

'And why did you burn the will?'

'It was on the desk. He had been reading it . . . I am not a qualified lawyer, sergeant, but I know more about the law than most people. I realised that, if I destroyed the will, Rodger's widow must have an interest of one-third in his estate. I felt sure that I could influence Elizabeth sufficiently, for her to allow me to participate in the business to some extent. The rest you have already surmised.'

'So, you did kill Edgar?' Bragg said.

'Of course. He too was in my way . . . But he was verminous. He was quite prepared to meet me at the cellars, to conspire against his brother. I had no more compunction than if I were stepping on a scorpion.'

The recollection seemed to fill him with sudden anger. 'Stand up!' he ordered. 'And back slowly to the wall!'

Bragg got up. He could feel sweat on the back of his neck. He measured the distance between them with his eyes. Even as he did so, Newby stood up and stepped away into the middle of the room. Bragg shuffled backwards. The gun was levelled at his head. There was a strange smile on Newby's face; a crazy, gloating smile. Bragg's heels hit the skirting board.

'Now stretch out your arms against the wall,' Sir John ordered. 'And legs astride.'

Bragg did as he said. He could be blown to kingdom come any second. His throat was dry, his brain refused to function. As if through a summer mist, he saw Newby level the gun at his heart. He took a despairing gulp of air . . . Then Newby gave a cackle of laughter, swung the gun to his own forehead and pulled the trigger.

EPILOGUE

'So, Malpas went home like a lamb, Bragg?' the Commissioner said, with a sly smile.

'Yes, sir. I think he was too worried about what his friends would think, if the business about the punch-bowl got out.'

'A pity, in some ways. I would have relished putting down that insufferable Member of Parliament of his . . . And the club owner?'

'I have had a word with Inspector Cotton, sir. He thinks we should give the charge of receiving stolen goods a run.'

'Have we enough evidence?'

'We are going over to Dorking, later today. If we do find the wines in his cellar – and I gather they will be easy enough to identify – then it should be plain sailing. Ward, from Pendletons, is keen to go ahead. Though whether Edgar Newby's family will thank us, is another matter. I don't see how we will be able to keep his involvement quiet.'

'Ah, these barristers are very clever. A nod in the right direction, and only the evidence bearing on Palliser's actions will be led.'

Bragg pondered. 'Yes, I suppose so. It could not help Palliser, to show that he had involved Edgar in the affair.'

'Indeed. And I expect they will give his counsel the nod that he will get a lighter sentence, if they co-operate. So that just leaves Frederick Newby wrongly detained!'

Bragg laughed. 'Well, that is down to the coroner, sir. We could hardly release him on our own authority. I have sent Constable Morton over to explain matters. I expect Frederick will be freed before long.'

The Commissioner leaned back in his chair. 'A strange case,

Bragg,' he said. 'What on earth was it about? Sir John Newby seemed to be such a sensible sort of chap.'

'I think he was sensible enough, in his own way,' Bragg said musingly. 'I reckon it was all to do with tradition.'

'You could hardly say there was a tradition of murder in the Newby family,' Sir William said. 'Even though we have collected three corpses in a fortnight.'

'No, sir. Nevertheless, tradition means a lot to the Newbys. After all, there have been baronets stretching back to sixteen hundred and eleven. Of course, as a family they were not in with the nobility; they were tradesmen, but proud of it.'

'I am right in thinking that no Newby had ever been Lord Mayor in the past, am I not?'

'That's true. To that extent, Rodger was going to put them up a notch. But, as I said, the seeds of this tragedy were sown by Rodger's father, Sir Thomas Newby. Now, I am speculating a bit, but this is what I think happened . . . Not long after they were married, Sir Thomas's wife, Gertrude, became pregnant. As time went on, they discovered that she was going to have twins – and, as we know, they were to be boys. When her time came, she went into labour. But there was something wrong. The baby that should have popped out first was lying across the passage. Gertrude was in agony. She was getting the labour pains, but nothing was happening. The doctor tried to manoeuvre the baby into the right position, but couldn't manage it. There was only one thing to do, if Gertrude's life was to be saved – a Caesarean delivery.'

The Commissioner screwed up his face in disgust. 'Is this absolutely necessary, Bragg?' he asked.

'If you are to understand it, yes, sir . . . So the doctor takes his scalpel, and cuts through the wall of the abdomen – and, in those days, they didn't have anything stronger than laudanum to deaden the pain. Anyway, he then cuts through the wall of the womb, and takes out one of the babies. Then he reaches in, and takes out the one that had been causing all the trouble.'

'Where is this getting us?' Sir William complained.

'Oh, it is quite biblical, sir. You remember the bit about "The first shall be last, and the last first"?'

'Well?'

'The baby the doctor pulled out first ought to have been born second, in the natural way. Now, most people would regard him as the elder, because he would cry first; when the cord was cut, he could be said to have an independent existence before his brother.'

'We are talking about the baby christened John?'

'Yes, sir. And, because there was a doctor and a midwife present, that was how it had to be. John was the elder. There was nothing, short of his death, which could stop the baronetcy passing to him. But I think Sir Thomas never accepted it. He said to himself that, if nature had worked as God intended, then Rodger would have been the elder. So he made sure that, short of the title, Rodger would have his birthright.'

'That sounds very fanciful, Bragg,' the Commissioner said.

'Maybe. And it took me a long time to realise it. But I am convinced that Sir Thomas Newby regarded Rodger as his rightful heir. The Newby goldsmiths' business had always been passed on to the eldest son. This was the first generation where the pattern had been broken. But you can see it right from the start. Sir Thomas gave Rodger the education appropriate for an elder son of the Newbys. A day-school, so he was kept in the family atmosphere, wouldn't get ideas above his station. Straight into the business from there; a thorough grounding, then an independent shop to run. All exactly what would happen to the eldest son of the family.'

'And the other baby?'

'Well, in a sense, he was left to make his own fortune. It is common enough, with younger sons . . . Of course, on the face of it, John was the privileged one – sent to the best school in the country, holding an administrative post in the government of India . . .'

'But John did not entirely agree?' the Commissioner said, with his foxy smile.

'Not when he got older, at any rate, and realised how little he would have when he retired.'

'So he tried to force his way into the business, was rebuffed, and began a course of systematic slaughter!. . . You know, Bragg, sometimes I am glad that my share of this world's riches is modest.'

'Ah,' Bragg said warmly, 'it's the resources of the mind, the riches of the soul that count, sir.'

Sir William smiled to himself. 'Yes, indeed. I believe you are right, Bragg!'